THERE CAME A SHARP SQUEAL
AND THEN SILENCE....

George leaped to his feet, the unwary and innocent bystander who has blundered into the murder scene and is now seen by the killer. The shadowy form across the street emerged into the lesser darkness of the pavement and reared up on its hind legs, looking at George. From its bloody jaws hung the body of a common house cat.

The man felt faint as his own sudden standing up drained the blood from his brain. Was it a bear? Taller than he was when it stood, it had a rounded head and a long muzzle and small eyes set close to the head. The eyes were large and luminous, a night creature's eyes. George Beaumont, called Bo by his friends back home, alone in a strange town in the dead of night, felt that a dream had somehow extended into his waking life, that, dreaming and waking too soon, he had pulled this apparition into his world by mistake. He wanted it not to be there. The creature dropped the dead cat into the gutter and stalked toward him on its hind legs, fixing him with its eyes. . . .

Books by Robert Stallman

The Orphan
The Captive
The Beast

Published by TIMESCAPE/POCKET BOOKS

Robert Stallman

THE BEAST

(The Third Book
of the Beast)

A TIMESCAPE BOOK

PUBLISHED BY POCKET BOOKS NEW YORK

Another *Original* publication of TIMESCAPE BOOKS

A Timescape Book published by
POCKET BOOKS, a Simon & Schuster division of
GULF & WESTERN CORPORATION
1230 Avenue of the Americas, New York, N.Y. 10020

ISBN: 0-671-41383-X

First Timescape Books printing September, 1982

10 9 8 7 6 5 4 3 2 1

POCKET and colophon are trademarks of Simon & Schuster.

Use of the trademark TIMESCAPE is by exclusive license
from Gregory Benford, the trademark owner.

Printed in the U.S.A.

This book is for
Stumper and Betty

And that which thou sowest, thou sowest not that body that shall be, but bare grain, it may chance of wheat, or of some other grain: But God giveth it a body as it hath pleased him, and to every seed his own body.

—I Corinthians 15: 37–38 (King James)

Chapter One

May, 1938

My third year of awareness in this world approaches its end. I feel old and bored. Spring comes again with its brilliant days and cold nights during which I wander to the sheep runs along the Rio Grande and contemplate an easy night's meal. Often I do not touch them, preferring to spend hours loping across the mesa to the east or wandering upriver as far as the Reservation boundaries. During the day, Barry cares for his family, our family now, and works at his two jobs. I am known by Renee and Mina, and even the new baby looks at me with blank blue eyes when I slip into the bedroom at night. He is not afraid either. But I am restless. Barry thinks always of becoming separate from me. I feel like two creatures now instead of one.

This May night is cool, with a waning moon hanging above like a bent bow aimed at the mountains. Below the cliffs I walk along, the Rio glints and swirls its brown current in the familiar music of water noises. On the west side of the river ahead I sense a coyote, head down, lapping water. Without thinking and for no reason other than boredom, I begin stalking him, sliding down the steep banks in a flowing of sand to slip into the brown water. It carries me as I paddle slowly and land some ways downstream. The wild dog is out of range of my spatial sense now, so I begin trotting boldly upstream along the sandbars.

I feel alert, my spatial sense surrounding me with news of the river bottom: a family of birds over there, ducks in the reeds, snakes, gophers, rabbits of several kinds and, there ahead, just scrambling up the clay bank, my coyote, his draggle tail full of burrs and Spanish needles. He does not scent me, as the breeze tonight is coming from upriver. I wait until his form disappears over the edge of the bank and then leap and scramble straight up the caliche until I can crouch on top. The mesa is dotted with brush and prickly pear; no cover or rocks for hundreds of yards. My spatial sense picks him up trotting, nose down, at an angle that will bring him within fifty yards of where I crouch behind some of last year's tumbleweeds. Now I can hear the rustling sound of his pads in the sand, the stertorous snuffling as he scents and then clears his nose.

I am about to begin my rush when something warns him. He shies away suddenly, pausing and looking in my direction, standing stiff-legged, his head thrust out. I decide to charge him directly. Perhaps the stupid dog will drop dead of fright. As I come scrambling out from behind the mound of tumbleweeds, the coyote utters a startled yip and scrabbles madly in the sand getting under way. The chase is on. He gets a good leaping start while I am still yards away, and his long legs become a blur as he goes faster than a jackrabbit back toward the riverbank. I see him disappear over the bank on the fly, desperate enough to chance breaking his legs, I think, panting and leaping right after him. Below the spot he leaped from is a dry wash packed full of dead tumbleweeds into which the coyote crashed and has now almost fought his way through. I find myself in the same stickery mess, unable to stop my momentum, and have to thrash about considerably to get through the ridiculous things. When I get out I sense the coyote speeding down the sandbar toward the water. He thinks to lose me in the river. Just like a stupid dog. Thinks I'm a cougar, probably.

I hear him splash into the river, and, not waiting to get to where he is, I leap out and crash into the water, too, treading hard against the current. Now, Mr. Coyote, you'd better swim like a sonofabitch, because I'm holding my own down here, and the current's bringing you right into my arms. Upstream I hear the coyote panting and gurgling as he windmills those skinny legs through the water, trying to beat the current and make the shallows on the other side. I put more effort into it, making headway against the current, angling also for the far bank. The coyote hears me now getting closer as the current carries him nearer to me. Just to help him along I raise my muzzle clear of the water and utter a roar that would scare me if I heard it from the outside. The coyote thrashes even more wildly,

10

making less headway than ever, for now his fright has ruined his coordination.

As I am about to put on some extra steam and grab the critter, a driftlog with several yards of exposed roots almost catches my rear, and I have to let the current carry me down a ways. The coyote finds the shallows and begins leaping high through the water for the bank. My feet hit bottom and I go crashing after him, roaring like seven fiends. I see the poor thing wobbling with terror as he scrambles and clambers up through the sand, trying to get to the top and the willows that grow on the east bank. But I am stronger, can leap farther at one jump, and the sliding sand does not hold me back so much. Just as the terrified wild dog reaches the top, I am close enough to slap his hindquarters with one paw.

He goes spinning over into the sand like a top off its string, and I leap sideways, staying near but not landing on him. This is no jackrabbit. He has teeth, although they are nothing like my own. He lies on his back in the sand, his legs tense, fangs bared, great hard pantings coming from his muzzle. His eyes are mad with fright and determination. I stand there growling at him, looking down at the ridiculous little scavenger, a part of me wanting to bat him over and break his neck with a quick bite.

And then the most astounding thing in my whole life happens. I am crouched there over the panting and terrified coyote, one paw raised, and it is not a coyote but a snake! I leap back, my mind flashing warning: a sidewinder! And where is the coyote? The snake is writhing away into the brush before I realize what has happened: the coyote is a shape-changer. I leap into the bushes, dancing about to avoid the snake's fangs, stepping on the wretched thing several times, and then I see its head. I grab, fast as lightning before he can strike, hold him just back of his jaws and give him a few good shakes. His coils are around my neck now and I claw them off, toss the snake in the air.

An eagle, falcon, some large bird, takes the place of the snake, flops uncertainly in the air, and I knock it to the sand and pounce on it, where it becomes a jackrabbit, then a prairie dog, a turtle, a snake again, a lynx. And at that I seize the creature firmly in all four claws and send a strong thought:

Hold your shape or I will snap your neck.

The lynx is suddenly a panting coyote whose body I

hold tightly in my claws. I drop the creature to the sand and put one paw on its belly, claws extended.

Get it over with, damn you.

What are you?

The coyote lets his legs relax so that the paws droop over, the fangs disappear behind the lips, the head turns to one side, exposing the neck. He rolls onto his side, tongue lying in the sand that blows out with his rapid panting.

You are intelligent?

You think you own this desert?

The finding of this being has thrown me completely off. I cannot imagine what it means. The creature looks up at me out of dull eyes and then looks away.

You are of the Great Cats. I await your death blow.

I will not kill an intelligent being, I say to it. I must know more. *How are you capable of shape-changing?*

The dog looks up at me with a flicker of surprise. *I am from Outside, even as you are. You do not look like a young one. But you are toying with me.* The eyes go shut and the coyote pants, getting sand in its nose and sneezing.

How does this creature know these things? It seems to know more about my—our—condition than I do. My mind itches with curiosity.

You are a human also? I ask. *You have a Person?* *?*

What form do you wear usually to live in the world?

You play with me, Big Cat. Damn your arrogance. I have not made my conjunction, and now I will never make it. I am here, forever a coyote, an animal, living an animal's life. Go ahead, kill me. He stretches his neck out as if he were home in his den and closes his eyes, giving a great panting sigh.

I must ask you more, I say, my curiosity getting the better of my good sense. *What is conjunction?*

The coyote pulls his legs under him and eyes me strangely. I think a word of surprise comes from him, but then it is veiled. He looks at me from a resting position, his paws stretched in front of him.

You are *a young one, then.*

I am three years aware, almost, I say defensively. I do not like the condescending tone of this stupid wild dog whom I have captured fair and square. He is, after all, mine to kill.

And you have identified with the humans, the creature

says, as if considering my sins in the light of his superior morality. I am getting irritated.

You are talking nonsense, I say rather stiffly. *You are trying to throw me off. You are nothing but a kind of creature I have not run across yet.*

Yes, I am only an animal. He nods his head toward the river. *Like those out there.*

I want to know what this creature apparently knows, but I hate putting my own ignorance on display. The coyote flops his ragged tail, like a friendly housedog.

We are fellow Outsiders, he says in a conciliatory tone. *We should not destroy each other. And you are a young one who has not mated, and so you know nothing. I can tell you much.*

I hate his superior air, this draggly, desert panhandler. But I want to know more.

If you will not keep so tight a hold on me, the coyote says, *I can think and tell you about our world. You want to know about that, don't you?*

I nod and sit back on my haunches, sheathing my claws.

Are you comfortable now?

I nod, eyeing the creature with distaste.

Now I will tell you about yourself, he says, sitting up and trying to look intelligent. *Do you know of the moon?*

I know it is important, but not why.

You have no understanding of The Leap or when it will come?

I don't know what you mean.

You have not attempted a mating?

I have never met another like myself. I have many times shared the sexual experience of my Persons.

The coyote looks disgusted. *That is not mating. It is obvious you are a late bloomer. But first, about the jump, for that tells you where you will go and where you come from.*

I lean forward, trying to believe this miserable dog, fighting against my instinct that dogs are liars and flatterers and cheats. He is telling me something I want to believe.

You will fix on the moon and two stars, he is saying. *That star,* and he lifts his muzzle to point directly overhead at a bright star. *And the one over there, in the south,* and he points again, this time to one behind my head.

I turn, looking in the direction his nose is pointing.

Where?

There! comes his triumphant cry at the same moment that I feel a vicious bite on the side of my neck. I twist hard, my claws snapping around to kill the creature, but there is nothing there. A rush of wind goes by my face and I leap, but I am off balance. The big bird is already higher than I can jump and pumping rapidly upward into the night sky.

Stupid cat! comes the fading cry as the bird flaps away into the dark.

On the way home I feel afraid for the first time in my existence. Around me in the desert, in the world, perhaps, are others like myself. The world is more complex than I had thought. There had been times when my Persons felt that, and I had shared it. Once Charles wondered if he were unique in the world, and concluded that he was. Now I know how he felt, for I watch the desert creatures —the owl, the snake, the prairie dog—and wonder if they are shape-changers like myself, out for a night's run. On the bank of the river I stand in the late starlight, feeling the cruel bite on my neck and the mocking words of that rotten coyote, and I look down on the sleeping town of Albuquerque. How many are there in this town, I wonder. Where are the others like myself? Will I meet another like myself and mate? Or was that miserable dog lying to me? But he said when I first grabbed him that he had missed his conjunction and now would never make it. And what is The Leap?

As I slide down the bank and head for the adobe house in the north valley where Barry's family is sleeping, I feel more strongly the truth of those hints. Perhaps that is why I feel so bored and unsatisfied with everything. As I approach the yard where the car is parked under the big cottonwood tree, I resolve to be more aware of my own existence. I have, after all, for these last six months been too concerned with Barry and Mina and Renee—and now the baby. I have been turning into a house pet, I think with some mild surprise, a tame house pet. As I walk in through the back door and pad through the silent house to the bedroom where Renee sleeps with the crib beside the bed, I make this resolve: I will regain my identity. The coyote may have said some true things. I will find out.

I shift.

Barry crawls into bed beside his sleeping wife. From the

crib beside the bed a pair of bright eyes watches what has happened, but the baby makes no sound.

Barry flipped on the heater in the cold bathroom and ran some shaving water, listening to the sounds of his family around him in the house: Mina was getting dressed and talking to her goldfish, Renee had little Martin on the bed changing his diaper and from the kitchen came the smell of bacon and coffee. He hardly remembered the night's surprises, since he usually slept through the Beast's excursions, but there was a sense of unease inside him, and he recalled getting bitten on the neck. It still hurt this morning, although the skin was not broken. He put that out of his mind for a time. Today he would talk with the Indian, John Strong Horse, about the new series he was planning.

At the counter in the kitchen Mina ate cornflakes and added columns of figures on a paper beside her plate. Barry cleaned up some scrambled eggs and Renee sat comfortably in the sling chair she had pulled into the kitchen and fed Martin, her dress opened on one side. Barry looked at his lovely, dark-haired wife and grinned.

"I'm jealous," he said softly.

"Isn't he a darling," Renee said. "Sleeps all night already."

"I heard you come in last night," Mina said, still adding figures. "You were growling."

Barry looked at his stepdaughter. "That wasn't me, sweetie," he said patiently. It was an old joke. He got up, wiped his mouth on a napkin and kissed Renee on the cheek.

"You know how much I love you?" he said.

"Harder than thunder can bump a stump up a hill backwards," she said, reaching up to pull his head back down and kissing him on the mouth. "Be smart and wonderful today."

"My dear wife, I am never any other way," he said.

" 'Bye, Daddy," Mina said, still adding figures. "Tell Benny I'll be out in two shakes."

He kissed Mina and walked out the back door into the cool New Mexico morning. It would be nice and hot today, he thought, getting into the Model A sedan. He called to the little Spanish boy who was swinging on the tire that hung from the cottonwood. "Hey, Benny, she'll *venira muy pronto*."

Downtown in the Liberty Bar, Barry sat in a front booth

where there was some light and the noise of the swamp cooler back of the bar was not so deafening. He watched a stooped old Indian, his paunch hanging over his belt, come rocking along the bar, holding out his jewelry to the men seated there. He wore a maroon velvet blouse and the colorless Levi's of the town Indian, and had silver and turquoise bracelets up both arms and a big concho belt under his belly. The Indian rolled like an old sailor, as if his feet were rounded on the bottom and his knees would not bend.

Barry was startled by the young man who appeared from back along the row of booths and slid in opposite him.

"Old Jimmie's an interesting story, if you like hard-luck tales," the young, black-haired Indian said.

Barry reached across and shook the young man's hand briefly. The Indian's touch was cool and firm, the skin smooth. "How are you, John?"

"Good. Your family?"

"Everybody's well," Barry said, grinning. "How you fixed for big stories? I need a Pulitzer to convince my editor I'm worth my keep."

The young Indian was watching his elder counterpart approach along the line of booths, holding up his arms to show the bracelets, mumbling to the people having their lunch. He was not selling anything. Barry was about to speak again when he smelled the old man's breath and felt a touch on his arm.

"Gen'win Navajo rings?"

"No, thanks," Barry said, somewhat embarrassed.

The old man threw a look at Johnny as he passed by, saying something in Navajo. The young Indian answered in a low tone with a single word.

"I wish I could understand that," Barry said, for something to say.

"Old Jimmie just wished my asshole would come out on my forehead," Johnny said, grinning.

"What'd you tell him?"

"Oh, that he was an impotent chicken."

Barry laughed. "I thought you were all brothers in the tribe."

"That old fart's no brother of mine. No, he's a half-wit," Johnny said. "Everybody knows he's not right up here," and he tapped his forehead.

"Hey, John, how about some firewater?"

After they had sipped their bourbon for a time, Barry

16

thought he could get back to the subject. "So what's happening over at Yellow Mesa?"

"You want something to write about?" Johnny was looking down into his drink.

"That's my job."

"You do that illegitimate children thing at Isleta last summer?"

"You know I did. Had my name on it." Barry felt a flush over his pride in that series. It had been syndicated all across the country.

"Yeah. I liked that. You know the Commissioner came up with some new money after that?"

"I heard." This is like the trading post, Barry thought. They walk in and stand all day before they'll say they want something. I just have to wait him out. The talk went on through that drink and halfway into the next. Barry was getting impatient in spite of himself. It was almost two o'clock.

"Here's your story," Johnny said suddenly.

"I'm listening."

"You've heard of the Native American Church?"

"Yeah, I think so. It's a sort of tent revival—hogan revival, I guess, isn't it?" Barry felt a letdown. If this was the story, it had been done.

"And you know about peyote?"

Barry's irritation almost burst from him. This was adding up to nothing. "The drug, yeah." He tossed off the rest of the drink, prepared to leave. Well, it had only cost two drinks.

"You haven't heard of Navajos eating peyote, though."

Barry's interest flickered. "Go on."

"The Church is having a revival up in northeastern Arizona. The People are getting saved again, this time by the little brown buttons." Johnny said the words in a monotone, almost in a whisper.

"That's illegal, of course," Barry said, signaling the bartender. "Have another?"

"No, thanks. This's not my poison. Anyway, if you want to see something happening to the Navajo that's never happened before, come along with me when I go home tomorrow."

Barry was still disappointed, but it might be something. "You're going tomorrow. We got a fresh baby at home, I don't know if—"

Johnny shrugged. "It's a good story."

"Okay," Barry said. "I can make it for a couple of days, if I can get Frank and Judy to look after my family."

"I'll get you into the Church," Johnny said, "and you can be as snoopy as you want." He smiled. "We welcome converts."

"I'll have to get a new angle," Barry said. "Peyote's been around for a while, I think." He didn't know, actually, much about it, but it seemed he had read something not so long ago.

"Sure, the plains Indians, the Paiute, the Cheyenne, the Mexican tribes, but never the good old middle-class Navajo. We're getting it now"—he leaned forward, his dark eyes looking intently into Barry's—"and I'm in it. But I'm afraid of it, too."

"Breaking up the clans and such?"

"You know about the big livestock massacre a couple years ago?"

"I don't recall it," Barry said. Not surprising, considering he had only been in this world, as far as he could remember, for less than two years.

"Thousands of sheep and goats," Johnny said, his face becoming hard. "My uncle was there, up north. He and some others wanted to get painted up, kill some white men."

"And that wouldn't work," Barry said. "So they're getting back to the spiritual thing."

"Right. And let me tell you something else. It works."

"Yeah, I imagine it does. Get yourself full of dope and you don't worry about a bunch of dead goats or an ineffective Tribal Council."

"More than that," Johnny said mysteriously. "But you come along. I'll show you. Or, rather, Little Brown Father will show you." He reached in the pocket of his Levi's jacket, pulling out a round, wrinkled cactus button. He grinned. "Have a bite?"

Later, on his way up the hill to the University of New Mexico library, Barry sorted out the possibilities: one, the Indians getting pushed around again; two, the Church filling the power vacuum; three, the shame of the good Indians being seduced by peyote. But first he would have to find out about that cactus. On his way into the library he paused to look across campus at the almost completed new library with its nine-story tower done in pueblo style. Now there was going to be some stack of books, he thought. It looked somewhat like pictures he had seen of Devil's Tower, a mountain somewhere in the Northwest.

In the old Reference room with its few students hiding in their books at the long oak tables, he found several earlier references to the drug peyote. There were the usual hysterical missionaries afraid for the souls of the Indians who were scandalously enjoying themselves; then he found an article by Huntington Cairns in the November *Atlantic Monthly* for 1929, over eight years ago.

As far as Barry could find out, it was the only article of any worth on the drug in the last ten years. And there were none referring to the Navajo. The article was titled, "A Divine Intoxicant" and quoted some diary passages from a Padre Bernardino in the year 1529:

Some danced, some sang; others wept . . . and some did not wish to sing, but seated themselves in their rooms and remained there as though meditating. Some had visions that they were dying and shed tears; others imagined that some wild beast was devouring them; others that they were capturing prisoners in warfare; others that they were rich; others that they had many slaves; others that they had committed adultery and were to have their heads broken as a penalty; others that they had been guilty of a theft, for which they were to be executed; and many other visions were seen by them.

He found that it was called *peyotl* from a word in the Nahuatl language, and sometimes it was called mescal, though it should not be confused with the Mexican drink of that name, that its use had extended at one time as far north as the Canadian border, and that the missionaries had fought it with no less than their usual zeal. And then he read some rather surprising accounts of peyote use by several famous men in America, including William James, Havelock Ellis and the author of the article. The accounts, except for that of James, who had got nothing but a bad stomachache for his scientific ardor, were fantastic. No drug that Barry had ever heard about produced that kind of response. The experimenters were scientists and seemed to be in their right minds. He read the accounts avidly, realizing there was little or nothing in the popular press about the effects of the drug. The U.S. Government had

19

recently been complaining about hemp—marijuana—smoking, but that seemed such an oriental pastime. An account by an experimenter named Weir Mitchell drew his attention:

> Gorgeous colors and wonderful shapes floated before his eyes. One vision impressed him deeply: "An edge of a huge cliff seemed to project over a gulf of unseen depth. My viewless enchanter set on the brink a huge bird claw of stone. Above, from the stem or leg, hung a fragment of the same stuff. This began to unroll and float out to a distance which seemed to me to represent Time as well as immensity of Space. Here were miles of rippled purples, half transparent, and of ineffable beauty. Now and then soft golden clouds floated from these folds, or a great shimmer went over the whole of the rolling purples, and things like green birds fell from it, fluttering down into the gulf below."

The other two accounts vied with this one for variety and sumptuousness of visual images. Barry smiled and leaned back as he finished the article, noting its typical nineteenth-century tone:

> Even where robustness of health is present, the subsequent physiological effects are too costly to admit for the civilized man, if not for the savage, more than one or two experiences with the drug. But to experience its intoxicating qualities even once is to look ever afterward upon the external world with at least a keener appreciation of color.

So, the savages could put up with stomachache and nausea, but the civilized man would, of course, back down if it came to Alka-Seltzer and aspirin.

There could be more than one article on the use of stuff like that, Barry thought, getting up to leave the library. White civilization dispossesses the Indian of his property again, forces him to turn to euphoric drugs; retreat from reality for the red man. As he rode back down into the valley in the warm afternoon, he could feel that power inside becoming aware. The Beast, too, looked forward to the trip into Navajo land and perhaps even a more sub-

20

jective journey with Little Brown Father. At that thought, Barry felt the power move and rise in him. Yes, it was interested.

"You need anything at all, or anything goes wrong, just call Frank," Barry said for the fourth or fifth time as they put his suitcase and a hamper of food into the Model A sedan.

"Have you got the water bags tied on tight?" Renee asked. She was holding little Marty on her hip in a comfortable, motherly way. Barry stopped to look at her, amazed at how she had encompassed the pregnancy and birth and care of their son. He filled up with admiration and love for his woman at that moment and walked over to put his arms around her.

"Sweetheart, it's going to be a big break for us," he said, holding her tight while the little round face of Marty slept in its blankets. "It's a good story, and it'll go even better than the one last year."

"You just take care of yourself and don't get scalped," Renee said, kissing him all over the face.

Mina was trying to get in between them, and they both hugged the little girl at the same time.

"I've got to go now, Daddy. It's the last day of school," she said. "You and the Big Pussycat can always call me if anything's wrong, you know."

Barry looked at the little girl, with her wide, serious eyes, knowing what she meant, although he had not participated in that sharing of minds that she could somehow do with the Beast. Not wanting to think now about the complexities of his double life, he picked her up and swung her in the air once before hugging and kissing her on the lips as she wanted. He kissed Marty on his bald head, rubbed his cheek against Renee's once more and got into the car. The soft, popping exhaust made him think of that other Model A whose destruction had lighted a whole mountain afire last summer.

He pulled the gearshift into first and looked at his family standing under the big cottonwood in the bright morning air, behind them the adobe house, solid and lovely under the trees, like part of the earth itself.

"I'm a lucky guy," he said, so that Renee could hear him.

"Goodbye, dearest Barry," she said.

21

Chapter Two

November, 1937

The last desperate people have visited the miraculous grave and gone away, most of them the same as when they came. This one sleeps on a doorstep like a homeless child. I watch him from a stairwell across the street and think whether I should help him. He is very sick, and even at this distance I sense that he will soon die. Lilly urges me, but then she is always eager to save people and would have me working in a clinic if she could. The man is huddled in his overcoat and leaning against the iron railing of someone's front stoop. He is a large man in middle life, thick hair under his hat, a tired face, strong, graceful hands that are now relaxed on his lap. Dried mud crusts one arm and the bottom of his coat.

Will you help him?
Why this one from so many?
He is here.
All right, Lilly, we will help.
Let me take him home.
No. He would not understand.
You will frighten him.
He must change. This begins it.

I do not allow the shift my Person wishes. If we are to help this man, he must reverse his own descent toward death, and my appearance on this misty night will give him a shock. I will make it seem an accident.

In his dreams, George Beaumont found himself again in the line of people. The cold November afternoon stretched away into infinity, and they marched somewhere in the mud, like soldiers going to their deaths. They kept their heads down. The destination was known.

His eyes snapped open, his whole body bristling with fear, breath suspended. What sound had wakened him? Huddled against the iron railing that was now warm with his own warmth, he felt like a part of the building suddenly come aware. There. Something moved in the shadows across the narrow street, a form so sinuous it could only be an animal, a huge animal slipping from doorway to cellarway to stairs. George felt the hair on his neck standing up, his stomach tight with fear. That was the sound that had pulled him from sleep: a low moaning. The shadow suddenly moved so fast that George thought it had disappeared and reappeared farther on. There came a sharp squeal and then silence.

George leaped to his feet, the unwary and innocent by-stander who has blundered into the murder scene and is now seen by the killer. The shadowy form across the street emerged into the lesser darkness of the pavement and reared up on its hind legs, looking at George. From its bloody jaws hung the body of a common house cat.

The man felt faint as his own sudden standing up drained the blood from his brain. Was it a bear? Taller than he was when it stood, it had a rounded head and long muzzle and small ears set close to the head. The eyes were large and luminous, a night creature's eyes. George Beaumont, called Bo by his friends back home, alone in a strange town in the dead of night, felt that a dream had somehow extended into his waking life, that, dreaming and waking too soon, he had pulled this apparition into his world by mistake. He wanted it not to be there. The creature dropped the dead cat into the gutter and stalked toward him on its hind legs, fixing him with its eyes.

Bo could not move from the spot.

I will not harm you.

The man staggered as if he had been struck in the face, the words like a physical touch inside his mind. But he felt the agony in his side moving again and knew he was not dreaming. As if from a distance, his mind noted the details of the scene: the Beast with its gleaming teeth and blue-gray fur walking toward him, a vision not to be credited by the waking mind, and the man in his dark overcoat and hat standing with his arms hanging down. The Beast was like a huge cat but tailless, with almost

23

human forepaws and blunt fingers where he could imagine retracted talons.

You are sick.

The voice felt feminine to Bo's mind, as if a woman were speaking, trying to keep him from being afraid. The fearful muzzle came close to his face. Huge, luminous eyes peered into his own.

You have been to Malden cemetery seeking a miracle?

Bo nodded, his mind still at a distance.

The sickness will take you into death soon.

He nodded again, thinking of the long line of people standing in the November rain, the hopelessness in his mind, the pain with him now.

I will help you if you do not betray me. Will you keep my secret?

Bo hardly understood the words, although they came into his mind as clearly as if carved in stone. He looked at the Beast uncomprehendingly and nodded. His choices had been narrowing in these last months, until now he had none.

We cannot stay in the open. Come with me.

There was a time of walking through the dark, following the creature that paced before him on all fours now like a lion or other big cat escaped from a zoo. But it was a sleek blue-gray, and its haunches moved so smoothly it seemed to glide rather than walk. Bo was aware that, although the creature did not turn its head, it kept him somehow in its perception, and in his mind he felt the inexplicable touch that he thought of as feminine, a comforting, like a smooth hand against his cheek.

The pain in his side was bad now. He had to limp, almost to cry out with the agony that spread across his abdomen. And then it became so intense, as it did sometimes, that he had to squat down on the sidewalk and hold himself. Hell, what did it matter, he thought, looking at the huge cat that had stopped to look back at him. Let it kill me, he thought, squeezing the flesh of his sides with both fists, wanting to cut himself in half, to leap into a river and drown.

A little farther and you may rest.

Bo nodded, walking on doubled over. His senses dimmed for a time until he felt the animal's paws helping him lie down in a musty place. It was mildew and rotten wood, a fetid smell, but one that had been rotten for so long, it was harmless, almost a smell of good, rich earth. He lay

24

on straw or dry grass in a cellar or barn, some stone enclosure that was very dark. He did not care.

November 6, 1937

Dear Mary Louise,

Don't worry about me. I'm alright and have found a wonderful doctor here who is helping me. I won't be home for a while, but I think I'm getting better. Tell Doctor Goodnaugh that I can't come to the hospital for the exploratory operation because I'm under another doctor's care here. He won't probably like that, but tell him anyway. And we'll pay his bill as soon as I get back. Tell him that, and it ought to keep him out of your hair. I went to the cemetery like I was going to, but it wasn't any great shakes. Just a lot of sick people, some of them sicker than me. I was really lucky to find this doctor that is treating me now because I feel lots better already. You can write me if you want in care of General Delivery, Revere, Mass.

Your husband,
Bo

November 12, 1937

Dear George,

Come home right now. Doctor Goodnaugh is furious and said he might even get the law on you for disobeying his orders. He said you shouldn't have gone out there to Boston and that your mind is going bad when you start thinking about miracles. He said only medical science can help you and if you don't come home you will be dead in a month. Oh George, please please please do what the Doctor says. You know you are really sick its not like measles or something and you're surely going to hurt yourself worse going to some quack we don't even know there in the East.

Please George. Oh now you've got me crying again and I didn't want to cry. George you are so mean to me I cannot ever believe it. Your mother used to tell me you were always selfish, and now you're doing it again even in your sickness when you should be more careful. You know how I worry about you anyway, and what is Kneipe's Jewelry

going to do without you? They called again yesterday,
I think it was Mr. Kneipe himself this time, and I
told them you were so sick you went to Boston to
see a specialist and weren't back yet.

Please George, come home.

Your loving wife,
Mary Louise Beaumont

The little room was always clammy, no matter how
much he used the bathroom heater he had bought to make
it warmer. The plaster walls seeped with moisture under-
neath the faded scrolls of wallpaper, and he could always
feel a draft from around the window sash. Outside, a few
flakes of snow whispered past the glass, and he could
sometimes see a bird sailing down the wind, heading in-
land. He was seated in the middle of the hooked rug that
was the room's one luxury, facing the east as he had been
told, his legs folded Indian style and his arms relaxed so
that his palms rested upward on his knees. He breathed in
slowly, feeling the air deep down behind his stomach,
slowly building like a clear, blue column of sky inside
him, cleanness inside him, he thought as he continued to
inhale until he felt his rib cage expanding to the sides and
the air filling him to the very top. A count of twelve, then
hold for twelve, then exhale slowly so that it was twelve
slow counts to get it all out again. Think of the middle of
your body, the Beast had said. Think of the blazing center
of life in the middle of your body. Bo tried to keep his
mind on his middle, trying to imagine a blazing fire right
at his navel. Sometimes, when his gut hurt so bad, it
wasn't hard to imagine it was a fire.

After he had finished and had lain back to rest, he
wobbled to his feet and sat on the sagging bed. It creaked
and swayed down under him like a hammock. Oh, God,
he felt worse, if anything. The pain was with him all the
time now, and his thirst was getting so bad he would
drink half a gallon of water without stopping, using a
quart milk bottle and filling it again and again until his
stomach felt bursting. He would walk gurgling around the
little room from door to window and back again, trying to
say the formulas the Beast had given him, trying to think
of them as real things, as he had been told. It sounded
like the Coué stuff. Every-day-in-every-way, and Coué
was dead. He said the lines aloud, trying to make them
clear, willing his body to listen: "This is my body. This is

26

myself. I want to be well. Love is my healer. Love is my spirit. I love my life."

He said them over the required number of times and stopped, panting from saying the brief lines forcefully and with proper emphasis. For a moment he felt tears behind his eyes as the pain surged back into his consciousness. It wasn't going to work, and he was going to die in this little furnished room in a strange city, tricked by some supernatural creature that was probably just a hallucination anyway. But he remembered the hypnotic words of the Beast: *You must not despair, for that is your death*. Bo sat up and began saying the ritual to combat despair: "Life comes first. Learn to live. Live forever."

The words were only sounds, but he felt some ebbing of the pain if he concentrated on them hard enough. He must have said them over for ten or fifteen minutes until they sounded like waves against a shore. As he concentrated, his breathing eased from its tight panting, and he felt the pain getting farther away. It was just as bad as ever, but it was not so close. Now he did not care so much. He kept saying the words until his throat was dry, and then he said them in his mind. Or, rather, he allowed them to go on in his mind, for they had established a sort of circular track that was almost musical, sailing around effortlessly, making a circle around him, a charm, inside which he sat, breathing easily, the pain held at a distance while he was safe.

On this Thanksgiving Day, George Beaumont, called Bo by his friends but not by his wife, sat on the sagging bed with its patchwork quilt made of the leftover lives of old ladies in cold parlors. He suffered from a metastasized cancer that an exploratory operation would have revealed as hopeless. The surgeon would have looked up from the opening, his hooded eyes would have met the eyes of George's doctor, Randolph Goodnaugh of Chicago, and the surgeon would have shaken his head and pointed one rubber-sheathed finger down at the abdominal cavity, now exposed. The other doctor (and two surgical nurses and six interns sitting above the operating theater) would look down at the white and gray nodules and strings of insane tissue that filled the patient's body. Dr. Goodnaugh would feel the dropping sensation he always felt when death stood near him and pointed with its bony finger, the sensation he had felt once when, standing at the edge of a high balcony, he had resisted the urge to jump. He would shake his head, now swathed in operating-room linen, look at his colleague and golfing friend with weary eyes (he was, after all eleven years the surgeon's senior) and then turn away. The surgeon would close up, being perhaps a bit less meticulous with the stitches than he might have been, might even allow an intern to suture, since it was all going to be undertaker's work soon anyhow. And another round would have been lost in the eternal battle of medical science with death.

George Beaumont sat on the bed, mumbling a string of words while his insides went crazy and the pain screamed at him and screamed at him and he managed for a time not to hear.

Then Bo felt suddenly free of pain. In a lightness inconceivable to a middle-aged man, somewhat overweight and big-boned anyway, with size thirteen shoes, he stood up in the center of that charmed circle of words. He stood up and found himself floating against the ceiling like a freed balloon, looking down on himself sitting on the patchwork quilt, himself sitting there saying some words over and over. Bo watched the man on the bed for a time before he realized he not only had stood up, he had floated up and was against the ceiling of the little room. There was a mild buzzing nearby, as if he were next to a beehive in summer, the buzzing getting deeper as it, or he, approached. The body on the bed grew smaller, farther away, the room elongating upward like an elevator, an elevator going up into the sky with Bo fastened to its underside and watching as the body on the bed got smaller and smaller. The buzzing roared around him now like a cataract. There came a lurch, as if he had been bumped by a moving vehicle. It did not hurt, but it sent him off into some strange direction, so that he was heading down into a dark place. And as he entered the darkness that was like a soft tunnel around him, that was like a soft black tubing that just fit his body, his own voice said, "Bo, you're dying."

The surge of fear he felt then added speed to his flight into the dark tube that stretched ahead of him as he sped along. The buzzing sound was left behind now, getting faint as his speed increased through the darkness. Was he going to hell? George Beaumont felt his past life, not seeing it exactly but feeling it as if it were somehow imprinted on his flesh. Scenes emerged full of sensation, smells, sounds, the very taste of pancakes in the morning at Uncle Day's farm, the smell of the first cow he milked, the feeling of the dive off a tree limb into the summer river, the crying out as he fell from the wagon and the wheel went hard over his arm and broke it, his mother lying in the white bed with her eyes darkening and her hand in his going suddenly not alive, and his father crying and stomping around the room, the kiss he felt with his whole body as Bunny Mecheam put her lips to his, the sound of the high-backed Oldsmobile and the feel of its leather seats as it ran grandly through the streets of Whitethorn and across the hump at the railroad tracks, how perfect and pure Mary Louise looked at the wedding, the work in jewelry, the casting, learning to cut precious metals, and the quick flashing scenes of his son, the pregnancy with Mary Louise wailing about death every day and lying always in her bed, how he hoped it would be a boy and it was, and the growing up, softball and flying kites in the valley by the old Duchesne farm, the face that was so like Bo's own that sometimes at night he would go in and look at his son asleep and think it was himself become twelve again, and still he could not say his son's name, even in his hurtling to death or hell, whatever it was, he could not say the name, as if that magic talisman kept the past somehow secure, prevented that last scene from appearing, the drowned face and his own screaming.

"Oh, Charles!" the scream extended ahead and behind his course through the tunnel like an explosion. He emerged into light so intense that it stunned him. He stopped suddenly, brightness around him like the inside of a star. The agony of his son's name vibrated away from him, radiating like heat from a cooling stone, and Bo felt a peacefulness beginning to replace the agony, a serenity that included all joy and all pain, all life and death, all beginnings and endings and the spaces of life in between so that peace filled all the corners of the universe and no event, no sickness, no tragedy or triumph could be other than peace-giving. He felt the nearness of God, as he came to rest in the presence of some Being, perhaps in the center of that Being who now understood so completely the processes of living and suffering and dying that it could instantly and for always supply all wants, answer all questions and doubts, reassure him for the whole agony of loss that is called living.

Bo felt the peaceful light surrounding him, and then, as the thought formed in his mind, the name of his son, which

he could never say in his life, came to his lips and he
spoke it, calmly this time. The brightness faded in front
of him and he saw the meadow where they had played
baseball, the elms and oaks on the far slope, the barn off
to the left and a few Holsteins standing near the fence
watching the man and the boy with wonder as they hit
the ball and caught it and ran.

But out of the brightness over them, whether it was
sunlight or the great Being who was Peace, came a com-
manding voice that spoke his name in a firm tone, from
a great distance but with a command like a gong sounding
for the final ceremony.

"George Beaumont."

Bo felt the pull on top of his head where the sun had
just been warm, where the sweat was mixed with his black
hair. The pull came from above and jerked him from the
meadow where Charles stood. Bo's last sight of his son was
the boy's face smiling, his arm waving, as if it were only
an interlude, as if Bo would be right back.

"George Beaumont!"

Bo felt the sucking back into the darkness, felt the pain
coming at him like a roaring, now thundering mass of
rock, like an avalanche of rock down from a cliff approaching him as he was pulled back through the dark, and
he tried to scream, but the wind was too great in his open
mouth, and then the darkness of the world again, what
seemed darkness after that supernal light he had visited,
his body on the bed swaying and saying words to itself.
The fall into weight again snatched him down into the
pain so that he screamed as he entered it, like falling into
scalding oil. He screamed, and it sounded in the little room
where a woman with short, dark hair and great frightened eyes was shaking him by the shoulder, screamed
"Noooooooooooooo!"

"George! Bo! Come back. Be here, now!"

The shaggy head of graying black hair bent over the
chest. His body shuddered, lips moving with sounds that
were no longer words. George Beaumont returned to his
life and the pain that twisted his hands into knots in the
flesh of his abdomen.

The woman, who was small and younger than he by
almost a generation, hugged his shoulders, stroked his
tear-streaked face, spoke words in his ear.

"It's despair, Bo," she said, rocking him back and forth

30

as she sat on the bed beside him. "You know despair is bad, and it will take you if you let it."

"I saw him."

"Yes, I know. Now come back and live again."

"We were there, in the pasture."

"You're not ready to die yet, Bo," she said, taking his face between her hands and forcing him to look at her eyes. She had large, luminous green eyes—her best feature, she had often been told.

"You're not ready to go yet, now are you?"

"I've got nothing to say about it," he said, clutching his pain to him. "This thing is going to kill me, and all the crazy exercises and not eating anything, and the magic words . . ." He paused, looked at the woman with rage building up in his face, twisting his mouth into a sneer. "All this . . . shit!" he spat out. "Get away and let me die."

"I won't," she said, her face frightened but her voice steady. "You're doing well, Bo, whether it feels like it or not. You're going to beat it, and it will never come back." She tried to pull the man's head to her shoulder, but he stubbornly resisted her and would not look at her face.

"Anger is good," she said, sitting back on the ragged quilt. "It has energy, and that's what you need."

"What do you care," he said, his mouth still held tight. "What the hell is it to you?"

"Life is good, and we have to live it all we can," she said.

"You keep coming here and checking on me, bringing me that goat food I have to eat." He looked at her as his pain ebbed for a time. He seemed to be trying to see beneath her skin. "I don't even know your name."

"Now, that's better," she said, smiling so that her face fairly radiated. One might have said that, even more than her eyes, her smile was the best part of her visible personality. "My name's Lilliam, with an *m* at the end, and people who like me and who I like can call me Lilly."

Bo grinned now in spite of himself. Her smile was so happy.

"Well, I'd like for you to tell me if that animal, that thing I made a deal with, is all in my mind. You know what I mean?" He felt embarrassed even mentioning it, but she had to have some connection with it.

"Oh, now you're worried about going crazy. It's real. I know her very well, and she's got your best interests at heart. She really likes people, you know." Lilly had slipped from the bed and was taking things from a string bag she had put down on the rickety pine table beside the hot plate.

"She? It's a female? What kind of thing is it? I thought it was a lion escaped from a zoo, but I never saw a blue lion, and it puts words into your mind."

"I don't really know much about her," Lilly said. She turned to Bo with a small bag in her hand. "You're going to like this. It's wheat germ."

"I'm hungry all right, but not for that junk," Bo said, looking at the bag she had given him. He opened it and poked into the grains with a tentative finger. "This's nothing but bread crumbs. How can I get well eating like a mouse?"

"You're not going to eat much of it, you know," Lilly said, stirring a bit of milk and what looked like flour into a pan.

Bo got up and walked over to the table. He was a foot taller than the woman and, although he had lost fifty pounds in the last few weeks, was probably still sixty or seventy pounds heavier. Standing beside her as she mixed a white powder into the milk, he felt protective toward her; but there was something about her that was very strong, too, something he could sense. Bo wondered if anyone had ever tried to get funny with her. She might know some secret technique or a magic word that would really wreck a man who did that. She had a—what could he call it—a way about her, a presence, as if she was so certain who she was that no one and nothing could ever harm her. He also liked her looks when he had leisure from the pain to think about it. She wasn't pretty, really, but she was fetching in a way he could not recall seeing in a long time.

"What's that stuff now?"

"It's not ready yet," she said, smiling as she saw his nose wrinkling with disgust at the smell. "But it's going to be yoghurt."

"Ye gods," Bo said. He liked standing beside her. "You already got me doing Yoga and now I have to eat yoghurt too." He laughed briefly and was rewarded by a dazzling smile from Lilly.

"But you can't have much."

"Yeah, I know. We're talking to my body, right?"

"That's right, sending messages it can understand. No

more cigarettes or cigars or pipes, no more coffee or alcohol, no more meat and, especially, no salted meat." She made a face that Bo thought with some surprise only made her cuter.

He went back to the bed and sat down, feeling exhausted. He found himself watching the slender, small woman as she worked to prepare his meal and set the yoghurt aside to work. If it wasn't that he was feeling so punk, he would actually be attracted to Lilly. He felt a faint stir of attention somewhere far down and turned his mind away quickly. Jesus! Here he was, a dying man, and thinking about doing it to his nurse. He looked up, surprised, as she sat beside him with a plate in her hand. He looked for an instant like a guilty child.

"This is very good soup," she said, catching the look on his face but putting it aside to think about later. "It has lentils and other good messages for your poor body."

"As usual, there isn't much of it."

"Enough for now."

He ate the soup willingly enough, thankful that the pain was gone so he could enjoy it. The soup was just warm, not hot, and it tasted like soybeans and needed salt, but he knew he couldn't have salt, either. There was no more than a cupful altogether and it was soon gone.

"That must have been a telegraph message," Lilly said. "It went so fast."

"You don't have to treat me like a little kid," Bo said, wiping his mouth on his handkerchief.

When the woman was silent, he felt he had to say something else.

"I feel better this afternoon—now, I mean." He was afraid as he said it, afraid the pain would begin again. He knew it would, that this was only a short vacation during which the world seemed real again and there were other things than his wretched, dying guts.

"You've been getting better right along," Lilly said quietly. "But"—and she paused and looked at him with such open sympathy that he almost reached over to touch her—"there's still a long way to go."

"I just want to know if you think I'm going to make it?"

"I'm sure of it. But it's all got to be gone through if you are to live right afterwards." He would remember the compassion on her face as she said that, remember it when the pain was so intense he was sure he would die.

"Times like this, I mean, like now when I haven't got the pain, I feel like it might really be true," he said, and in his voice he heard himself that undertone of childish fear. That was why she treated him like a kid. He felt like one, like a poor little kid with a bad pain wanting his mommy to make it well. He decided he would try to get rid of that tone.

"What about you, Lilly?" It was the first time he had said her name, and it sounded strange and exotic to his own ears. "What do you do to stay on the sunny side of the street?"

"Oh I'm just another working girl," she said lightly, happy that his voice had lost its fear for a while. "I take a streetcar downtown every day and put books together. I work in a printing plant."

"You have a family, I guess," he said, trying to remember if she wore a wedding ring. He hadn't noticed, and now she had her hands in her lap and he couldn't see her left ring-finger.

"I live with my folks," she said, and stopped, as if there were something further she did not care to say.

"Your parents, father and mother?"

"You're very curious for a sick man."

"I didn't mean to get personal. I haven't got any right to pry."

"That's all right, Bo. I call them my folks. Actually, they're my very good friends, Dan and Polly Carruthers. My parents are dead."

"You got a boyfriend, I bet."

"Oh, there are men who ask me out once in a while. I'm not a wallflower."

He wanted to go on with the questioning, wanted to ask her more about the boyfriends, but he caught himself. He was acting like a man half his age, for crissake. What about his own Mary Louise back in Whitethorn, taking care of the house and the bills on his savings, trying to make ends meet and not knowing what was going on or where he was even. He felt a pang of remorse about his wife. She had always tried so hard, and . . . the death had been hard on her, too, harder since she couldn't have any more kids. He guessed she couldn't have any, but that had been pretty much a dumb question for the past few years, since they didn't even try much anymore.

"Are you feeling okay?" Lilly asked, looking at him closely.

"Just thinking about home," Bo said, and at that moment he felt the faintest creeping in of sensation in his side and knew the pain was coming back. He lay back on the bed, his hands pressed to his stomach, ready for it to begin again.

"I don't guess you could get hold of some aspirin or something," he said, his eyes closed.

"I'm sorry, Bo." Lilly's voice came to him out of the darkness of his closed eyes. "If we're going to win, we've got to do it alone."

"I thought probably that was it."

He was startled by a cool, soft hand on his cheek. "Now, Bo, here's a thing our animal friend told me you should do when the pain gets bad." Lilly's voice went on softly as she stroked his forehead, and although the pain returned inexorably as she spoke, it had that distant quality again, as if her voice were somehow shielding him from its full impact. He was paying close attention to her words, as he always did when she gave him instructions, but he seemed to be listening without trying, with his whole self rather than with just his ears and mind.

". . . stretch the stomach out, you see, by bending back in that position I showed you a couple of days ago. And then you breathe in the short way, always through the nose, never through the mouth, ten breaths, then you come up to sitting again. Got that?"

He nodded, grateful for her voice, her interest in him, her certainty around him when he himself was so uncertain that he might die just from being uncertain.

"And you will do the chants, as you have done before," she said, her soft voice almost lulling him totally away from the pain. "But . . ." and here she reached her other hand to take his face in both her hands so that he opened his eyes and looked at her. She was very close to him. He could feel her breath and smell how nice it was. The pain was far back, but still there. ". . . if you leave your body again, Bo," she said, very serious now and intent, looking with her deep green eyes directly into his so that he felt faint, "then you must say your own name and come back." She shook his face lightly between her hands. "You must come back. It's not bad to leave it for a time, but you must come back right away."

"I thought that was a dream," Bo said, his voice weak.

"It was real enough," Lilly said, sitting back with her hands again in her lap. "But it's not time for you to go

35

yet, and in your condition you might just make it across that way and not be able to get back."

The pain surged into his guts again as he thought of that dream, what he had thought was a dream, his son in the meadow, the peace.

"I wanted to stay."

"You can't go that way," Lilly said, her face all serious now.

"If I die, then will I go there?"

She was silent so long that he grew afraid: afraid that there was nowhere like that, that his boy was gone and he himself would only go into the empty grave and be like a candle that is blown out, nothing more. The pain was bad.

"I don't know about that," she said, finally. "But I do know that if it isn't your time, if you can make it but you give up, I know that's bad. I don't know any more than that."

"Even if it's terrible?" He felt tears squeezing out of his eyes in spite of himself. He didn't want her to see him cry, although he cried a lot when he was alone.

"It's going to be better soon, Bo," she said positively. "I'm going to make it a little better right now."

"How can you do that?"

"It's a trick, and it's not good to use it all the time, but we need something right now to help." She looked into his eyes. "Just listen and trust me."

"I do," he said, and it was true.

"Close your eyes and relax. Let the pain have you, let it have you, you can move away from it for a time. That's right. Now let your hands go loose, that's right."

She talked to him, just talked for a few minutes, and the pain got off to a distance, sending him messages like crazy; but now he had time to decipher them instead of just getting torn up about the way they were written. The pain became like a long paper tape, like the ticker tapes they showed the big stock market boys reading before they jumped out their office windows. He could take the pain in his hands now like a long white tape and read what it said, or, rather, could almost read it. There were words there, some of them in red and some in what looked like a foreign language. They were more than print on paper. They rose up off the paper and flew toward his eyes as he tried to read them. They were flying into his eyes before he could make out what they said, but then he realized

36

they were flying into his mind directly so that he could read them there, and while he was trying to put them back in order so they would make sense there in the big red room of his brain, he fell asleep.

After a long time he dreamed, as he often did, that the Beast came again. She was looking down at him with her big green eyes, and there was such compassion in those eyes that Bo imagined it must have something to do with love. But then the Beast raised one huge paw that had almost human fingers but also long ivory claws and, with one swift downward stroke, plunged the claws into Bo's stomach. He tried to scream, thrashing about to keep the terrible claws from tearing into him, but he could not get away. And then he watched quietly as the claws sank into his body. What he felt then came not from the claws but from the pulling away as the pain itself tore loose. It flowed up into those ivory channels that grew a clear, translucent red as the pain seeped up into them, out of his body and into the blue-gray arm.

The Beast seemed to be smiling.

Will he remember this?
As a dream only. You have done well.
He almost died today.
He still wants to die with part of himself, but now he will be better.

I find the human will, unlike my own, is capable of turning upon itself, a strange act that I cannot entirely understand. The man who lies on the bed as I assist in his healing watches me with blank eyes. He has been acting out his sorrow, and his will is so strong it has transformed his body into this artifact of grief. I have learned to care for these creatures. They have, in their madness, that quality I need for my life.

I leave the sick man's room, treading lightly down through Mrs. Peavey's house in the early morning hours. Lilly is asleep now. I will have a run to refresh myself and neutralize the poison I have taken in. The streets are lit at distant intervals, and the houses are dark along my way to the beach. I smell the ocean, its fecundity and exciting battles. Salt spray lightly coats my fur as I pace along the rocks looking for a way down to the water. The surf is quiet tonight, low rollers breaking far out in the bay as I reach the dark sand and feel the dampness that prickles my fur and excites me. I will swim. I run fast along the shallows, splashing a long line of spray behind me, dive into the cold rush and swim out into the bay. The water submerges my ears momentarily, and I hear the creatures swimming, scuttling, writhing in the water around me. My spatial sense reaches below, and I feel the sandy bottom and the life there with a brilliance that is pleasure over my whole skin. I am complete, delighted with my muscular body that surges through the freezing element. I feel about in the dark water for something more substantial than the shellfish I could scoop up or the somnolent flounders in the sand. It enters the sphere of my spatial sense like a palpable shadow, lazily casting about for its own late-night snacks close to shore, a thick-bodied fish half as long as I am. I tread the cold water in slow time with the fish's own movements, feeling out with my mind to touch that cold, intent brain, listening to it with my own. I have for a long time lacked singleness of will that would bring the fish helplessly to my jaws, but I can feel its intentions by relaxing into its mode of being. I tread lightly, just enough to keep my nose above the low waves and follow the fish as it moves in near the bottom. Now it is swimming just beneath me, and I turn to follow it to more shallow water. It seems unaware of me. I feel its mind that is like a cold, carven jewel giving off a single ray of intelligence: the endless search to fill the jaws.

Now I can feel it sensing the shallows and about to turn. As it swings back I move so that it will pass under me and wait, swaying upward with each incoming wave. I feel the smooth rounded body coming so close under me that my hackles rise with pleasure and—now! I dive and snatch it cleanly with both sets of foreclaws, digging deeply into its solid flesh as it gives a mighty heave and pulls me under. I go with the big fish, letting it drag me to the bottom and there put all four sets of claws into the thing and give it a quick bite behind the head.

Leaving the water, I carry my head high, the weight of the big fish coming onto my neck muscles as I splash out of the surf. I do not like sandy fish, so I carry it up instead of dragging it until I get to the rocks. There I drop it and give a couple of good, satisfying shakes so that the saltwater flies around me. The fish is firm and cold on the outside, warm and bloody on the inside. It is so good I have to pause and dance around it several times after taking bites. At one point I lie on my back, holding the fish

38

with all four paws and gnawing it as a human child sucks its bottle.

After my meal I clean myself thoroughly and feel utterly washed free of my night's work with the sick man. There is no danger to myself in healing sick humans as long as I do not take in their wretched emotional twists by mistake. The physical poisons are easily overcome by a few hours of simply enjoying my own existence.

Later, on my way back along the beach toward the town, I feel a pulling sensation, as if something inside me were tied by a long cord to a distant object that moves away. It is like the pull I sometimes feel from one of my former Persons who again wants to come awake but cannot rise enough to speak. I pause and search in that emptiness where my Persons still wait—all but the youngest, who has passed on to her own destiny. But none of them is aware. They wait, held in my necessity, and do not speak. The pull is from something in the near future, something coming that is even now altering my next days and nights. But I cannot tell yet what it will be, and it does not feel dangerous.

I roll in the sand to shut out the strangeness and become whole again. The grains get all the way down to my skin, feeling itchy and good. I roll, kicking my legs and twisting my head like a cub, then stand up and shake, whirling the grains in all directions. Whatever is coming will announce itself in time. To the east, out over the ocean, I see the sky beginning to pale. I turn back toward the town.

Chapter Three

Barry drove over to Rio Grande Boulevard and turned left. He would pick up Johnny Strong Horse at a cousin's house in Alameda, and they would take route 44 up toward Jemez. The day was bright blue and clear as usual, but there was an ominous haze high up in the eastern part of the sky, a faint yellowness that stained the northeastern sky above the Sandias. Damn dust storm coming, he thought, and felt a drop in his spirits. If it's a bad one, we'll have a time getting there.

The address in Alameda was a little, square adobe hut, unplastered, with crooked vigas sticking out over the front door and single window, looking as if it were slowly dissolving back into the caliche clay from which it was made. A rickety screen door opened and Johnny stepped out, black cowboy hat in his hand, blue shirt, Levi's and a single band of scarlet around his head to hold the hair back. Very Navajo-looking today. He might be any Injun on the reservation, Barry thought, looking at the high squared-off cheekbones, the impassive, wide mouth, the dark eyes that were expressionless at the moment. Johnny tossed an old wicker suitcase into the back seat and got in.

"Dust comin'," he said, glancing at the sky.

"It'll be at our back, I hope," Barry said, pulling out onto US 85 and heading north. They turned left at the Coronado sign onto the lumpy, tarred New Mexico 44 that led off northwest toward the dark blue mounds of the Jemez mountains. A low mass of cloud blended in with the mountains and made it impossible to tell where earth stopped and sky began. Barry settled down for the long trip, trying to keep the speed around thirty-five but finding that somewhat slower was more comfortable on

40

the wretched road. They traveled in silence for a few miles as the road gradually angled more and more north until they were quartering the approaching yellow cloud, which was now clearly visible as a gigantic standing wall of dust reaching up for miles into the clear morning air.

"Doesn't seem to be much wind this morning," Barry shouted over the noise of the car and the open windows. "Wonder what's carrying that dust storm along?"

"Texas real estate men," Johnny said, looking up at the advancing wall of yellowish dark that was closing off the morning sun. "It gets raised up over there in Texas, Oklahoma, and maybe the wind is all up high. Sometimes it comes with no wind at all, just like a big piece of hide being pulled across the top of a drum."

"We got a dust bowl of our own here," Barry said, making conversation.

"We had one here a long time before the Okies got it," the Indian said.

The morning was turning yellow, filtered through the cloud that stretched over half the sky now, and Barry thought regretfully of the beautiful morning they had started out in, ruined now. Well . . . he gritted his teeth and then grinned. They would be plenty gritty soon.

They had been bumping along for less than an hour when the first dust began settling out, flying in the windows in stinging handfuls that made them roll up the windows and close the windshield that Barry had cracked open for the breeze on his face. Breathing became a distasteful chore, each breath smelling of dryness and dirt, seeming to have less air in it than it should. And with the windows rolled up the heat became oppressive, so they cracked them open and more dust swirled in. They both began coughing. Visibility closed down as the main part of the cloud rolled over them, the blue sky entirely gone now, and the world around them narrowed into a miserable few yards of desert and rocks and scrub pines. The closed-in landscape moved by them more and more slowly as Barry had to shift down, unable to see more than a hundred yards, then fifty, then less in the yellowish gloom. He shifted again, cursing.

"Patience, my friend," Johnny said with a smile. He pulled a big blue bandana out of his pocket and offered it to Barry. "Here, want me to tie it around your face? Keep out some of the dirt."

Barry glanced at the Indian's impassive face, thought

of the dust gathering up his nose and down his throat and in his eyes. "What we need is a couple of divers' helmets," he said. He grinned. "Yeah, tie it on, Jesse, and we'll take that express car."

After the smooth brown fingers had tied on the bandana, Barry felt better, more adapted. He looked over at Johnny, who had produced a white cloth and was tying it on his own face.

"I see you came prepared for this," Barry said. "I wish I had thought of it, but we haven't seen many dust storms in the time we've been here."

He caught Johnny's rather strange look, a look held too long, so that he finally turned his head. They did look like bandits, he thought, glancing in the rearview mirror.

"We had plenty of dust couple years ago," Johnny said, with the same inquisitive look at Barry. "You remember."

For a couple of minutes, Barry was so intent on negotiating a series of curves on the old road that he did not catch the full meaning of the last words. And then it struck him. A couple of years ago, before he was even on the earth? Was this another person who had known him before the Beast had taken him over? He knew, or he wanted to believe, that Barry Golden had not suddenly come into existence one warm June night in Michigan two years ago. He looked over at Johnny to see if he could jog some memory. Had he known the Indian before? He had not been able to verify his existence since last summer, when it all came together, when it had seemed possible to become a being separate from his Beast. The man was about his own age, he thought, but then he didn't even know how old he was.

"Goddamn! Watch it!"

The horsemen appeared as suddenly as if they had been dropped out of the dust cloud above them, and Barry, lost in his thoughts at just the wrong moment, had almost smashed into them. He swung the wheel hard, too far and too hard, so they missed the rear end of one horse by inches but skidded across the humped tar road sideways and almost turned over as their wheels hit sideways in the soft sand. Barry had swung back hard, and the wheels grabbed and straightened. In three seconds it was all over, and they were back on the right side of the road again.

"You get bumped in that mess-up of mine?" Barry asked.

"No, I hung on. But I sure thought we were going to be up that horse's ass."

"I'm sorry. Got to quit thinkin' while I'm driving." The question could be put off until later, he decided, squinting through the dust.

It was well after noon when they entered the more difficult road that wound through the Jemez mountains, and Barry decided they might as well stop for lunch without trying to get to Cuba. Probably what he had in the hamper was better than anything they could get in the little mountain town anyway. He would have liked a beer to unclog his pipes, though.

They pulled off at a wide place in the road and Barry got the hamper out of the back seat. The two men walked a ways off the road and sat down among granite boulders and piñon bushes. In the hamper were ham and cheese sandwiches, fried chicken pieces wrapped in waxed paper, potato salad and coleslaw, homemade biscuits, cheese, apples, oranges, bananas, Cokes and a quart thermos of coffee, along with little extra touches like salt and pepper shakers and napkins.

Johnny grinned, looking into the hamper. "You got a first-rate squaw there, friend."

They ate the chicken, gritty with dust but delicious, and washed it down with coffee with cream and sugar hot from the thermos. Up in the mountains the air was not as warm as it had been in town, and Barry thought if it were just a clear day they probably could have seen the Rio Grande valley from this spot. The dust continued as a windless haze, thinning now somewhat but still pervasive, so their shirts and shoes and eyes were all packed with it, and when Barry put a finger in his ear to scratch it, he found a drift of fine dust there, too.

As they started up again, it seemed darker than it had been, although Barry's watch showed only two o'clock in the afternoon. Johnny said it was either another duster on top of this one and they'd get some wind pretty soon, or it was going to rain.

"All this dirt and it's going to rain?" Barry said incredulously.

As if to answer his question, a deep-throated bark of thunder sounded out of the hills around them just as they came around a bend and found themselves in the little town of Cuba. They gassed up the car and had a beer in a rickety barroom decorated with antlers and dusty fish on plaques. On the road again, the rain was falling heavily so that dust turned to mud and visibility was reduced again in the murky darkness that the afternoon had become.

"Just what we need," Barry said, peering through the mixture of yellow mud and water that streaked the windshield. "A shit storm."

"Clean up the air, anyway," Johnny said.

And eventually it did. They had run on out of the mountains, coming to flatter and clearer land where the trees got small again and the road took longer hills and curves and fewer tight little turns around giant boulders. About six in the evening, the sun appeared from behind great masses of dirt-colored cloud and the land emerged in long vistas of down-sloping mesa and valley. They were nearing Farmington, and the air was almost clear again. It seemed they had been traveling through a strange other world where the atmosphere and the planet had not been clearly separated. Now the westering sun cleaned everything, and the blue sky came back out of the east. It felt as though they had made a long journey through a dark and miserable tunnel to emerge into this bright, sweeping world of towering clouds and long miles of valley and watercourse lined with trees.

"We turn off to the left at the bottom of this hill," Johnny said. "It's a long pull over a horsetrack 'til we get to Yellow Mesa. We might could stop once we get across the north-south highway."

"Suits me," Barry said. "I'm pooped out from looking through a mile of 'dobe dirt to see the damn road."

West of Farmington, the land turns bald and empty again, a desert of rock and ledge with a few trees huddled around the widely scattered damp spots, but the scenery is terrific. Barry stood in the early-morning clearness, his blanket still wrapped around him, and looked north to Shiprock mountain, which gave the area its name. It did indeed look like an old fashioned battleship, frozen for eternity in a stony sea.

"Do your people see that as a holy mountain?"

"Every mountain has something holy about it," Johnny said, throwing his blanket into the back seat of the car. "But yeah, that's one of our big medicine places."

"You aren't as sarcastic as that around home, are you?"

"I'm not sarcastic now," the Indian said. "You're taking it that way."

"I mean, you do still feel the holy places have something real, something important about them?"

"I never thought otherwise."

"Well, Johnny, sometimes you talk like a person who has left the tribe, and sometimes you sound fully Indian. It's hard to know which guy I'm talking to."

"It's true, I get more Indian as I get back into home country, but I'll always be Navajo, and that's all there is to that."

The road to Yellow Mesa wound upward through every kind of country Barry had ever seen in the Southwest and some he had never thought he would see anywhere. For a while it was rocky, with ledges sticking out of the road, if it could be called a road when it was so much like the landscape around it that Barry didn't know if he was on it or off it or had lost it miles back. And then it angled downward gradually for miles, coming out into a dry wash valley in which there were cottonwoods, willows, piñons and cedar; there might be a group of hogans and summer shelters along the streambed where a trickle of muddy water still ran from last night's rain. Then the road would wind past the end of a volcanic mesa with its rubble of black and yellow stones that looked like sponges, and it would angle upward again until they were in high hills of cedar and pine and vistas of distant blue mountains on every side. They were on a down slope approaching flat land with evenly spaced tufts of coarse grass and yucca when Johnny noted they had passed over into Arizona.

"We on the reservation now?" Barry asked.

"We've been on it since yesterday afternoon."

Barry wondered at the vast empty spaces, where the sheep could find to graze, how the people—any people— could make a living in this emptiness.

They entered an area of greenish blue dirt that swirled up around the car wheels so they had to close the windows again. The ground had turned a poisonous yellow color that looked as if it had been boiled and a sour crust allowed to form on top. They rode through this cracked desert for several miles where not even cactus would grow, looking at the seared hills and empty arroyos before the track climbed out again onto an upland that stretched for miles with the flat-topped mesas off in the distance. Johnny pointed ahead and to the left at one far-off mesa that seemed lower than the ones around it.

"Yellow Mesa," he said.

It seemed to take them longer after they got within sight of their goal than before they had seen it. The mesa would disappear as they drove down into a hidden valley, and at times it would be lost among the other mesas so that the angle changed and Barry could not have said which of them it was. Certainly at this distance it appeared no more yellow than the rest of them. And then, coming around and out of a wash, they caught sight of a building about half a mile ahead, a genuine pitched-roof building with trees around it and a corral behind it.

"Tumbling Rock trading post," Johnny said, grinning. "Now you'll see some Trading-Post Indians."

As they came to a halt in a swirl of dust in front of the cement-block building, Barry saw about a dozen Indians, most of them male, young and old, lounging along the length of the building. They all seemed interested in the car but said nothing until Johnny got out, took his hat off and rubbed the sweat out of the band. A couple of them waved their hands and grinned.

"*Yahtahay,*" Johnny said. And they answered almost gleefully, it seemed to Barry.

"*Yahtahay,*" and one said a few more things in a language full of unexpected sounds. Johnny walked over to a couple of young men leaning against a hitch rack where a horse harnessed to a wagon was tied. He spoke with them for a minute and came back to where Barry was emptying a water bag into the steaming radiator of the Model A.

"I hope they've got water here," Barry said, flopping the empty bag against his leg.

"Yeah," Johnny said. "Over between the house and corral there's a pump that works once in a while." He stood awkwardly between Barry and the Indians, looking as if he wanted to say something that he was embarrassed about. "We better pick up some more grub here, too."

"Why? We're almost there, aren't we?" Barry said, somewhat impatiently.

"That's true. Yellow Mesa is only a few more miles, but my family are all moved to summer range now, I just heard. There's nobody at the Mesa camp."

"Gone?" Barry said, tired and thinking of some insane migration that came over the Indians in the spring. "Gone where? Where could they go in this place?" He had almost said, "Godforsaken."

"Not really so far, but it could be one of two places and

46

I'm not sure which one they went to. I'm betting on *tsay-ih*, though."

"They just picked up and left?"

Johnny grinned. "They do it every year."

The inside of the trading post was as rough as the exterior: uneven plank floor; several counters, worn smooth along all the edges from people lounging against them as a few of the men and women were doing; buckets, trace chains, harness, horsecollars, lanterns, pots and pans hung from the overhead beams; on the walls were several large sheepskins stretched out. Behind the main counter hung a tawny hide that must once have held a cougar together. One woman sat on the floor against the wall rocking a fussy baby in her arms and crooning a lullaby. In spite of the warmth of the day, all the women Barry saw wore the store-bought blankets around their shoulders. He wondered why they wore the cheap ones when they made such beautiful blankets themselves, but he forgot to ask.

They bought a few supplies and some small gifts for Johnny's family from the trader, a short, grizzled man who spoke as little as did his dark, blanket-wrapped customers. Most of the Indians seemed as if they had just waked up and found themselves in the store, with no more idea why they were there than if they had been dropped into a grocery store on Mars. Barry watched them as Johnny picked out candy and some toys he knew would go well with the children. When they had climbed back into the car and bounced on their way again, Barry asked, "What are they doing there? Most of those people looked like they didn't want to buy anything anyway."

"Oh, they buy things, all right. They spend all their cash money, usually. But it's bad form to let the store-keeper think anything he has is at all interesting." Johnny smiled. "You ought to be there when one of my mothers gets to bargaining over a rug *she's* selling. Then you'll hear something interesting."

"*One* of your mothers?"

"Sorry. That doesn't make sense to you, does it? Well, it's like saying 'one of my female relatives on my mother's side,' and there's no word for it except aunt, and that's not right, either. So I said it that way."

"Hey, now that everyone's left home for the summer, where are we going?"

"Let's try *tsay-ih,* the north canyon, and hope I'm right.

If I'm not, it's only a few miles back to where they'll be, and we'll make it by tonight whatever the case."

He looked out over the land to the left of the road. "See that big juniper by itself?" He pointed to a small tree that was notable because it was the only tree for miles. It looked to be about a quarter of a mile away. "There's a road off to the left there. Not a road, really, but it's not too bad."

"Not too goddamned good, either," Barry said a few minutes later after they had rumbled down stone ledges and through sand-filled washes and even over the remains of a brush corral that suddenly appeared in their way.

"Well, it's not so bad on a horse." Johnny grinned, holding on to his hat as the car gave a mighty buck over a boulder.

Once they pulled carefully around a horse and wagon, the wagon incredibly holding together through the teeth-rattling journey over the stone outcroppings. The man and woman and the four children all waved, and Johnny shouted a few words of Navajo.

When they got into an area of junipers and stunted pines, they stopped to eat dried meat and canned fruit and some of the cheese that was left in the hamper. It was getting on toward evening again, and still the land went on, the mountains getting bluer and more distant as the sun slid down the sky, and still no sign of human habitation. Barry was beginning to feel disheartened as the Model A reluctantly climbed a long rocky slope when Johnny put a hand on his arm.

"Go slow here," he shouted above the roaring of the motor. "And watch."

Barry allowed the car to slow but shifted down and kept grinding up the slope until they had come to a flattened-out place, and then he almost threw them both through the windshield, jamming the brake down with both feet, killing the engine and grabbing wildly for the nickel-plated emergency brake in the middle of the floorboards. They rocked to a stop some five or six feet from a yawning chasm in the earth.

"Jeezus!" Barry said, his shaking hand still on the pulled-back emergency brake. "When you say slow, you mean stop."

"White man take life too fast," Johnny said, grinning. "Welcome to *tsay-ih*, or, as you call it, Canyon de Chelly."

"Wow, what a welcome," Barry said, getting out of the car and walking around to make his legs stop quivering.

The chasm opened out into a steep-sided canyon with a green valley at its bottom almost a thousand feet below. The road that was not a road at all but a horse trail simply stopped at the edge of the canyon and a faintly discernible track led off to the left and disappeared down a narrow passage between two sandstone buttes. Barry stood in awe, looking into this perfect gem of a valley, with trees green and lovely in its depths, some fields of grain already sprouting and a flock of sheep coming back from downstream for the night. The huge, bellied-out sandstone cliffs were reddened with the lowering sun. They hung protectively over the settlement he could see on the valley floor, the little brushy shelters and a few permanent hogans spaced back from the stream. The last sunlight had left the canyon floor now and glared brilliantly on the eastern cliffs.

"Pretty, huh?" Johnny said, picking his suitcase out of the back seat.

"Does the rest of the world know about this?"

"Yeah, but they don't like the road," Johnny grinned. "But there are forest service people down at Chinle. They take a few tourists around the lower end of the canyon, but they seldom bring anybody up this far."

They shouldered the stuff that had to be carried and left the Model A where it sat. From the trail below it appeared to be a flat-faced little blackbird, spouting steam, ready to leap into space and flap its fenders across the canyon. The trail was beautiful in itself, Barry thought, stepping down the gentle slope that wound back and forth between hummocks of rock and little pinnacles of volcanic basalt. They walked down out of sunlight into the reflected brilliance from that great spinnaker of stone that swooped out from the other side. As they emerged on the last slope before the valley floor, Barry looked up at that ruddy cliff with the long curving black streaks showing its outward bulge over the valley, and he felt that washing away of discontent, that loosening of the worried mind, that total agreement with our own selves that we call a religious feeling. He stopped and stood, the suitcase and hamper hanging in his hands, just looking at the cliff. Down in the valley the sunlight had been drawn upward for the night to leave a softening of shadows over the willows that bent slightly in the breeze, and from somewhere in the canyon he began to hear the sounds: first was the regular stroke of an ax far away, and then there was a song, the words high and drifting in the breeze, words in an unknown language but speaking an unmistakable joy in life. He stood and held the weight of his baggage, looking at the valley and listening, the cool wind of the approaching evening running over his skin, and he wanted it. He could not have said what it was he wanted. Not the Indian way, the savage life, not just the startling and isolated setting, but the combination of the long journey, the trail down, the evening sun lifting its colors up the cliffs, the long floating music drifting up the valley. He listened to the song, clear and joyful as a hymn sung by a single angel, like a lark at heaven's gate.

Chapter Four

Two weeks before Christmas the wind from the north-east stopped and the sky bloomed with cumulus against a pure summery blue. Bo walked out under the empty trees just to breathe the air. It was like spring again in the little square park with the statue of Paul Revere in the center. Feeling convalescent and new as a wet butterfly, Bo sat on an iron bench and watched the armadas of cloud sail away into the north. They were like ships, he thought, and his mind relaxed with comfortable fantasies of cloud sailors and fishermen in misty rigging. He felt good again. After so long being in pain or expecting it and thinking of the imminent destruction of his life, Bo felt ecstatic in a quiet way just to be sitting in the sun and breathing. He thought languidly of a cat sitting in the sun with its toes tucked under and its tail wrapped around. A blessing, that's what it is; a blessing just to be alive.

"You're very good at following the doctor's orders, Bo," the familiar voice said. He turned his eyes, which were dazed from looking at the sky.

"Your orders are easy to follow, Lilly." Looking at her smile was better than a whole month of June. "Sit down, take a load off," he said, feeling sheepish and rather shy.

"I've got a present, a special treat," she said, pulling at something in her coat pocket. She brought out a lovely red apple, a Washington Delicious that made Bo's cheeks suddenly smart with saliva. He hadn't eaten real food, he thought, for a month, at least.

"You wouldn't be kidding. I can really eat it, the whole thing?"

Lilly laughed and held the apple by its stem before the older man's face. "Can I tempt you, dear Adam?" She did a little dance step and then sat beside him still holding the apple.

"You sure can," he said, taking the apple and turning it over a couple of times. When he took the first crunching, delicious bite, he thought he had never tasted anything so heavenly. It brought back a scene from years ago when he had been working at a resort in Wisconsin and had led a troop of young campers back from a too-long hike. The apple was the duplicate of the one he had grabbed from the mess-hall table that hot afternoon. Strange how vivid such memories were, he thought, greedily biting again into the apple, how everything came back as if it had been stored there just for that purpose.

"Goodness," Lilly said, watching his progress. "I'm afraid when you finish that poor apple you'll begin on me. Such an appetite."

"You'd be hungry, too," he said, sucking back the juice, "if you'd been eating no more than enough to keep a sick rabbit alive for a month or more."

But as he finished it, he wondered if the pain would begin, as it had so often whenever he ate anything. It still grabbed him sometimes, though at longer intervals in the past week. Lilly could evidently see the concern on his face.

"I think it'll be okay," she said, wiping at a spot of juice on his chin with her handkerchief. "But you *are* messy."

"I still can't believe it," he said, sitting back and putting one arm along the back of the bench behind her. "And what am I going to do? I can't just stay here."

"Would you like to go into Boston, see Paul Revere's house?" Lilly said, seeming to misunderstand.

"No, I mean I just got to thinking again about home and my wife." He felt ashamed for some reason to mention Mary Louise, as if he were being unappreciative, or even a traitor.

"Oh, yes, I knew what you meant," she said, her eyes cast down now. "Bo, I'm afraid you'll misunderstand what I'm going to say now."

He felt a sudden weakness in his guts and tensed himself for the pain. But it was only some unfamiliar emotion making his stomach feel butterflies. He could not have said why he felt that way, but an image he didn't understand flashed into his mind: a shy young boy being cajoled by a loving older woman.

"I want you to"—the young woman paused, feeling for

52

words—"to not go home for a while." She looked up at the man's face. "I want you to stay here with me."

Their eyes met then, and the two people on the park bench saw something in each other that made them both look away at the same instant.

"You mustn't misunderstand, Bo," she said. *"She* wants you to stay until you are really cured, and I . . . well, of course I want you to stay, but it's not like I want you to . . . to . . ." She stopped.

George Beaumont felt suddenly more like his own age and realized something of what was going on. He felt a flush of shame at the way he had been acting. What in the goddamn hell, he thought. I'm playing the kid here, letting her do all this. He straightened his back, looked at the young woman and grinned.

"Well, if I wasn't smarter, I'd say you were trying to propose to me right here in public." He put his arm around her shoulders and turned her to face him. "Gosh, Lilly, I know what you mean. You don't have to go through all that."

She looked up at him, an expression halfway between gratitude and frustration on her face. He felt for the first time since they had met that he was in command of the situation. It was a strange feeling. She had been nursing him, telling him what to eat, when to go out and for how long, how much to sleep, for crissakes, when to go to the toilet even. And he had forgotten that she was only a kid, maybe only twenty-two or -three, and it had made him feel like an even younger kid to have her mothering him like that; but, of course, he was older and should know about these things. His grin began to feel a bit strained.

"Well, what do you say we do take a look around this place. I never been much out of my home state anyway."

"Okay, Bo," she said, and her look was grateful now. "I'm not a native, but I can show you some churches and old houses, and I know a place where we can get the best Italian salad outside of Napoli."

They took a train into Boston and did a portion of the North End, Faneuil Hall and the Old North Church, which had announcements in front in Italian, but then Bo was feeling shaky. They found the restaurant, where Lilly said he could have one glass of wine and the antipasto with garlic bread, nothing with meat sauce. It was fine, the bright, summery day with no sea breeze at all so that Boston might have been a thousand miles from an ocean.

It was like early spring rather than late fall, and the Christmas decorations seemed funny anachronisms from a long-vanished culture. The food was great, Bo said, and he felt every bite, every swallow a tiny miracle of its own as it produced nothing but a warm glow in his middle, no pain or even discomfort. All of that in the past months might have been a nightmare, something that had happened to someone else. And Lilly was so comfortable with him that he kept forgetting they were not engaged or married, or going to be. When he thought that, he almost choked on an anchovy bone and had to hide behind the big napkin the waiter had tied around his neck.

When he raised his red face, she was looking at him with such compassion that he felt the surge in his blood again. He reached over to pat her hand and found himself holding it instead.

"It's . . . uck . . . all right. Just an extra big bone in that sliced fish." He grinned. "Boy, those Italians. Who'd ever think of puttin' fish in a salad?"

"Say," he went on heartily, "this wine is really givin' me a buzz. You better watch yourself, girlie." But he felt weak enough to be carried back to his room. The walking around had worn him out. He had not realized how weak he had become from the past month of fighting. Yes, he thought, I was fighting for my life. He had to pin his trousers together now, and his shirts had to be cinched up at the neck with the necktie or they looked like they belonged to his big brother. He had lost perhaps sixty pounds, and, although Lilly said he looked better without the extra weight, it made him feel unaccountably light and strange in his clothes. Even his shoes felt loose. He imagined that he looked like a bum. And that brought thoughts of Mary Louise, for she had always objected to his nickname, saying it was a tramp's name, not a respectable man's.

"Bo, you really look tired," Lilly said. "Let me call a taxicab to take us back, okay?"

"Hell, we can't do that. It's miles and miles, and it'll cost a fortune." He felt for his wallet. "I got to think about finances, you know." This was a stupid thing to say, what with Lilly buying most of what he had been eating for the past month or so, but he was worried about it. He had money at home, but even though he had brought more than he needed back in November and had wired the bank for more since, he was acutely aware of the money going out and none coming in.

"Sure we can," the young woman said, squeezing his hand. "My treat."

"You're always doing that, Lilly," Bo said, and his voice sounded querulous in his own ears, like a little boy again. But he slumped back in the chair and grinned at her. "You're awfully good to me, kid."

"I've got a good job, and that's something these days," she said. "And I've saved some, too." She looked so happy to be doing for him that Bo decided to quit being an ass about it all. She wanted to do it, wanted to be saving his life and feeding him, and hell, he needed it. He had always believed in doing things for himself, and now for the past six weeks somebody had been doing it all for him; and he had been taking it. Well, let it be that way, dammit, he thought. I need her. And he didn't think beyond that, as he would have before he got so sick; think beyond the help he got to the debt incurred, to the repaying of the obligation. A friend, that's what she was, a real friend, and that's what the by-God-hell friends were for.

One night later on he dreamed again of the Beast. In his dream the moonlight filled his room with liquid light. A colorless, shadowless aura seemed to be coming from all sides instead of through the window like real moonlight, and in that mysterious glowing field the Beast came stalking into his room on its long blue-gray cat legs. It stood beside his bed, standing straight like a man, or . . . no, he remembered, it was female, like a tall woman dressed in blue-gray fur. Now its blunt fingers were unbuttoning the pajamas he had bought at the local Sears Roebuck so he wouldn't look so awful sleeping in his underclothes when she came in—Lilly, he meant. And the Beast ran those fingers over him; not just his stomach, but his chest and legs and head, trailing its blue-gray paws so as just to touch his flesh. It left a tingling path along his nerves. He looked down at his naked body and saw traces of light wherever the paw touched him until his body was a series of gleaming streaks, as if She had illuminated the arteries and veins, the nerve networks, made the flesh itself transparent. And when he looked up again, the face of the Beast was close to his own; the muzzle with its gleaming fangs seemed to smile at him, and the eyes were shadows into which he looked and saw flashes and sparks far away. He kept wanting to ask, in his dream thoughts, "What are you? Why

55

have you done this for me?" But he could not move, not even his lips. Only his eyes followed the movements of the Beast as it faded into the clear moonlight, backed away from him, diminishing in perspective as if it were being pulled away on a track, until he could only see a faint touch of blue-gray in the surrounding luminous ether. He tried to call out, to cry for it to stay, to say he was grateful, that he wanted to do something in return, but it was gone.

When he awoke his head was propped against the headboard as if he had been sitting up all night. He looked straight out the grimy little window and saw that it was snowing. The room was cold, but he threw back the covers and undid the pajamas to look at his long, gaunt body. He looked for the streaks of light, but of course it had been a dream.

He had just put his feet on the rug when the door exploded with a hail of thumps and knocks. For an instant he was so stunned by the unaccustomed noise that he thought the house must be falling down around him. Mrs. Peavey, the landlady, never knocked, always called out softly, did he want his bed made, and things like that. And Lilly sort of scratched, very softly, although he always heard her. But the rain of blows on the door now could only be made by someone who did not know how small the room was, or who thought its occupant was stone deaf.

As he stepped the two paces to the door to open it, he felt anger rising in him. Who in the goddamn hell knocks like that at the door. He swung it open, prepared to be rude to a vacuum cleaner salesman, and found himself facing three men: two shorter than himself, wearing fedora hats and chewing cigars, the other quite a big man dressed in blue, a policeman.

"Mr. Beaumont, George Beaumont?" said one of the fedoras, the cigar bobbing to the words.

"Yes," George said, bewildered and feeling a twinge of fear in his stomach.

"Anyone else in there?" the other fedora said, pushing against George so that he had to back into the room.

"What do you mean?" George said. "Who the hell are you guys, anyway?"

The other fedora pulled a badge from his pocket. "Private investigator. Rawlins Detective Agency outta Chicago." The badge disappeared into the pocket again.

Bo looked at the big blue uniformed cop who stood at

the threshold like a statue with an apologetic look. "What is this?" he said to the cop.

"If you're George Beaumont," the cop said, "these guys have a warrant so I have to pick you up." He seemed reluctant but determined.

"Nobody else here," the other fedora said, knocking cigar ashes on the hooked rug.

"Crummy joint you picked to hide yourself away in," said number-one fedora. "You do *look* sick, like the lady said," he continued, giving Bo a once-over.

"Better get dressed," the cop said, coming through the door and looking around as the other two men had.

"What the hell are you guys looking for?" Bo asked, feeling so outraged that his fear could not surface.

"We know you been having a little . . . ah, shall we say, love nest here with a young lady of anonymous name," said fedora number two. "And we have been engaged by your legal and deserted wife, one Mary Louise Beaumont of Whitethorn, Illinois, to locate your whereabouts and haul your ass back." The man leaned against the wall and gave Bo a sarcastic smile. "That answer your question, big shot?"

"But you can't walk in here and force me to go back," Bo said, fear beginning to sound in his voice in spite of himself. "I got some rights, too."

"You ain't got rights," fedora number one said. "What you got is a wife." He laughed over at fedora number two.

"I got to stay here," Bo said, listening to his voice shake and feeling, as from a distance, the foregone conclusion of his helpless entreaties. "My doctor isn't done with me."

"His doctor isn't done with him!" fedora number one said, tilting back the hat to reveal a large expanse of bald forehead. "Listen, wise guy, that little broad is a pretty cute doctor, but she ain't the one that ain't done with you. The one that ain't done with you is your legal spouse, baby. And when she's done with you, you gonta *need* a doctor." The two detectives, or whatever they were, guffawed.

He was detained at the police station in Malden for most of the day until he could see a judge and be released on his own recognizance. He was then presented with a subpoena demanding his presence in court at Rockford, Illinois, on the Thursday after Christmas, to answer charges of gross neglect, mental cruelty and desertion brought by Mary Louise Beaumont in a divorce action. Bo could not believe his eyes when he untangled the legal jargon and understood what was happening. The two private investigators disappeared once the subpoena was served and witnessed, but they left a few parting thoughts for Bo to ponder. One, his wife had a case for desertion if he was not seeing a bona fide doctor here in the East and if he was not dead by the time the court action came up; and two, they had gathered evidence of a love tryst (fedora number two called it a "triced") involving George and one Lilliam Penfield of the city of Revere, Massachusetts, with pictures of himself and the young lady (as fedora number one said, "pitchin' woo") in a local park.

He was left to find his own way home and had to take a taxi, finally, since he could not figure out which streetcar went near his rooming house. He arrived late, cold, angry and somewhat stunned to find Mrs. Peavey cleaning out his room.

"Mrs. Peavey," Bo said to the short, energetic woman making his bed. "I won't be leaving for a couple of days yet."

She spoke without turning around, snapping the sheets across the slumped bed. "You are."

"I don't understand."

"I say you're leaving, Mister Beaumont." She looked around. "I guess that's your real name? Or is it an alias name you're using?"

"This is all a bad mistake," Bo said.

"Exactly what I'm thinking, Mister Beaumont." Mrs. Peavey turned around, hands on hips, her face red. "That little baggage told me you was her long-lost father, she did."

Bo was stunned again. Her father?

"And I find out I'm running a house of ill fame here. Shame, Mister Beaumont, shame!"

"That's not true," George began, but he gave it up. Too much.

He put the few things he had into his suitcase and found himself back on the street. It was getting dark, and snow was coming down steadily. He felt like Little Eva starting across the ice. Mrs. Peavey had stoutly refused to take a message for Lilly and said the woman would not ever get into *her* house again. George decided he would wait right there at the curb until she showed up, since she usually came around after work on weekdays.

When she did not appear by the time it was quite dark

and George was afraid of being frozen to the sidewalk, he walked the three blocks to the streetcar line and rode into Malden to look for a room at the little downtown hotel. There were three Carrothers in the Malden phone book and one in the Revere book. One number did not answer and the other three had never heard of Lilliam. By the time he went to bed that night in another saggy little bed in another fusty little room, Bo felt as if life had betrayed him once more. But he was tired. He slept.

Next morning there was snow on the ground and gray skies that meant probably more snow coming. Bo sat in a diner on the main street eating scrambled eggs, and wheat toast (no coffee, no jam) and trying to assemble his life. While the world turned predictably on toward Christmas, which was now only two days away, George Beaumont had three strikes called and was still standing in the batter's box, in the snow—that's what it's like, he thought. The pain is gone, so I guess I'm on the way to being alive again, he thought, putting events in order of importance. Number two, Mary Louise is divorcing me; number three, I can't find Lilly. He wanted a cup of coffee or a cigarette, or both, but the thought of going back to what he had been before, with pain and fear in every waking minute, made his mind turn away from those lost pleasures. And, finally, his funds were on the edge of extinction.

He wondered idly what Mary Louise would reply to a telegram asking for a hundred dollars from the savings. Maybe Mr. Kneipe would loan him something. Ha, with him going off sick just as the holiday business got to its peak the first week in November? Fat chance. The thought of a divorce rested heavily on his mind, making his body slump as if it were really a physical weight that Mary Louise had placed on his head. There hadn't been much love in the last few years, sure, Bo was thinking. But he had loved her, and there had been Charles and the good times; but then they lost him. It was two years ago and more, the end of June when it happened. And now they almost didn't speak anymore. Maybe the divorce was the right thing. He certainly didn't feel any sense of present loss, as he felt because he couldn't locate Lilly. Mary Louise was his wife, and Lilly was a kind young woman who had nursed him away from death. He was certain the cancer would have killed him if the Beast and Lilly had not saved him.

He had to appear in court in a week, which meant he

59

had to leave here probably the day after Christmas at the latest to get back by train, since he would have to go the cheapest route possible and would have to find a lawyer. The thought of being in court added to the weight he felt in his head. They would cut him up good in court, especially with the "evidence" those two gumshoes had with their picture of Lilly and him in the park that innocent time, all the innocent times. And at that, Bo started to get angry. Damn them, they not only wouldn't believe what had happened to save him from dying, they would think he was a middle-aged scoundrel out seducing a young girl, and they hadn't even hardly touched each other, not even a kiss. And at that thought, Bo felt mad enough to put his clenched fist, which now rested beside his empty plate, right through the counter.

"Merry Christmas, friend!" said a hearty voice at his elbow.

He turned to find a gaunt, rouge-colored Santa Claus standing beside his stool with a red bucket and his hand out. The man's false beard hung from his ears with ratty abandon, and the eyes were appropriately twinkly, aided no doubt by the liquor on Santa's breath. Bo felt like flooring the dope.

"What, not a Scrooge so early in the morning," Santa boomed so that the other diners turned to look. "Help the children of St. Boniface with a nickel or a dime. Do without that extra cup of coffee just this one morning!" The man's voice was as obnoxious as his breath, but he was persistent, and the other people began to look at Bo with distaste for not contributing. He gave in and fished out some nickels left over from last night's phone calls.

"Thank you, sir, a few nickels for the poor children. Thank you so much for your philanthropic largesse."

Bo was about to make an angry remark, but Santa moved on down the line, extorting money from the rest of the patrons, the waitress watching sourly as most of her tips went into the red bucket.

Christmas, Bo thought. He wanted to get something for Lilly, even though what he felt for her was a gratitude larger than any gift he could afford. There must be a way to find her. The other Carrothers in the phone book, maybe. He left ten cents under his plate and slid off the stool. She was standing almost behind him and he almost knocked her down.

"Going shopping?" Lilly said, looking up at his astonished face.

Bo felt his features go in several different directions before assembling into a lopsided smile.

"How did you happen, I mean how'd you know I was here?"

"You're not so hard to find," she said, putting her hand through his arm as they walked for the door. "After all, there's only one hotel in Malden, and this is the closest diner to the hotel and it's breakfast time." She looked up at Bo with such a joyous smile that he forgot to pay the cashier and had to be yelled at before they got out the door.

While they rode the streetcar into Boston, Bo filled in what had happened since yesterday morning while Lilly listened attentively with an occasional searching look at his eyes. He was a little surprised that she was not more upset at the charges the detectives had made or the fact that he would have to leave soon after Christmas to attend the divorce proceedings. She seemed to have an unshakable aplomb, an attitude of serious attention to all these matters, but one that also said that she considered them of less importance than did the rest of the world.

"You know," Lilly said, looking at him thoughtfully, "it might not be as serious as all that. Your wife may just be telling you that she feels hurt and neglected."

"You don't send out detectives and subpoenas and judges just because a guy doesn't bring home flowers every night," Bo said morosely.

"Well, she certainly shouldn't have involved those people," she said. "But I'll bet if you call her on the phone she would listen."

"Yeah, I thought about that, but I don't know if I want to talk to her now." Bo felt bad saying that, but it was true.

"So maybe what's happening is something you really want?"

"What? A divorce? Hell, no." Bo sat there watching the Charles River as they crossed the bridge, thinking that at home there might be ice in the river already.

"Are you feeling well now, Bo?" Lilly said softly.

"Sure," he smiled over at her. "It's like all that pain never happened at all. I think sometimes it's going to be pretty hard to make people believe that I was that sick when now I'm all cured."

"You'll have to get along with that, I suppose," Lilly said. "They will say it was all in your mind, or that you had something that only looked like cancer and wasn't. You have to be accepting of their way of looking at it."

"That's something else," Bo said, and paused while the trolley bell clanged a number of times. "If you and, and Her, can cure a thing like that, why you could set up clinics all over and save the lives of thousands of people." He had not thought through what he was saying but went on anyway. "And think of the money you could make. Why, you could really make it big, besides saving all those lives."

He was surprised by the look on her face. She seemed almost sad for the first time since he had known her. He felt instantly guilty that he had mentioned such a thing, but puzzled too. Why wouldn't it work?

"Bo, it's not the same for everybody," she said slowly. "And I'm afraid a lot of times it wouldn't work out as well as it did in your case."

"What d'ya mean?" he asked, wanting to take that sad look from her face and not knowing how. "Look what you did for me. I was dying, really dying, and you saved my life. I know how sick I was. Why, look at me now. I've lost so much weight I look like somebody else, and I feel different, and I'm not eating all that junk anymore, and I feel, I feel like . . ." He stopped, wondering just what it was that he wanted to express. He did feel different. He felt like a new person, a really alive person. And before he had felt . . . what?

"You know," he said with new animation, "before, you know, when I was so sick, I felt like an old man." He grinned and put his arm around her shoulders and squeezed. "And I'm not an old man at all. I'm only forty-five—be forty-six next month—but that's not old."

He was rewarded by her face losing the sadness and a smile beginning. She reached up suddenly, grabbed his head and pulled it down and kissed him quickly on the lips.

"You're a *young* man," she said, almost in a whisper. "Because you can be whatever you really want to be."

Bo felt as though he had received knighthood. Her lips sent a glow through him so pleasurable that he felt goose-flesh all over his body. He grinned broadly and felt like dancing. What a good day it was, by golly, a good day.

They held hands on the street going from one department store to another. Bo advised her on jewelry, what was a good piece and what was only cheap casting, pointing out well-set stones and that some costume jewelry looked better than the real thing because it was made with care. And when she was off looking for some napkin rings for a woman friend at work, Bo bought a gold-filled ring with an opal, a tiny one, but as beautiful and fiery as any he had ever seen and set with exquisite care in a ring that must have been made by someone who loved precious metals. It was a great buy, but it took most of his going-home money, and he thought, well, so I have to hitchhike if Mary Louise won't send any money, the hell with all that.

"You're invited to Christmas dinner, of course," Lilly said to him as they were standing in a packed elevator.

"I don't even know your folks," he said, feeling his stomach go fluttery.

"They know about you, though," she said as they got off at another floor. "They know you've been very ill and have to watch your diet, and they know you're away from home."

"I'd like to get them something, but . . ." he said, wondering what sort of people he'd have to deal with.

"Sure, now look, Daniel loves chess, but he can only play at home because he just has the big pieces Polly got for him years ago. Now there are little travel sets that he would enjoy. He could take it to work with him."

Bo watched Lilly's face while she rattled off gifts for Daniel and Polly, the older couple she called her "folks." She had told him that she had met them a year before and they had taken her in.

"Polly has everything possible in her kitchen, so she might like something to read, or hankies, or a set of playing cards."

Bo was trying to remember and make up his mind at the same time. He was unsettled at the thought of meeting Lilly's people, but it was exciting, too. He had to keep reminding himself that he was probably not much younger than them, that he was not going to meet his best girl's parents but a nice couple who were good friends of his good friend.

It was dark and snowing again when they finished and climbed aboard the trolley to get back to Malden. They had agreed to go to Bo's room to wrap the packages and eat some cheese and crackers and apples they had picked up. Bo was tired. He usually hated shopping, especially Christmas shopping, when everybody you knew already had everything they needed and you knew that you, and all of them too, were just out spending money because it was the Lord's birthday. But he had really been interested today, taking such care with everything, arguing with clerks about quality like a housewife, laughing with Lilly about the toys she got for the kids who lived in the other half of her building.

Lilly showed him how to tie a decorative bow and how to make even clumsy packages look neat. He had never cared for wrapping, either, but now he found that it was fun, too.

"I think I must have been a real wet blanket at Christmas," Bo said, sitting amid the paper scraps eating cheese.

"Why, you're full of Christmas spirit, Bo," Lilly said. She was making curls of ribbon with the edge of a scissors.

"Usually about this time of year I am full of it," he said, grinning. "Old Panther Sweat, mainly. But now I'm happy as a bug in a rug and don't even feel like a drink. In fact, the thought of it kind of turns my stomach."

"That's a smart stomach you've got, then," she said. "There, now, isn't that professional?"

"You're just great, Lilly." Bo looked at her, feeling a lump in his throat. "You really are Christmas."

She put the package down and walked on her knees over to him, put her arms around his neck and leaned back to look at him.

"You're going to love Dan and Polly," she said, her eyes bright.

"I think I—" He stopped. He had almost said he loved her, and he wanted to say it yet, but he knew he shouldn't say that. It shouldn't be that kind of thing, but he felt it was. She was close to him and smelled so good, and she was looking into his eyes in a funny way. He put his arms around her waist and put a little pressure on her. She responded so easily it felt as though she was part of him. Their kiss was long and slow and very sweet.

"Jeez," Bo said, his breath catching in his chest. "I'm shaking like a little kid," and he laughed a little.

"Bo, I feel very close to you now," Lilly said, looking into his eyes, her head on his shoulder, arms around his neck. "You are becoming a part of my life."

"I don't feel really alive unless you're around," he said,

his breath still catching in his throat. "I want to say all kinds of love things to you, but I think it's not right. I mean . . ."

"Don't think about that," she said. And she very deliberately kissed him on the lips again. He felt her small hands on his back, moving in little movements, the fingers spreading and releasing, and he felt her body coming in closer and pressing against his, and then it was no use thinking about anything. He really kissed her this time.

As they lay down on the bed, he started to say something about how he was afraid of doing something wrong to her, but she smiled so sweetly, touching his lips with one finger, that he stopped. He didn't say a word about anything outside the room for a long time after that.

She is so wonderful, Bo was thinking as they slowly got to know each other there in the dim light on the hotel bed. The traffic noises outside had almost stopped now, and it seemed they might be entirely alone in the world on this night before Christmas, the snow on the streets and in the dim trees and on the rooftops here in the eastern United States. Maybe the rest of the world would let them alone after all, he thought, feeling her smooth hands on his chest. A tingling sensation spread from wherever she touched, and he very gently ran his hand over the line of her hips, shaking with excitement but calm at the same time.

"Oh, Lilly," he said in a husky voice, "you're so beautiful."

She looked at him, and her face had a depth in it that he had never seen before, as if she were young and yet very old, very much aware of exactly what he meant.

"Don't you know that you are beautiful, too?" she said. "Now I want you to undress me."

He believed for a long time afterward that he was in a dream. Time did not pass, but appeared and disappeared as it did in dreams. He imagined they were somewhere out of time and space while they caressed each other and kissed and sometimes even laughed softly. It was a long time, he thought, but no time had passed at all, and then it got very intense, with passion rising up in both of them so that they became entangled, their bodies loving each other, hands working to touch the tenderest and the hardest places, their breathing coalescing and separating, eyes shut or widened with joy.

Bo had sometimes had trouble with sex in the past, sometimes thinking Mary Louise was unhappy with the way he did it. And there had been times when he couldn't do it at all or when he wanted it too fast and he was afraid of making her upset. He worried about performing, as if he were called upon to make a perfect brooch or incise a perfect inscription on each occasion. He thought of it as something like the necessities of a jewelry job, which made it like work. But when he thought about this night afterward, which he did over and over again, he remembered no time that he was uncomfortable or worried or even feeling such a thing was possible. Lilly seemed to fit in with his own emotions so well that there was never any sense of being on trial as there had sometimes been with his wife. He didn't think of performing at all. In fact, he thought later, he probably didn't *think* at all.

"Oh, yes, Bo. That's it, that's it," she was saying at some late time in the evening as they made love, created love between them with their feelings for each other that expressed love in their bodies. "Oh, now, it's now," she was saying, and in his own rising emotional force, he saw something in her face that amazed him. She seemed to be undergoing a transformation, her face taking on all the features of every woman Bo had ever looked at with love or lust or longing, becoming each and every woman he had ever dreamed about. His breath came faster now as they worked together, their bodies entwined, her lips opening and closing but no words coming out, his eyes watching the transformations with love and an absent amazement he would not think of until later.

And then, as if she could feel the exact moment inside him when the climax began, she looked straight into his eyes and her body jumped against his and she cried out with a high gasping, her nails digging into his sides and back, arching against him as she cried out again, louder this time, her mouth open, and he crying out with her, his own climax taking his breath.

And then there was a cry that turned to a growl.

What happened then Bo would never be certain of, but he knew it was not an earthly creature who held him between her legs, whose pelvis was surging against his own, whose body contained him with such passionate heat as he reached his peak and cried out. His eyes had closed for a second or so as he came, and then the cry became a roar and the claws raked his back and he felt the animal pelt around him as if he had been wrapped suddenly in a close, hot tiger skin. He opened his eyes, his body still

66

jerking with spasms as he climaxed into the woman's body, and found himself wrapped in the great blue-gray Beast's embrace, the muzzle full of teeth inches from his face and the growling of the Beast making the room reverberate like the lion house at a zoo. The embrace was complete and total. Bo could not have moved from it if he had tried. He looked on as if from a distance, his body still in ecstasy, and he could only feel the muscular body of that great catlike Beast, who could have torn him apart with a single movement. He felt his whole body embraced by a creature so much larger than himself, so different in feel, in texture, from the small woman to whom he had been making such passionate love, that his mind simply did not reason for those moments. He only felt. He did not think. The Beast contained him, held him, its muzzle swinging back and forth, the great green eyes opening wide and closing down to slits with its own pleasure.

And then it was over.

The Beast was gone and Lilly's own soft, feminine body lay with his, her eyes closed, breath coming in long, irregular gasps and slowing now. Bo lay beside her, and his mind slowly began coming back. It had been one of those dreams. But he felt a small trickle of blood and looked down at his side, where a long scratch ended in a puncture that bled slowly. No fingernail could have done that, and he felt the scratches on his back, too. He probably looked like he'd been in a cat fight, he thought, surprised at his own acceptance of this unnatural thing. And then it was so absurd that it became funny—the sudden feeling of possessive sexuality, what was called "the conquest" becoming its opposite, the possessor being possessed by a sexual partner so much greater in size and power. It was too much for the mind to take in. Goddamn, I guess, Bo thought and put his face into the pillow beside Lilly's head to smother his suddenly uncontrollable giggling. How the hell can it be funny, he was thinking. It's crazy. But his happiness could not be shaken, even by the certain feeling that there were three of them in the bed.

Lilly turned her head to look at Bo. She saw he was shaking.

"Bo?" She tried to turn his head from the pillow and finally took a handful of his hair.

He raised his red, grinning face to her. "I'm sorry, but all at once it seemed funny."

She laughed softly and pushed his face back into the

pillow. "My goodness, I thought you were crying." And she thought how wonderful it was to laugh at it. It *was* funny. The shift had caught her just coming past her own climax and had blanked her out for several seconds, although she was still present in some way and could feel Bo's reaction to his suddenly fur-pelted paramour. Maybe that was what the French meant by *ménage à trois*, she thought, feeling there were three of them, that there were always three of them when she and Bo were together because She had saved his life and was always there just under the surface.

The man and woman rest now and speak quietly of their love while I feel myself a part of both of them. It is a complex harmonic of three conscious lives that I feel building at this moment, the singing of each set of vibrations matching in key but not in pitch. I have experienced sexual joy from within the human form before this time, but now a new sensation fills me. It is an expansion keyed by three interlocking minds: as if three stones were dropped at once in the water and the ripples meshed, united their force instead of cancelling it. The burst of energy that hurled me from my assumed form at that moment of passion has now become something different, something much larger, more my own. I feel as if my whole universe were expanding.

The cracking of a shell. Light flashes around my submerged self as if I were emerging from a dark sea. The understanding that overtakes me makes all other events surround this moment. So. Now, I do understand. I withdraw into the darkness of myself to consider this change.

A long time later he heard her sigh. "It's not just the two of us, Bo," she said.

"Yeah, I feel that."

"Did you know before?"

"No. Well, I guess maybe I thought about it when I was sick," he said, trying to remember if he had ever come to that conclusion.

"Oh, She scratched you," Lilly said, touching the place on his side that had now stopped bleeding.

"Biggest hickey I ever got," he grinned. "Best, too."

She laughed a short little laugh, but then her face became serious.

"You know that I'm not just an ordinary working girl," she said, sitting up and looking at him. "It's real, Bo."

He opened his eyes and looked up to see the woman he loved sitting against the head of the bed. Just seeing her smooth and perfect body made him start getting excited all over again. But she was asking him something.

"What? I'm sorry," he said.

"I'm afraid you'll think about what happened and some-time later you'll think how horrible it is."

"It's not horrible," he said, seeing the pain come into her face. "It's just something that's part of you." He was not thinking clearly yet, but something in his mind was beginning to feel the unbelievable, the supernatural un-reality of his situation.

"No, that's not it," she said, pulling the sheet up around her shoulders. "It's not part of me. I'm part of it."

"What d'ya mean?" Bo said, wanting the scared feeling inside him to go away. He spoke too loudly. "You've just got this thing that happens to you, like."

"I've only been alive for a year, Bo."

"Now, wait a minute," he said, a coldness in his throat. "You're younger than me, but not that young." The joke didn't work.

"She's the real one. I'm just something She uses to get along in this world." Lilly held up her hand for him to wait before speaking. "She's kind and good and loves humans, but She's just using me—like a mask or a cos-tume. You know what happened when we made love and when both of us were so . . . so ecstatic. She couldn't hold on to me because She was enjoying it, too. She's always there with me, some times more than others, but always." Lilly closed her eyes.

Bo tried to listen, but his mind wanted to say that this was nonsense, something they should forget.

"Lilly, this is just dream stuff. We love each other more than anything, I know that now, and if you've got some-thing . . . well, wrong, we can fix it up or ignore it. You're so sweet and kind and loving." He tried to make his words say what he meant. "You've just got this . . . problem."

"I'm not a real human being," Lilly said, almost in a whisper.

"Don't say that," he said, his voice getting angry. He could not stand the sudden drop into emptiness that she presented. "You're the most real person I ever knew." But at the same time he felt that third presence, not as if he saw it in Lilly, but as if it were there beside him, stretched on the bed, long and blue-gray and terrifying in its power. He knew it was true.

Now the parts were reversed, with her the weak one and Bo the strong one. He was unready to accept it, fumbling in his mind, trying to understand this change to a world different from the one he had always known—and, on top of that, this big catlike thing that he must accept as real.

"You're the realest person I ever met in my life," Bo said, hugging her clumsily.

"No, no." She went on in a low voice, like a child admitting a fear. "Less than a year ago I stood on the street in front of Dan and Polly's house looking at the number and thinking that I had to make these people like me. And that's the first thing in the world I can remember." She pushed her head away from his embrace to look at him.

"It's that cat-thing that isn't real, sweetheart," Bo said, not believing what he said, remembering the embrace of that muscular body and the sound of the roaring that must have stood some hair on end elsewhere in the little hotel.

"I don't even know why She's here," Lilly went on, her voice low and abstract. "She brought me here so I could live with Dan and Polly. I do love them dearly, but I told them all sorts of lies about myself, lies that just came to me, and I'm not a liar. I never have been. . . ."

"Well, so you've got amnesia or one of those psychological things," Bo said.

"No, it's not that. This Beast uses me for something She needs. I'm not angry against her because She's kind, and She healed you, and that's not the first time. Last summer there was a little Italian boy who fell from a fire escape behind the theater, and She made him breathe again and made him live. He was dead, Bo." She looked at him as if there were some thought in her mind she could not articulate.

"She brought a kid back to life?"

"The boy's head was all flat on one side where he hit the pavement. When I touched him, he was so limp." She shuddered, holding the sheet tight around her neck. "He was like a . . . like a rag bag. Oh, it was so terrible. I knew he was dead. And then She came out and carried the boy back to the hole under the chapel in the cemetery where She used to stay and She healed him, made him come back to life. He's alive now, lives a couple of blocks away from Dan and Polly."

"And She did it for me, too," Bo said, thinking back about the dreams. "I used to dream She was in my room at Mrs. Peavey's, and—"

"Those weren't dreams," Lilly said. "I remember each time, but I don't know what She was doing or how. I told you things She told me to, the exercises, the diet, and the words to say. She told me all those things."

"But you're the one that did all the work," he said, trying desperately to take the distant look away from Lilly's face. "You pulled me back when I died, remember? When I saw my son?"

"I never know, really," she said. "Sometimes I think I remember doing that myself, going out of my body to somewhere beautiful and being in the center of a great light, where it is so peaceful."

"Yeah, yeah!" Bo said suddenly. "That's what it's like. You've been there, too. You must be human, because that's heaven, I know it is because my boy's there." He was not aware of making sense or not making sense, only that she looked more like her old self as she tried to remember.

"My birthday party," she said in a low, absent voice.

"Huh?"

"The car. We were all singing 'Alouette,' and Rudy was driving." She went on as if telling a story about someone else, her voice growing stronger as she went. "It was my birthday." Her brow furrowed. "I was twenty-one, and we were drinking, drinking from a bottle without a label . . . because even though I was twenty-one . . . I couldn't drink . . . because of . . . Prohibition." She looked up at Bo with her eyes round.

He didn't get her meaning.

"Bo! When was Prohibition repealed?"

"Why, let's see, a couple years ago. It was in 1933, wasn't it?" He looked at the woman wonderingly. "But there's some states still dry, you know?"

"Bo, I haven't taken a drink of liquor in this year of my life. That's a memory. I know it's a memory." She clapped her hands and grabbed his shoulders and kissed him. "It's a memory from at least four years ago. Do you suppose the Beast really has taken me over and I'm a real person with a real life somewhere? Am I just kidnapped?"

He was so happy to see the blankness gone from her

face that he would have agreed to anything, but it seemed natural that she would have lost her memory. For that Beast to have created her was stretching things too much.

"Sure you are, Lilly," he said, hugging her. "Sure you are. You've got a home and real folks somewhere, and maybe brothers and sisters and maybe even a husband." He stopped, looking down.

But then she lay down and put her face on the pillow again. She rubbed her palm over the pillow, and he could see she was thinking of something else.

"It won't work, even so," she said. "How can I be real if I *don't* exist when She *does?*"

"Well, look, maybe it's just like She, uh, comes over you some way, like you were putting on a coat or something. Maybe it's really you in there all the time. Like what they used to call werewolves and things like that."

She looked up at him, and a smile began to grow around her eyes.

"I'm living now," she said, reaching up to take his face in her hands. "And that's what I'm always telling you to do, isn't it?"

"Sure, and we'll let tomorrow take care of itself, right?" He eased down beside her and kissed her lightly.

"I'm not going to talk like that anymore, Bo," she said into his ear, hugging him to her. "Tonight is for us to enjoy, and tomorrow is Christmas Day, and we're going to Dan and Polly's house and make turkey dressing and eat Polly's fruitcake and open presents." She moved her body against his. "Would you mind if we loved each other again?"

Bo didn't mind at all.

Dan Carrothers stood five feet six, which, as he said, was one inch more than Polly. He laughed. "One inch taller and forty more around." He was the only completely bald man Bo had ever seen, and he wore a fringe of beard that was gray and black speckled and made him look a bit like an old sea captain. He worked as chief linotypist at the same printing plant where Lilly worked. He had gotten her the job there, he told Bo while they sat in front of the fireplace and cracked walnuts into a bowl. But she had done so well in the first months, they had given her two promotions. His face wore a smile when he talked about Lilly or about Polly, his wife. He liked his women, as he called them.

"Good cooks, too, both of 'em," he said, cracking two walnuts in his hand.

"Yeah, I know Lilly is," Bo said. "She's kept me alive through that sickness. Though I don't suppose yoghurt and wheat mush is any indication of what she can really do." There was a thoroughly safe air about their home, as if anyone coming in was automatically under some protection, and accepted too, as Bo found out. Neither Dan nor his jovial-looking wife had asked him questions about where he was from or who he really was. They accepted him because Lilly did, and Bo was grateful not to have to evade queries about family and such. They allowed him to lead, making him comfortable by talking but not interrogating.

Polly came in with flour on her apron and a smile on her ruddy face. Bo thought that for a woman of sixty she was certainly alive looking. Her hair was pure white and done up in a loose series of braids that made her look like a white-haired little girl. And although she had wrinkles in her face, they were what Bo called happy wrinkles and not the downward turned lines that made a face look dragged and old.

"You men finished those walnuts and pecans yet?"

Dan offered her the bowl. "How about some eggnog, my little cabbage?"

Polly stopped and put her floury hand on Dan's gleaming head. "I hope you don't mind this man's sense of humor," she said. "He has called me everything under the sun since we've been married, and now it's got down to the vegetables." She patted his head so that flour prints stayed on his bald pate. "Cabbage indeed, you old rutabaga."

Bo saw Lilly standing in the dining room doorway, an apron on, her black hair done in small curls around her face. They looked at each other across the width of the living room and smiled. Bo felt a fluttering around his stomach. Maybe it was around his heart. He knew that it felt good, anyway.

"You play chess?" Dan said, almost apologetically.

"I'm not very good."

"That's what they all say," Dan said, grinning ear to ear, "before they whip the pants off me."

The men sat before the fire and played the game while the women finished in the kitchen and came back to the living room, where they worked at some small sock monkeys Polly was making for the boys next door who were coming for dinner. The turkey cooked slowly through the morning, the dressing filling the little house with savory smells that complemented the piney odor of the tree and the wreaths and the candles that were burning in the two front windows. Outside it was getting ready to snow again with a low moaning of wind through the eaves and telephone wires in the street. The fire made snapping noises and the women giggled occasionally while the men sat and pondered their moves, Dan drawing his pipe out and sticking it in his mouth but never lighting it.

When the boys arrived a little after noon, the house became noisy and rollicking with packages being unwrapped, cries of delight at the funny presents, tears at the nice ones. The heap under the tree dwindled while the pile of paper and ribbons grew and Dan kept circling around to pick it up and stuff it into the fireplace, and Polly kept telling him he was going to throw away the card from Aunt Cathy or the instructions for her new mixer. The boys, eight and nine years old, had brought some of their new toys from home, but they found more at the Carrothers'. There was a metal biplane with a propeller that really turned around and a pilot in the cockpit, and a sulky-harness racer that you could wind up and let go to buzz off through the wrapping paper like a mad team of mice.

Bo watched as Lilly unwrapped her ring and was rewarded by her bright-eyed smile that turned to tears as she put the ring on and it fit exactly. She held it up for admiration and then came over to kneel down by Bo, who was sitting on the floor with the kids. She kissed him long and hard in front of everybody.

"Now you have to open mine," she said, handing him a small, flat box.

Inside was a beautiful wallet of expensive leather with his name engraved in small neat letters along one edge. He opened it up and found in the card holder a picture of Lilly with that lovely smile on her face.

"Wow," he said, holding it out. "Look at that, and it's in color, too." He hugged Lilly and kissed her again. "I love the picture," he said into her ear. "I'll never be without it."

"She got that done and tinted especially," Dan said, looking across at Bo with what seemed a wistful expression.

74

Dinner filled the house with tasty smells and the table with heaps of food and drink. As they all got settled in their chairs, Bo noticed them looking expectantly at Dan, so he did too and folded his hands in his lap. As the older man began to speak, they bowed their heads.

"Dear God in Heaven, for what we are about to receive we thank Thee with all our hearts, and for this Christmas when we can be together in love and health, we thank Thee, too. Dear God, we are glad and grateful to have Bo and Lilly with us today in their happy state, and we are thankful for the boys, Eugene and Dale, who are the sparks of the future and beloved of Thee in Thy goodness. And God, we wish on this special birthday of Thy Son Jesus Christ to ask that you continue to give us health and each other, that we may continue in love for all the days of our lives."

He stopped and looked up. "Amen."

The meal proved as good as it looked, and although Bo could only have small portions yet, he did eat more than he had for months, even some of the mince pie and ice cream afterwards.

Later they talked in the living room after the boys had gone home, and when it got dark they invited in the carolers who came down the street singing "Good King Wenceslaus."

"I'll never forget this day," Bo said to Lilly at the door. It was after midnight, and the Carrothers had already retired. Outside in the dark the wind began to pick up and the snow grew thicker.

"Do you have to leave tomorrow?" Lilly said, her arms tight around him.

"Yeah. That thing I got to be at is Thursday, and I got to find a lawyer, and the trains are slow. Connections are bad up to Whitethorn." He did not say that the train depended on money from his wife, if she would send it, since he thought she probably had the bank account under her lock and key now. But it didn't matter. He would get there one way or another.

"When will you be back?" Her voice was so soft he could hardly hear it.

"Right away," he said confidently, feeling at the moment that it ought to be simple. He could get there and get the court stuff over and tell Kneipe that he had to leave town, and then he would come back and look for a job in Boston or one of the little towns like Malden.

Surely somebody around needed a good manufacturing jeweler who could cut stones and engrave and cast and do all kinds of things. He had talked a long time about it to Lilly, and they had agreed it sounded like a good chance. But now, as he stood there in the dim hallway, having said his thanks and good-nights to Dan and Polly, hearing beyond the door the deep moaning of that wind and snow, he had a sudden falling sensation in his stomach. For just a moment he thought of the old pain again, but then he felt Lilly in his arms and knew it was just his apprehension and fear of leaving her.

"You don't worry at all, sweetheart," he said, sounding false in his own ears, sounding like an actor in a movie.

"I'm not worrying, Bo," she said, putting her face up to his for the kiss. "I just want you to know that I love you."

"I love you, too, Lilly."

And after that he walked away into the snowstorm that was getting thicker and colder now. He looked back as she stood in the lighted doorway with the door cracked open to watch him, and he waved with what he hoped looked like good cheer. That night in the little room he packed his stuff again in the old suitcase, decided to wait until a decent hour in the morning to call Mary Louise and lay down on the bed. He lay there thinking a long time before sleep finally took him without his knowing it.

The train was an hour and a half late, and Mary Louise Beaumont had been standing or pacing for two hours at least. Now, with the train in the station, steam clouds around it and people getting on and off the little steps the porters put down, she told herself for the five hundredth time that she was going through with it. Her husband was among the last three or four to get off, and, although he carried the suitcase she had bought him twelve years ago, she didn't recognize his face or his stature.

Mary Louise," Bo said, thumping the suitcase down on the wet platform. The cold rain blew under his hat and made him shiver.

"George, George," Mary Louise said in wonder. "What in God's name has happened to you? Oh, you're not the same person. You . . . oh, you're so thin and you look taller." The woman stared up at him, her fingers knotted over the little cloth purse.

"I'm well now," he said, wondering if he should hug her or take her arms or something. He felt numb.

"Oh, you can't be, you're so thin—why, look how that coat hangs on you. George, you'll have to go to the hospital . . ." she faltered as she looked into his eyes, seeing there a strangeness she could not remember in him. ". . . right away," she finished weakly.

"I don't need a hospital now," he said, picking up the suitcase. "You had lunch?"

"Yes, well, I mean no. Oh, George." The wife of twenty years looked at the husband returning in disgrace, the man she had thought would only come back in a coffin, and she didn't want to be cold and bitter with him. She felt old habit sway her toward him, make her want to take his arm, even to be angry with him. But she thought then of the detectives' report, the young girl he had been seeing there in the East, and she hardened her expression. Her voice lost its high, wavering tone.

"Come on home, now, and we'll have something there. We got lots to talk about before tomorrow." She turned and took a couple of steps before looking back. He followed.

She has always been strong, George thought as she drove them home through the familiar streets of Whitethorn. In this place, this home where we grew up and lived our lives, she and I have had a pretty solid life. He felt a numbness in his face, as if he had drunk too much or just got back from a dentist. Was it possible he still loved her? He looked over at her as they waited at the only stoplight in town. She had put on a few pounds, but she was still a damn pretty woman. But things had been so bad these last couple of years since the accident. He looked away, the numbness making it hard for him to think about all that.

He sat at the kitchen table in the house they had lived in for fourteen years and were still paying the mortgage on. The old life wanted to close around him, to make him comfortable and wipe away the strange and the supernatural. But it could not remove Lilly from his mind. She was there, a part of the new life he felt inside.

"Hey, Mary Louise," Bo said as she got things from the refrigerator. "I can't eat that meat loaf. You got any cream cheese?"

"Can't eat meat loaf?" She turned to him, her face so like old times that he caught his breath and looked away.

"It's part of my being cured," he said. "I'm a vegetarian now."

"A vegetarian?" She put her hands on her hips and looked at him. She wanted to say something else, he could tell, but she put the meat loaf back and got out the little jar of pineapple cream cheese and the loaf of wheat bread.

They sat at the table, and, if he let his mind relax, Bo could imagine it was three years ago or more and they were waiting for Charles to come home from a baseball game on a Saturday afternoon. But it was the dead of winter now, their son was gone and it was all changed.

"So you're going to untie the knot?" Bo said.

"You've already done plenty of that yourself," she said, taking little bites of her sandwich as she always did, picking it up and putting it down as if it were too hot to hold.

"I think I ought to explain a few things," Bo said, feeling even as he said it the impossibility of explaining anything.

"Oh, you don't have to do that," she said lightly. "Heavens, if there's one thing *everybody* understands it's the middle-aged man going off and having a fling."

"Well, now, you've got a right to think that, but it wasn't that way." He felt she was insulting him and was surprised to find he was not angry. A few months ago they would have been into a big fight by now—but, of course, it looked that way. He couldn't really blame her.

"I meant about my sickness," he said quietly.

"Well, it's pretty obvious you didn't have cancer, isn't it?" She bounced up from the table to get the coffee.

"I did," he said. "But I got cured, and I don't think there's any way in the world I can explain how, 'cause I don't know myself."

Mary Louise put the coffeepot down on the trivet and sat slowly. She looked at him with a softening of her expression. "Did you see a doctor there, George? Did you?"

"No, not a real one. I mean, not one with an office and such." He gave her a quick, agonized look. He didn't want to hurt her any more by talking about Lilly, and he certainly couldn't talk about the other thing. "She's just what you might call a natural doctor," he finished lamely.

"*She is,* huh?" Mary Louise said, picking up the coffee-pot and spilling some as she poured. "Well, Mr. Morrisey says you will have to be checked by a *real* doctor"—she paused, the angry look coming back into her eyes—"as he says, to ascertain the extent of your culpability."

Bo felt stung by that, but, after all, he should be dead

78

by now. "They can sure look if they want," he said, and then as an afterthought, "but no cutting."

"Now that I've had a chance to get a good look at you," she said, "I can see you're not sick. You've lost a lot of weight, but you look healthy as a horse."

"I suppose the fact that I'm not dead makes me guilty," Bo said, feeling the numbness leave him and some of the old anger rise again.

"If you remember, George, you left here almost two months ago against the exact advice of Doctor Goodnaugh, and leaving me thinking you were going to your death in some strange city."

"I had to do something," he said in a low voice, his anger subsiding.

"Doctor Goodnaugh is the finest specialist this side of Chicago," she said, her hands folded on the table, "and he advised the exploratory operation, and that's when you jumped up and ran away."

Well, he thought, you couldn't argue with the goddamn facts. Mary Louise wanted to know what the hell was going on, and she would never in this world be able to. Even at this moment, when she was needling him and pushing at him, he thought of her with affection. She was a damn good woman. Well, that was over.

"I suppose you went to Boston and got cured by a miracle?" She said the last word with a mocking upward inflection.

"Yeah, I guess you could say that, but it wasn't—"

"George Beaumont," she said sharply, "you don't mean to sit there and insult my intelligence by telling me you got healed by some plaster saint or sacred bones? I suppose you've joined the Holy Rollers, too, besides becoming a vegetarian?"

"No, it wasn't anything like that. That shrine in the cemetery only made me feel worse." He felt sick inside now, recognizing the emotional response of his body for what it was and not fearing a return of the pain in his guts. That was all over, too. But he couldn't let her think he was just pulling off shenanigans.

"No, there was a person there who helped me, and now I don't feel the same, or even eat the same things." He really wanted to say something to his wife about the new way he felt about life. If there was just some way to tell it without involving Lilly.

"That's a new way of saying it, anyway, you—you

betrayer." She put one hand angrily to her face and began to cry, sitting there very stiffly and crying with one hand pressed against her cheek.

Bo found himself beside her, his arm around her shoulders. "Honey," he said, "Mary Louise, I'm sorry about all this." It was the first time he had touched her since he had come home, and the old feelings washed over him so that his eyes watered, too. But he felt her stiffen under his hand, and she twisted around in the chair, pulling away from his arm.

"Who is this little doctor of yours?" She turned a tear-stained face toward him, her mouth pressed into a line. "Some blonde—no, they said she was dark, some little floozie you found that put you back onto the road of life."

He stood there in the kitchen, unable to answer. Wasn't it possible to love two women and want both of them to be happy? He felt as miserable about all this as he could, but there was the fact, and they were going to have to deal with it. There was no way he could make it clear, and he was just going to have to go through this—to put Mary Louise through it.

"Pretty cute, George!" Her tone was harsher than he had ever heard. "Telling me and everybody else you had cancer, and making us go through all those tests and doctor's visits, and Mr. Kneipe giving you time off and everything right in the busy season, and all you wanted was to get away and act like you were at a Legion Convention." She jumped to her feet, looking at him with sudden hatred. And then her face seemed to dissolve in tears again. "Oh, George, George, how could you do it?"

He stood there like a tree stump, numb again with the distance he felt from even himself. Yes, he had done it all right. His wife stood six feet away from him beside the table with their coffee cups. They might have been deadly opponents ready to draw their knives or pistols. Still, there was nothing to say. He felt that any try to explain further would only make her more angry, would only make him look worse. They would just have to suffer it out. He hated doing it to her.

"Well, you're going to pay for your fling, George Beaumont, you're going to pay plenty." Her angry face came close to his and receded as she strode back and forth, her hands making strange gestures as she struck at him with her words.

"Mr. Morrisey has shown me my rights as a betrayed wife. He has been my best friend in the terrible time I have had these last two months." She came close to him again, trying to make him look at her. "While you were out there in Boston having your little love nest. He is a good, sweet man."

Bo felt the sting of that and realized with wonder that she was playing up the lawyer, pretending she was falling for the guy just so he could come back at her. He looked at her agonized face as she wailed and waved her arms, the sound of her voice like winter waves against the rocks. Perhaps for the first time in their married life, he really felt how much she loved him, even after what he had done. He shook his head. He could not bring Lilly into it, and Mary Louise would not believe the other stuff. He wanted to say to her that he still loved her and wanted her to be well, but that he couldn't stay with her anymore. But he said nothing.

The day in court on Thursday, the thirtieth of December, nineteen hundred and thirty-seven proved to be a series of preliminary legal skirmishes between Mr. Morrisey and Bud Hopps, an old friend of Bo's who also happened to do an occasional divorce action. The judge listened with half-closed eyes, his hand occasionally making a note on a large pad, and then called for the couple to "approach the bench."

"Mary Louise and George Beaumont," he said, reading the names from a paper in front of him. "This is a serious matter you are bringing to my court, and I want you both to consider your actions calmly and with thought for the future. Marriage is a legal as well as a holy institution, and the dissolving of the legal bonds will give rise to certain effects that will change your lives. Now, it may be," he said, leaning over the high desk, "that you have had a deep disagreement, but you can, after more serious thought, reach a position where this action will not be necessary." He looked up at Mary Louise's lawyer, a thirtyish man in double-breasted dark suit with a cinched collar and a narrow tie. "Mr. Morrisey, counsel for plaintiff, has suggested your differences are deep and irreconcilable. Mr. Hopps, counsel for defendant, on the other hand, does not dispute the differences but holds for an amicable settlement."

Mary Louise stole a look at her husband, who stood looking up at the judge, listening with a solemn expression.

She could not get over the change in his appearance, and he acted so different. She felt a moment's panic as she thought that he had met someone who did that for him, but then she thought, he probably believed he really was dying; now he's like a man reborn. He connects that with this girl in Boston. She listened again to the judge.

". . . but I do not hear from defendant that these differences are unamenable to arbitration. You, George, as a mature man with a solid career in your town, should consider the seriousness of your actions. . . ."

Bo listened, but inevitably the judge's talk got away from him. There were too many legal terms, and it sounded like a detective story he had read once and been bored with. It boiled down to the judge doing his duty in trying to get Mary Louise and him back together, and that was impossible.

They walked out of the courtroom at different times, as if each had separated from the other and taken up with a lawyer instead. Bo and Bud went out to have a beer while Mr. Morrisey and Mary Louise retired to his office to plan more strategy. The next court date was in thirty days, much to Bo's amazement. He had thought things would simply be got through with and he could go back to Boston. In the little bar on Broadway, he had a ginger ale while Bud had a beer.

"She's going to skin you, Bo," the lawyer said.

"If that's what she wants, let her have it." The ginger ale didn't taste like much, either.

"Bo, I don't know what's got into you, but you act like you don't care if she gets everything—house, car, bank account. How about your tools down at the store? She can have them, too?"

"Aw, Bud, look," he said. "She's had a hard time, and I've gone and made it worse. I don't care if she gets everything. I'm leaving here, anyway."

The lawyer whistled through his teeth. "I'm going to see you got enough left for my fee, old friend, and anything over that is all yours."

January 6, 1938

Dearest Lilly,

This is terrible business going on here. The courts are going to be slow, with no chance of settling things until the end of this month. Old Kneipe down at the store wants me to train a new man, and he isn't too keen on giving me great references because he said I left him in the lurch. You see, sweetheart, they all think I was shamming about being sick, and now they are all down on me for doing that. Well, that's what you said would happen, I guess.

But I'm not down, not really, sweetheart. I'm thinking about how I'll be able to leave right after the court thing is over and I'll come out there again and we'll have such a good time and find a nice place where we can set up housekeeping and be real people. I want you to get ready for that, Lilly, because I'm so happy about loving you I am really a changed man. There's nothing these people can do to me that will change anything between us. You can bet on that. Please write me soon, and remember, I love you more than anything in the world.

All my love,
Bo

January 4, 1938

Dear Bo,

I was hoping for a letter again today, but don't think I'm nagging you. It's just that I want to tell you some of the things I've been doing here to get ready for your return. I'm happier than I've ever been, even if that is only a short while—you know what I mean. "She" is restless, and says we may not stay here much longer. I don't understand why she would have to leave, where we would go, but I do catch an ominous note that perhaps I will not be going with her—and, there again, you know what that means for us.

Well, anyway, I'm looking for apartments closer to Boston, and I've already found a couple of beauties. Each of them is rather expensive, but with both of us working we'll have plenty. I like the one that has a view of the river and the bay from a big double window with a window seat. I just love window seats in cozy little apartments where two people can sit and sip tea. I have also bought some supplies already, Bo. There's a set of cups and saucers to drink the tea out of and a little throw rug that will go anywhere. I just had to buy it because it was your favorite color: deep indigo blue, just the color of the night sky. You'll love it. I hope there's a letter today, but I know things are no doubt in a terrible mess back there. I can't imagine what it would be like to go through something like that, and I'm so sad for you now, Bo. I love you very much, and I want you to get back as soon as you can. Think about me, Bo. I love you.

Lilly

January 12, 1938

Dearest Lilly,

I got your letter right after I mailed mine the other day. It was so great hearing from you, sweetheart. I know I'll like whatever setup you decide on, so you go ahead. But remember, I can't get there until around the first of Feb., so don't count on me until then. Wow, a view of the river and the bay. That must be a swell place you picked out. You know, sweetheart, I am really different now. I don't get mad at people anymore, not even at Mary Louise's dopey lawyer. I tried to tell her he was just playing up to her, but she won't listen to me anymore, and I guess I don't blame her for that.

Well, there's not much to tell, Lilly. Things are just dragging on here with me sleeping in the back bedroom and taking my meals out and trying to train a young cluck at Kneipe's who can't tell the diff between a graver and a bar of silver solder. Just remember, sweetheart, I love you more than anything. It won't be long now.

All my love,
Bo

I run along the rocky beach every night now since the change began in late December. The wind is always cold and full of icy spray, the rocks covered with a glaze frozen into pinnacles and streamers that glitter in the moonlight. Each night as the moon approaches full, I feel more strongly the call from The Other. What it may be, or from where, I have no more notion than I used to have of my reason for being on earth at all. That, at least, I know now. The change, or, as I feel it inside myself, the awakening, revealed answers to questions I did not know how to ask. Lilly's favorite poet returns to my mind as I wander, abstracted in almost a human way. My joy used to be only that of the birds in the poem that says,

> *I am content when wakened birds*
> *Before they fly, test the reality*
> *Of misty fields, by their sweet questionings; . . .*

I questioned by no more than my own existence, by the joy of supple muscles, the leap into still water, the fury of the chase and the kill. But now, I feel; as in later lines, like those maidens

> *who were wont to sit and gaze*
> *Upon the grass relinquished to their feet. . . .*
> *The maidens taste*
> *And stray impassioned in the littering leaves.*

The poetry speaks to something deeper than my joyous senses and love of movement. It is like the call that comes each night now and makes my fur erect, my head turn to find the source of that sensation, as if something were always just out of range, just on the edge of my spatial sense, so that sometimes I leap wildly across the fields after it. It is far away in space and I am not yet sure where.

The surf crashes. Spray hits the rocks and streams away into the cold little salt pools. It is freezing, and yet I want to swim, to feel the grasp of the water around me. The moon moves across, visible only at rare times in the spaces between the racks of low-flying scud off the ocean. Each night as it passes into the west I feel the pull more strongly.

Now. It is almost a voice, almost a name. The image comes of a creature like myself, but as yet unawakened. It sends messages without being aware. It is still unformed, still in love with the sensations of life. I listen. It is the one I must find. There are others who send to me from the bright mirror of the moon, others I might find more easily. The night is filled with cries now. They echo and reverberate in a chamber of my mind I did not know I had. It is like a noisy crowd clamoring for my attention. But there is only one who is right, the one who calls from great distance, calls unconsciously, and I listen to him, his voice alone like the song of some night bird singing in the darkness, his eyes not yet opened. I listen. Soon I will know which way, and then we will go. This is why I am here, the learning and joy are steps to this necessity and the knowledge of where we will go afterward. I listen, the freezing wind ruffling my fur; the voice sings, sings in its own darkness.

January 13, 1938

Dear Bo,

I have to hurry. She's wild to leave and hardly lets me hold the pen. She got a message last night. We have to leave, or she said she will go without me. Oh, dear, Bo, I don't know what to do. She said take all the money I had and get a ticket to St. Louis. But maybe further than that. She won't let me finish. I love you. I love you.

Lilly

21 Jan '38

Dear Bo,

In answer to your letter concerning Lilly, we have to just say that we don't know much more than you do. One morning she got out of bed, packed a suitcase no bigger than a hatbox and went out the door crying like she was fit to die. She couldn't more than kiss us each goodbye before she ran out the door. She used the word "compulsion," and Polly and I think she must have something psychologically wrong. Not that we think she's off her head or anything. Certainly she is the sweetest girl in the whole world, and we love her like a daughter. But she was being dragged away, and that's no exaggeration.

We have talked about it and decided she is of age and we can't call the police to drag her off the train like a criminal. She mentioned St. Louis, but we don't know any more than that. You know, when she showed up at our place more than a year ago, she said she was a drifter with no family and a lot of sad things in her life. But she never told us anything specific that a person could use to find her, no names or addresses. We feel pretty darn helpless, too, Bo. You can believe that if we hear anything, we'll send

86

you a telegram. And we'd appreciate you doing the same. Our sorrow we share with you.

God keep you,
Dan and Polly

The train rattled slowly through more suburbs, the snow-covered backyards and fences repeating endlessly as the train rumbled over crossings, past the dinging bells and flashing lights, the crossbars like poison signs drifting past, cars stopped at the crossings with plumes of white exhaust and impatient faces in the frosty windshields. Lilly was too warm in the overheated coach, but she could not rouse herself to take off her coat. She had been on the train for three hours now and had eaten nothing, not even breakfast. She wondered at the numbness she felt inside. Something had tightened up and would not let go.

We have not been in conflict before, Lilly.

Lilly answered by thinking out the words rather than whispering, as she sometimes did. There were people sitting all around her.

You are taking me from the people I love, all of them.

My own necessities must come first.

Why do we have to leave?

It is time, my time to . . . I cannot say the word. It is my time to find another of my kind and to join with him.

You are going to mate?

It is nearly the same as your mating, but we must have achieved a particular stage in our growth. It comes on suddenly, and must be done.

Can't you do it in Boston?

There is only a particular one with whom I can join. We must journey to find him.

Well, how do you know he is in St. Louis?

I do not. But I received a communication last night from that direction.

Oh, God, this is funny. You might put an ad in the paper.

Lilly could not hold back the tears now, and she was laughing at the same time. She fumbled in her purse for a handkerchief, found it and, as soon as the tears began she let go with sobs that she could not hold in. The woman next to her looked on with a kindly expression.

"Are you all right?" the woman said. "Shall I call the conductor?"

"No, please. I'm all right," Lilly said. "I'm leaving home is all."

"Yes, that's such a sad thing," the woman said, smiling. "But then you have the homecoming to look forward to, you know."

Lilly tried not to think at all, concentrating on one of the ritual chants the Beast used sometimes to make inner peace. She said the words in her mind, aware that the Beast was close to the surface and listening but unable to help her.

Why are you so kind to other people and so cruel to me? I'm the closest one to you.

There was a long silence from inside, as if the Beast could not find an answer.

I have been kind.

You have healed other people, saved people from getting hurt, and now you take me from the only people I have ever loved.

I have been kindest to you.

I don't know what you mean. Lilly almost said the words aloud in her growing anger.

I have given you a year of life.

I want to know if I'm a real person. She asked the question suddenly, although it was the biggest question, the one she had never dared to ask. And yet, if this was to be the end of her, if the Beast was on its way to some unthinkable coupling with another of its kind, then she might never return to life, never have the chance if she did not ask now.

I did not know until recently myself.

Please tell me. I have to know about that.

When my change occurred . . . it is like the beginning of estrus for you . . . I knew about my Persons, but I had not known before.

Tell me!

I would rather not.

Am I just part of your mind?

When I called you up, you were not what is called real.

You mean when the first thing I can remember happened, when I was suddenly standing there outside Dan and Polly's?

Yes. When I spoke your name for the first time.

If I was not a real person, how did you know, how did you . . . make me real? Lilly felt coldness come over her in the hot train coach. If she was not real, if she was only a fabrication of this creature, then there was no use to even think about Bo, about a life, or about love.

I called you up from the . . . from what is available in the adjoining space.

I don't understand what that means!

Lilly was ready to speak aloud at this point, feeling that coldness inside her and wanting to know, wanting the terrible truth, as maybe Bo wanted to hear from that doctor that he had cancer, just to know it at last.

It is hard for me to explain to you because you have no concepts for this space except in religious language, which is prejudicial. But I will try because I understand your anguish and I share it, as I share all of your life, and because I am very sorry that you must return to that place when you do not wish to.

You mean I will just stop, just go out like a candle?

No, of course not. You are a Person, an Entity.

Please explain, please tell me about this space.

It is necessary that you understand that when I tell you, you must accept. You must not attempt foolish actions. You know that I will enforce my control to save myself, that I will call up another Person if necessary?

I know. I'll listen. She felt cold in her bones now, seeing with one last desperate memory Bo's sweet, wondering face as they made love.

I called you up from the newly dead.

"Oh, God!" Lilly screamed. "Oh, God!" She tried to stand up in the coach, hitting her head on the baggage rack and unaware of the pain, her eyes wild. "Oh, God!" She dropped her open purse and her hands clutched at the woman beside her, who thought she was going to be sick and was scrambling out of the seat to make room.

Lilly clawed her way out of the seat and staggered down the aisle, her eyes unseeing, the words sounding in her head now with a warning from the Beast inside, a warning that was emotional rather than in words. *Take care,* it was saying. *Take care, or I will replace you.* She bumped into the small, frightened-looking conductor, who held her by the elbows and tried to look into her stricken face.

"Here now, Miss, here now, what's the matter? Are you sick?"

The message got through to Lilly's mind, and, unable to do more than stand and look at the little man in front of her, she got enough control to say some words: yes, she was sick, and would he just help her to the ladies' room, and yes, he said, of course, and he would stand outside and she should just call out if she needed anything, and yes she said, just help me there.

Inside the hot little cabinet, she sat on the stool and breathed deeply, not thinking, breathing in the three-phase movement of the Yoga complete breathing exercise, and then she did the tranquilizing breath through each nostril for three times. At the end of that, her mind came back.

You tell me I was dead?

You were.

And I'm going to be dead again?

You will continue in that place from which you were called. And I think now, although I am not sure, that you will wait in that place until I have completed my transition here.

I will stay with you somehow, is that what you are saying? Will I be aware while I am . . . while I am dead again?

I do not know that, but I know that when I shift, you return to that place and wait to be recalled while my hold on you continues. I mean that you do not have memory of your former life until my need of you is finished.

I don't understand that. I just want to know if when you "call up" someone else for whatever strange purpose you can have, will I be dead again?

You will be in that space adjoining, as I said, until my transition is complete.

"Goddamn you," Lilly hissed between her teeth. "Tell me a straight answer, you filthy monster, you terrible thing that has torn me from death itself, you rotten beast —tell me if I will be dead!" She found herself tearing the handkerchief to shreds.

It is my belief that you will return to that state. Yes, you will be dead.

Chapter Five

As they slogged through sand toward the camp, Barry could see none of the usual hogans, only a large brushy pile that looked like a close-woven set of bushes such as one might find in a forest. Alongside this pile of brush a woman in a long green skirt and dark maroon blouse was chopping at some tough pieces of piñon branch. Johnny called a greeting in Navajo and she dropped the axe and turned, her hands on her hips, looking, Barry thought, like any poor mother watching her son approach, except that this was probably not really Johnny's mother but one of her sisters. She put her arms around Johnny, then took his face in her hands, shaking his head until his hat fell off. Johnny laughed and squirmed like a five-year-old, and Barry stood, suitcase and hamper in hand, grinning, wondering what to say or if it made any difference.

Johnny turned, his eyes sparkling, held out his hand for Barry to come closer. The young Indian said a few words in Navajo and the woman nodded, although she did not smile. Her face was almost round, high forehead, clear eyes in nests of wrinkles and with a wide, strong mouth. She looked, Barry thought, like she could handle things.

"My mother, Betty Chee," Johnny said.

"How do you do, Mrs. Chee," Barry said. "I don't know if you can understand me, but I am honored that you will receive me here."

"I speak English some," Betty Chee said. "You friend of this one"—she pushed Johnny, smiling at him—"you stay with us long time."

"Thank you very much, Mrs. Chee," Barry said, setting the suitcase and hamper down. He looked at the wood, the

91

gray, twisted, tough wood she was hacking at with the dull axe. "If you'll let me, I'll chop the wood?" He heard himself sounding silly, and wondered what a guest did in Navajo land, anyway.

"Inside. Be at home," the woman said, picking up the axe again. She had apparently not understood what Barry meant.

Barry stood in some indecision before the wall of brush. How did one get inside? He heard a snort of muffled laughter at his side, and Johnny pushed him around to the left.

"No, you don't go crashing through a wall," he said, pushing Barry around until a large opening presented itself. Inside, the shelter was roomy, floored with smooth, hard-packed sand, and contained a variety of cooking utensils and a tall loom made of straight posts tied together with cord and holding a half-finished rug. In several corners were some rolled-up blankets that must be for sleeping. On a sort of shelf made of poles cleverly entwined with the growing willows were articles of clothing, pots and dishes and sacks of flour and meal. In all, it was, with its roof almost but not quite closed to the deepening blue of the evening, remarkably pleasant, cool and perfect for its use in a land where rainfall was no problem. Barry felt snug inside it, like a bird in a well-built nest. In the center of the floor smouldered a small fire with ashes around it that told of it being used for many days. A cat was asleep in the corner beneath the shelf, completing the domestic scene.

"This is perfect," Barry said. "A summer house."

"That's what we call it," Johnny said. He sat leaning back against the blanket roll he had taken from the straw suitcase. Outside, the strokes of the axe kept on regularly.

"If this were Western civilization, one of us guys would be out there chopping that wood," Barry said, feeling genuinely uncomfortable.

"She does the cooking," Johnny said. "She would be insulted if I told her she was too weak to chop wood anymore."

"Where are the rest of your family?"

"The kids are probably bringing the sheep in about now," he said, lying back and tipping his hat over his eyes. "And the menfolks are either coming home from the trading post—not the one we saw," he added, "or maybe upstream at the sweat lodge getting ready for the ritual tomorrow night."

"They're going to have a peyote ceremony, then?" Barry said.

"How about not using that word in this house, okay?" Johnny said without moving. "My mother understands some English, and she's not in favor of the Church and the way they do things there."

At that point a man with his hat in his hand bent to come in through the low doorway. His eyes were hard and his mouth turned down in a frown as he looked at Barry. Barry stood up awkwardly, not knowing whether to shake hands first or not. But Johnny had got up at the same time and was smiling at the newcomer, whose face broke its frown as he saw the younger man. There was a brief exchange in Navajo, and the man slapped Johnny on the back several times. He was short-statured, with a gnarled face and a distinct stoop to his walk. He might have been anywhere from forty to seventy, Barry thought. Johnny said some more to the man, and he turned to Barry, this time with a smile and with his hand extended. Barry took the hand, felt the smooth, light handshake of the Indian and said, not knowing if he would be understood, "I'm very pleased to be here and meet you . . ." He looked at Johnny.

"Oh, yeah, sorry. This is my, uh, maternal uncle, Albert Chee. And this is Barry Golden," Johnny said, indicating Barry.

There was another exchange and Johnny shook his head, smiling. He talked at some length and then turned to Barry. "Albert was thinking you might be from the agency, one of Collier's people, and he was about to politely tell you to take your ass out of his house, but I told him what you were doing here and that you had nothing at all to do with the Indian commissioner or even the tribal council."

"What's all that about?" Barry said, sitting down again.

"You know much about the slaughtering of livestock the last few years?"

"Not from the Indian side of it."

"The U.S. Government decided a couple years ago that our people were overgrazing the land because they had too many sheep and goats, so they pushed the tribal council around until that bunch of half-whites put out an order that everyone's herd had to be cut ten percent. The big,

93

rich herders who live like whites and have suction in high places lost no animals at all, while the little guys, like my relatives here, lost more than their share."

"How do you mean, reduced?" Barry said. "I thought they put a limit on the number of animals you could have and then bought up the ones over that limit."

"If you can call it buying when they give you twenty percent of market value," Johnny said. He leaned over to Albert, who was sitting now listening with a puzzled expression, and said what must have been a brief resume in Navajo. The older man's face grew stolid again, and the frown turned his mouth down. He looked at Barry and said a long series of things in his own language, gesturing emphatically at several points. He concluded by spreading his arms wide, his face growing old-looking.

"He's telling about the burning of the goats," Johnny said. "Couple years ago I wasn't here, but Albert saw it. The government bought up more than three thousand goats for about a dollar and a quarter apiece and then took them out into a bit corral and shot them all dead. Bunch of whites with rifles had themselves a time doing it." He paused while Barry let that sink in. "And then they poured gasoline over the bodies and burned them all up. You can still see the big piles of bones and the ashes of the corral up north of here, right out on the mesa. Lots of our people saw it."

"Hell of a way to reduce livestock," Barry said. "But they do that nowadays, and not just with Indian animals. They burn wheat and dump coffee in the ocean to keep up the price. Did they explain that to your people?"

"You can't explain something like that," Johnny said, shaking his head. "My people don't waste the world like that. It's a sin, maybe the worst sin. And they don't care about keeping prices up. In fact, most of them can't imagine what makes the prices go up and down and just take it as part of being herders. But to waste life and meat and hides by burning them like that"—he turned and said something to Albert—"that's almost like doing it to people."

Albert nodded his head and said something in Navajo.

"Albert says it's the white man going finally insane, and he will be doing it to people next thing because there are too many on the range."

The conversation had distracted Barry, and he didn't hear the two little girls outside with their mother. Now

94

they all came in, the woman carrying wood to the fire and giving directions to the girls in a soft voice Barry could hardly hear. The girls were dressed like their mother, with fewer pieces of silver on their clothes; but the older one, who might have been twelve, had heavy strings of turquoise around her neck as her mother did. Barry saw, too, that the woman wore several silver bracelets, some with turquoise stones, and that the buttons of her blouse were silver dimes. Supper was a joint effort and consisted of mutton stew with fried bread, which the woman made by slapping the dough between her hands and then frying it in a skillet on a makeshift grill over the fire. Coffee completed the meal, and when they had eaten, Barry was genuinely surprised at how good it had been.

They sat around after the meal feeling torpid, Barry thinking he had eaten too much and made a pig of himself; but then they had kept pushing more at him, and he had simply tried to be polite. Now he felt as if he should hibernate for a week.

Johnny said something brief and, after Albert had answered him, turned to Barry. "Old Man Fisher, or Old Fisherman, I guess would be the correct way to say it, the grandfather, anyway, is visiting with the Begays up the canyon. My mother's sister's—ah, well, forget the relationship . . . a young woman who ran away from her husband's lodge up north is visiting there also. That's where the meeting will be held tomorrow night, if everyone gets there."

When it was quite dark and the mother had washed up the dishes in a tiny pan of heated water and they had drunk the last of the weak coffee, Albert Chee and Johnny and Barry walked along the edge of the stream that meandered through the middle of the valley.

Albert said something, pointing to a tall pinnacle of sandstone standing farther up the valley in almost the center of the streambed.

"He's telling you about Spider Woman, who lives on top of that rock there," Johnny said. "She taught the people how to weave rugs and blankets, and now she's all alone up there in that cleft rock. When I was a kid I remember Old Fisherman scaring me with stories of how she came scaling down at night to pick off unwary kids who wandered around after dark."

Barry sat on a stone while Albert and Johnny walked over by the horses hobbled in the grassy area near the west

95

side of the canyon. He wanted to let them have their own conversation, and he needed time himself to get things straight in his mind. He had taken a few notes, but mostly he was picking up the atmosphere and deciding what the background and setting in the article were going to be like. He had as yet heard nothing about the Native American Church, which was why he was here, supposedly. He leaned back against the rock and looked at the sharp black edges of the canyon overhead. The stars were brilliant, seeming to step out into space over the edge of the canyon and to peer down into this rift in the earth with particular care and brightness. He had never seen them so bright, perhaps because he had never looked at the stars so far from any city lights; here the blackness of the canyon accentuated their light. He wondered where the moon would be. Its transit across the canyon would be brief. In the moonless night, *tsay-ih* became a cavern whose roof was impossibly alive with stars. In the dense darkness he noticed smells more, the horses over to the left, the fire from the cooked meal as it died down, the wet smell of the little stream and the sand, the smell of his own body sitting against an odor of stone, an invisible stream of odors coming with a gentle wind that moved in the valley. His hearing, too, seemed to intensify. He could hear the girls and the Indian woman quite clearly, although their language was unknown to him. Johnny said that the girls knew English well but that they were shy of strangers, especially Whites, so not to expect much from them. They had said "Thank you" very nicely when he gave them the candy from the trading post, but that was all. He heard the cat give a screech and a rapid modulation of chatter from the woman. A horse was coughing over in the darkness, and another rattled its hobbles. Farther away past the shelter, the sheep were making sleepy sheep noises, little bleats and sighings. Behind it all the stream whispered in low tones, and leaves among the willows spoke a tiny rattling language of their own.

When he rolled up in his blanket that night alongside Johnny in the summer shelter of the Chees, he felt he had never been so comfortable. Listening to the breathing of the people around him, he thought of his family in their big house at home, blessed them with a silent prayer, thought of Renee so that her face, her hands on his shoulders, came back to him vividly. And then he slept.

I wake with suddenness and a tense excitement. I have shifted almost before waking, so eager am I to move as myself in this strangely new place. I note everything with heightened senses: the heaving sonorousness of the breathing humans in the dark shelter, their vibrations surrounding me, rippling in my spatial sense that seems newly alive with colors of its own beyond the visible spectrum. I sniff, and the full range of odors, the Indian scent, the embers of fire, the sheep outside, the food that remains, even the wool in sacks and the dozing dogs outside the shelter have a new significance. It is as if I had just wakened from a long hibernation, and, as I drop the blanket and slip out the door, I wonder if this can be true. Have I been asleep? I quiet the dogs easily and begin a cautious pacing down toward the stream, only to leap aside as an owl flutters by in the dark. I am tense, jumpy as a rabbit, and yet inexplicably and fanatically happy too in this place.

I smell the water and taste its flavor of cliffs and sandbars and willow roots, sip into me the clean taste of this place. And then I flash suddenly into a run, galloping down toward the bend in the canyon, running with joy as I have not done, it seems, since I was a cub, for here in the dark canyon with the moonless night over me, I feel properly myself, my own self again. I race across the flat sandbars, heedless of the wild tracks I am leaving, dash back and forth through the shallow water, splashing it around me gleefully, heading down the canyon where I sense there are no humans, where the walls close in on the valley and the close darkness is mine alone.

A rabbit occupies me for a minute or two, but I let him get away after getting close enough to toss him into the air. He squeals, expecting death, but I laugh under my panting breath and run on, the canyon slipping around me like a familiar street.

There is a coyote, too; I throw a quick thought at him as I give chase, but he does not answer. He must not be like that other one, but only a dumb animal. Him, too, I allow to escape, but not before making him try to climb a sheer rock wall. It is so funny that I roll on my back laughing and waving my legs in the air. I find a whispering willow and lie down to savor the night, getting back my breath. It feels so new and different here. My fur prickles as if a cold breeze had hit me, although the night is warm. I feel that someone is studying me, watching me, and I lie perfectly still, reaching out on all sides with my spatial sense. Nothing is there, right up to the solid rock walls on each side, which are, at this point, no more than a hundred yards apart. I sense the small animals of the desert, nothing else. The prickling remains, not unpleasant but like a warning sign that I cannot read. I lie under the tree for some time, listening. The nearby animals resume their night hunts as I still my breathing to hear better. A mouse begins improving his burrow not ten feet from me, and I sense a tarantula racing along after something, a dark, hairy shadow that appears and disappears in the rocks, and a bird over my head mumbles in his sleep. It must be only my excitement at this place. I relax and rise to walk on down the valley.

A mile further, as the valley widens again and I am walking close to the right side in the deepest shadow of the wall, I feel a tension building up in my body. It is not localized to spatial sense or hearing, or even feeling, but makes me uncertain. I stop, sensing around as I did before. But this time the feeling is different: danger. There is nothing dangerous in the life around me, but, rather, there seems to be an incipience, a possibility of danger, perhaps not even a real thing. I advance one step at a time, the vague feeling becoming more strong until I must stop to assess what it is. My fur is erect, my hackles up as if with fear and I feel a quivering in my legs. My senses tell me nothing except that there is a break in the canyon wall ahead, one of the old ruins of the pre-Navajo people who lived here hundreds of years ago.

I take another step forward. A blind terror seizes me, so that I cannot take another step, can hardly organize my mind to step back out of that zone of fear. I struggle in my mind to recall that feeling, and it comes back from more than a year ago. My fight with the farm woman, Aunt Cat, the mother of Barry's wife, involved the same feeling. It was the amulet she carried and lost in that brief grappling with the guard when she was trying to kill me. I remember waiting for her in the dark trees as she stalked forward, shotgun at the ready, confident that I could make her put the gun down. Then, as she got closer, the terrible fear that made my muscles let go, made my very flesh rebel against my mind and lie down in abject terror before her. The amulet had that power—whatever it came from, whatever it signified to me—and now I feel it here. But the fear is coupled with a perverse need to step forward into that terror, to give in to what is most awful, like giving in to my own death.

I back up another step on the dark sand, hearing it crunch beneath my feet, hearing the night wind forcing the leaves of the willow into speech, filling the night with unintelligible words, tree words. Is there another sound also, a speaking as of people far away, barely heard, speaking in a different language, but so low that I think it is not sound at all but the blood tumbling through my own veins? I step forward again, hearing the sand grains crunch. The terror builds around my heart like a grasping claw that threatens to squeeze but does not yet do it. I cannot help taking another step. The claw grips my heart, and I know that if I step forward again I will die.

But now the sound, the rasping undercurrent of vibration that was so faint, is growing more distinct, and it might be voices. I might recognize the words if only I could go closer. I will take one more step, only one. I step. Sounds intensify: sand crunches, wind howls in the willow leaves, water crashes across rocks behind me, a snake thunders along in the grass, and the sound of voices rises to a chorus of raging, a tumult of imprecations that assault me from every side so that I must take time to pull my consciousness together to think which way is back, so distorted is time and space in that agony of sounds. My heart seems to have stopped in midbeat, my breathing suspended as if I had been turned to stone. I try to scream and have no voice, but my mind pulls the muscles of my legs in a final attempt to go back; I fall back, out of range of that force. I am lying on the sand, twisted around, trying to crawl away. I crawl, the sounds becoming less painful, the voices vanishing, becoming the willow leaves again, the quiet lapping of water, the susurration of wind in grass. I take a sharp breath and howl like a cat on fire, like a bear leaping from a cliff, shaking with the nearness of death.

Sometime later I regain myself, sprawled on the sand, my muzzle in the water, panting into the shallow water as if I had just run twenty miles. I have not used my mind in this emergency, I think. Where I cannot go, Barry can. And then, as I am about to shift, I recall the agonizing thoughts Barry has had about his continued existence in this world. If there is an amulet or something like it in that forbidden area ahead of me in the dark, it will be Barry's first thought to secure it for his own continuation and my banishment from consciousness. Time does not usually matter as much to me as it does to him, but I feel a pressure on me now, an imminence that does not want to wait, should not be blocked by my Person and his concerns.

I stand stupidly in the dark, feeling around me with every sense I have, trying to fathom that aura of terror that lies no more than ten feet away, imperceptible where I stand, overwhelming at three or four steps' distance. I must block this experience from Barry's mind, the first time I have ever resorted to such tactics against my Person. I like Barry. He is closest to me of the humans I have assumed, but his survival instinct is strong, too strong for me to trust him.

I retreat up the stream, my night joy transformed into a tired feeling of defeat. The place has a magic charm on me—yes, more than a charm, a force indeed that might destroy me. I ponder that as I pace slowly back to the shelter. And, too, the feeling of being watched is still with me. Perhaps the Indian stories of spirits are not all superstition. And they speak of shape-changers also. I feel uncertain now for one time in my life, uncertain of my strength and ability and safety in the world.

I am forgetful and do not conceal my scent as I approach the summer shelter, and the horses and sheep stir restively as I come into their range. Putting everything out of my memory so that Barry will recall nothing, I slip into the shelter after making sure no one is awake, crawl into the blanket, pull myself into a tight white point of consciousness and shift.

The morning was cool and dusky in the canyon before the sun began to drop its fire down the sandstone walls, and Barry felt he had never slept so well. No wandering about as at home. Perhaps what he needed was to camp out on the ground. Renee would balk at that, he thought, eating the cornbread Johnny's mother had made in a pan over the little fire. Albert Chee seemed lethargic this morning and, in spite of several sharp verbal exchanges with his wife, sat rather morosely in the corner of the shelter after breakfast was over. The girls had quietly slipped out to take the sheep to pasture and were gone before Johnny and Barry had finished their coffee.

As they walked upstream toward an angle of the canyon where the lowering bluffs cut off any view beyond the bend, Johnny was unduly silent, so that Barry felt he should say something.

"You look worried this morning, old sidekick."

"It's my uncle."

"Albert Chee?"

"He's supposed to see about getting the wool to Red Rock Trading Post before the price goes down any more. But he says it can wait."

"Is that unusual?" Barry said, watching the rising sun inch its fiery light down the west side of the canyon, turning the dull stone to daylight orange.

"Yes, it is. He is not a lazy man. But my uncle is not feeling right." Johnny kicked at a stone and picked a handful of piñon nuts out of his jacket pocket. He held them out to Barry, who took a few.

"No, you put them all in your mouth," Johnny said, tossing the handful of tiny nuts into his mouth. "Then you crack them one at a time between your front teeth, spit out the shells"—he spit out two neatly split shell halves—"and keep the rest in your cheek."

Barry tried it, got shells all over the inside of his mouth and spit the nuts back out to crack one at a time.

"It's the slaughtering of the ánimals you think has made your uncle feel bad?"

"Sure, even though it's a while ago. How would you feel if you knew that anytime they wanted, the government people could come to your house and take your car away, maybe some of your money, too?"

"That's about what they do with taxes."

"It's not the same thing," Johnny said, spitting out piñon shells. "You people expect that. Your government gives you what you want, and then they take something in return. With my people it's not that way. The government took everything, and we tried to build it up again and then, just because their grazing-range figures don't agree with reality, they come and kill thousands of animals."

They were coming around the bend of the canyon, and Barry caught sight of a settlement up ahead, many of the brushy shelters and two or three hogans made of stones and logs sitting in a wide plain that the valley opened into. There were rickety stick fences around what looked like new cornfields with grain growing and perhaps vegetables also. It had the look of a settled community, people moving around at various tasks and even an old Ford truck sitting beside one of the hogans.

"There you are," Johnny said. "The whole Yellow Mesa camp and then some."

Barry felt a twinge of apprehension, seeing so many Indians in their natural habitat. He felt badly outnumbered and knew in an instant how the Indian must feel in the city, surrounded by alien culture and endless numbers of the aliens themselves.

"In that old hogan over there," Johnny said, pronouncing it *ho-ran,* "we will have the ceremony for Blessing."

"Doesn't seem to be anybody living in it."

"No. Whites don't live in their churches, do they?"

"Oh, of course," Barry said, feeling a hint of antagonism from the man at his side. Don't forsake me now, Tonto, he thought.

But it was all very friendly, so Barry should not have worried. He did not know that one of Johnny's little sisters had run down here last night and told all about the white who would be coming to write about the Church and how wonderful it was, and so he was pleasantly surprised by the welcome he received. It was like coming into a large party. He remembered only two names in the first group: Old Fisherman, of whom Johnny had spoken at length, and Sarah Lakuchai, a young, pretty woman in a cotton blouse and velveteen skirt somewhat shorter than those worn by the older women. She was a strikingly handsome Indian woman, Barry thought, realizing he was looking at her too long for politeness. Her hair was gleaming blue-black, and her eyes had a distinct slant that recalled her Mongolian ancestry. Her mouth, with its good-humored smile, inevitably reminded him of Renée's, and he caught up his thoughts guiltily, looking away and shaking hands with a woman who looked so ancient she must remember coming across the Bering Straits.

Some of the people spoke English, some could but didn't bother. Each person was busy at some task; some hoeing weeds or fixing fences so the sheep and goats couldn't get at the crops; some cutting wood and carrying it in from the slopes farther down the valley; some, doing traditional jobs like the women he saw at their looms. The older women were spinning yarn from wool using a simple stick fitted into a flat piece of wood they held on one thigh, while the younger women cleaned and carded the wool. He noticed there were fewer men than he would have thought, and Johnny said that many of the men were

102

working for the railroad, the Santa Fe, and some of them would be gone for months at a time.

"We usually have a celebration when the gang comes back to Gallup from working out on the line," Johnny said. "They are on the section gang, the old pick and shovel stuff."

Barry nodded, feeling somewhat chastened again. It was not his fault the country was still in the Depression. But that had not been what the young Indian meant. He looked at Barry with a grin and said something incomprehensible.

"You remember what fun that is, I guess." He slapped Barry's shoulder and said, "Remember old Asa, the foreman with no teeth?" And he laughed.

Barry was mystified by his reference to something he could not remember. Obviously he had known Johnny Strong Horse in his earlier life, and they must have worked on a section gang at some time. That would explain why Johnny and he got to be friends so easily; they had been friends before. Barry felt frustrated again, but the problem was such a common one by this time that he shrugged it away and grinned back at Johnny. He listened as the people spoke about the Church, those who could speaking English for his benefit. They mentioned the "Road Man" or "Chant Leader" who would be arriving to do the ceremony that evening.

The day passed swiftly with Barry listening and taking notes so that by evening he began to understand the enormity of what was being done to the Indian herds, the calculated deceptions of the government bureaucrats, the weak-kneed duplicity of the old tribal council members who were now discredited and the general apathy of those Indian enforcers of the law who saw themselves as dupes of the white. He heard more than enough during that day to smear the whole Indian Service from Washington on down, at least as seen from the bottom of the totem pole. As evening began darkening the canyon, he sat with his back against a cottonwood down near the stream and tried to think of what he would need from other points of view before putting together anything coherent for the lay reader. It occurred to him that he had the makings not only of an article but of a whole book. He pushed the excitement down and concentrated on the material at hand. Johnny's approach startled him.

"You heard enough sob stories for one day?" the young Indian asked, squatting down on his heels.

"I'll tell you, Johnny," Barry said, flipping closed the notebook, "there's a whole book's worth of stuff going on here. I'm surprised no one is down here writing it."

"You are."

"And that's not even the reason I came. There's the ceremony tonight," Barry said, giving a sigh. He felt exhausted already.

"It's all part of the same story," Johnny said. "But you can see that. The people lose heart, and the sensitive ones, or the weak ones, let go and begin seeing visions, like Wonowa, that woman with the long braid—remember? The one who said she had seen Banded Rock Boy?"

"Yeah. I was going to ask you about that. Has there been much of the visionary stuff lately? More than usual, I mean?"

"Sure. In my own clan I can think of three people who have seen various gods and spirits and—" Johnny stopped, looking down at the dirt.

"Go on," Barry said quietly.

"My own sister saw the tracks of Yei-t'so just this morning."

"What is Yei-t'so?"

"He's one of the terrible beings, the giants, monsters, evil creatures that prey on the people in bad times."

"What'd the tracks look like?" Barry said, making no particular connection.

"She said they were big cat tracks with long claws or fingers on them."

Barry came aware suddenly. So, the Beast had been out last night. He wondered at the blankness of his memory. Usually he recalled a dim, dreamlike set of images, but there was nothing that he could remember at all. He shrugged. "Mountain lion probably, or a bear."

"Yeah, there are black bear around, and once in a while a cougar, but my sister knows what their tracks look like. She said they were big, and . . . well, different. I believe her." The young Indian rocked on his heels, looked at Barry with a sheepish grin. "She wanted me to come see them, and I laughed at her. I shouldn't have laughed."

"So there have been a lot of visions and other evidence of the supernatural," Barry said, jotting items in the notebook again.

"More than I've ever known. We aren't an overly superstitious people, I don't think, not as Indians go, anyway, but I hear about somebody seeing Shell Woman or some

104

ancestor spirit every time I come home now. That's what worries me."

"Yeah. It's a sign of trouble, all right."

"And they talk about it in the Church gatherings. You won't be able to get it tonight because it will all be in Navajo, but if I can, I'll try to remember it for you. I can't keep up a running translation because it would be discourtesy to those singing or praying."

"I understand. But I wish you'd fill me in on what I'm supposed to do so I don't offend the powers that be."

"Okay. It's not complicated, not for a visitor, anyway. You can just sit still and not get in any trouble; remember, though, if you have to go out, go clockwise around the circle. Don't go to your right. You'll be sitting on the south side of the hogan, so if you want to go out, get up and walk past the Chant Leader, between him and the moon altar. Don't go out to your right."

"Why the big thing about going to the left?" Barry said, confused by the terms and wondering if he would be able to tell the difference between the Chant Leader and the moon altar.

"It's too complicated to go into everything, but the circle would be violated if you went the wrong way around; the circle has to stay complete during the ceremony." Johnny picked up a twig and with his other hand smoothed a space in the sand. "Now, here is the inside of the hogan," he said, scratching a circle in the sand, "and in the center toward this end is the fire, and behind that is the altar, shaped like a crescent moon that goes partway around the fire. There will be a man who tends the fire, Fire Man or Fire Chief, who uses a stick that he lays right here, pointing toward the door." Johnny looked up. "Don't stumble over that stick, either."

"I'm not going to move."

"Fine. Just sit still and enjoy it," said Johnny Strong Horse, grinning. "Now look here. Behind the altar is the Chant Leader, or Road Man he is sometimes called, and on one side of him is Fire Man and on the other is Cedar Man, or—what would you call him? Maybe the Incense Shaker. He also handles the drum at the start. So you have three main officials for the ceremony. Don't worry if you have to smoke a cigarette or get some of the smoke from the fire blown on you by Road Man. It's all part of the praying and asking for Blessing. And there will be some singing by everybody there, but it is all individual stuff—no group hymns, usually—and nobody *has* to do anything. So just take the peyote when it comes around—if you want it, that is—and smoke a cigarette at the beginning like everybody else." Johnny grinned. "And don't flip the butt out the door. Give it to Road Man and he'll put it against the altar."

"So I just pretty much do like everybody else?"

"You don't have to sing or ask for Blessing if you don't want, but otherwise . . . yeah, just follow me. And if you want more peyote, nudge me with your elbow three times and I'll ask for the sack. Usually it comes around plenty, so you don't have to ask." Johnny frowned. "You have to pass it a certain way, but—well, tell you what. When the stuff comes around, just take it from the person next to you in exactly the way he is holding it and pass it on that way, okay? And if they pass you the drum, use it if you feel like it, or pass it on."

"What happens if I do something wrong?"

"You can't, really, short of taking a crap on the altar. I'm just thinking out loud is all. It's pretty new to us, and even the Chant Leader is not always sure of what is correct. The important thing is to sit back, be calm and savor the experience. Trust in your companions, their friendship and you'll have a good evening out of it."

"Is this an all-male thing?"

"No, not at all. Just about all the women you met today will be there. They have as much part as we do."

Barry looked up to see that the sun had left the canyon and dusk was gathering among the rocks and against the western walls. A light breeze caught his sweaty skin, and he shivered.

Inside the hogan there was more space than seemed possible from looking at the outside of it. A dozen people sat around the shadowy walls, and more came stooping through the low doorway each minute, and still the circle of people around the walls had gaps in it. Barry noticed the people seemed relaxed and joked with each other, some of them laughing in low tones, but that they became quiet once they sat down. The fire was built up a bit under the crooked piñon branches that lay as Johnny had described them, and the man with the narrow face, who sat at the end opposite the door, began playing softly on the drum while Road Man, the ascetic-looking young man next to him, began a low chant in which Barry heard a series of repeated sounds. It was a low-pitched singing that went on while the final preparations were made and Fire Man settled the wood to his liking and returned to his place beside the singer.

Cigarettes were made from corn husk and Bull Durham, which made Barry smile as he tried to roll his own for the first time in his life. But he saw everyone else was serious, so he put his face straight and decided to be the observer who is invisible. The smoking went on, and one old man sang a short song—quite impromptu, it seemed—and then the butts were leaned against the altar, which was no more than a smooth mound of clay, flat on top and shaped like a crescent. Road Man was occupied in using a feather fan to waft fire smoke onto a woman who rocked back and forth and sang a few words over and over. Then he would go on around the circle and waft the smoke on another person. The drumming went on softly.

After a time in the firelit gloom, a sack and a small stick with feathers attached to it were passed around, and everyone began chewing, spitting out something occasionally, and Barry found himself with two of the brown buttons in his mouth, chewing the dry, fibrous cactus, spitting out the cottony center and then, when it seemed possible, swallowing the stuff. He sat still, wondering how long the effects would take to appear, but for a time nothing happened, and he became absorbed in watching the other ceremonies taking place in the low flickering light that lit up one face and then another around the circle.

The sack had come around again, and he had taken two more of the buttons before he recognized the young woman he had met that morning, Sarah Lakuchai, the one he had thought beautiful, sitting directly across from him so that the flickering shadows had hidden her face. Now he watched her as the flames danced lower and saw her eyes looking at him, their darkness seeming larger in the dusk of the hogan. Barry felt himself expanding, feeling good, feeling light and youthful and like singing a song suddenly. He repressed the song but could not help smiling. He felt so vigorous and potent, as if he might fly if he tried, as if gravity and the heavy earth were illusions he might pass through and beyond. Yes, they are illusions, he thought, gazing across at the woman's eyes that were larger now than he had believed possible. He drew away his gaze as one of the Indians passed in front of him. He recalled where he was and sat still, feeling he had almost gotten to his feet to sing something, or to begin a dance, he felt so good. Be calm, he told himself, determined to sit still and learn the mysteries.

The individual singing and drumming went on, and Old Fisherman sang with his head thrown back and the tears running down his cheeks through the wrinkles and furrows of age. Barry felt intense empathy with him, could almost understand his song, the words becoming images and emotional symbols rather than language sounds. Fire Man tended the sticks that burned, and the Incense Chief threw shavings on the fire at intervals. Road Man sang and moved around the circle, and at Barry's side sat his friend, Johnny Strong Horse, who was now singing in his language, a low-toned, repetitive song that again Barry thought he could understand, a sadness and a strength, a call for help. As Barry looked back at the fire, he saw without surprise the figures of the spirits emerging from the flame tips like uncertain and wavering fingers extended from another world below this one, reaching up slender gray fingers to touch this world.

He watched, fascinated, as the fingers formed on the flames and reached upward until they were as large as the song, until they said the song, were the song made visible and wavering up toward the dark smoke hole, making visible the young Indian's song, and Barry sat as one turned to stone watching the spirits undulate in their dark colors as the song seemed to go on forever—or was it someone else singing now? He could not have said, for his eyes were fixed on the spirits who swarmed inside the hogan, expanding its walls to great distances. And now the people on the other side of the circle diminished to insect size, to grasshoppers who sat and sang with their brown, glittering wings rubbing together, the spirits' song a visible thread of scarlet running out from each of their throats, forming a burning skein that circled the hogan while the eyes of the people opened wider. The eyes of the woman whose name was Sarah became larger than the smoke hole above him, larger than the hogan, opening to him a visible darkness into which he entered, leaning forward, falling horizontally across the earth as it passed away from under him, flashing into and through the dark portals so that he looked down, gasping as he fled out across the night land, fleeing with his clothes streaming behind him in smoke swirls that he heard with his ears and sensed with his skin in purple vibrations swelling around him like a net, a cross-weaving of threads in impossible colors singing to his ears, and a low-voiced thrumming that he watched as it swelled and fell under him while he sped through the dark of the woman's eyes.

If she held them open he would fall forever around the dark swell of the earth, the bright horizon receding behind him, the sharp-edged clouds whispering backwards, each one a precipitous ledge over which he flew without wings, being held only by her eyes, which narrowed, pressed in upon him until he could feel the tunnel through which he traveled, its veins and muscles touching his skin, its great throbbing music in his ears, the deep scarlet tunnel turning to the azure of evening sky at great heights, and the purples wavering in long curtains like the Northern Lights. He closed his eyes.

And was there, in the other world, the rounded land under him turning with music, an extension of himself. He was two, a blessed double being, the larger one and himself, the larger one crying out a song of blessing while they separated from each other like stereo images coming apart in the eye: tenuous, distinct, wavering as a wolf's cry becoming two separate cries, a chord heard singing across the rounded world, across the sudden bands of color that rose in place of suns, brilliant, more colors than existed in the world. The colors throbbed with sounds, vibrations that shifted around the two figures, a multitudinous network centered on each of them, interlocking, meshing so that they understood each other and, while they moved apart, remained a single chord of music, harmony as positive and unbreakable as a major and its dominant, moving apart until the interlocking nets began to break, the colors to separate from the banded spectra, and one of them had to open his eyes to fix on the world before it was too late, and Barry did.

The hogan flickered with the light of the small fire. The eyes of the woman across from him were fixed on his, staring as if looking past him, and Barry thought she had been there, too, and he dared not close his eyes again for a time. The vision began to break through, and he felt sudden vertigo as the earth tipped under him, the colors broke through reality, and around the moon altar and Father Peyote, small and brown in the center of the moon, came the flaming colors announcing their presence to his ears as magnificent chords and arpeggios that he saw, that he knew with more than senses. The vibrations made the world spacious, coming from all living things and lighting the things of space with the time-fixing vibrations of life. He opened his eyes wide and watched the moon altar shift its shape to a high and beautiful mountain range, snow cresting its top, and along the sides of the mountain, people. No, not people, creatures that moved in graceful couples, more slender than earthly cats or bears, now running on all fours, now dancing upright along the rock ledges, light as vapor, unafraid of the unscalable falls beneath them, the drifting long veils of vapor pouring like smoke into the valleys. As he watched, the figures changed to birds, wheeling over the moon mountain in great, paired circles, held fast in the streaming nets of vibration that interlocked and made of them all one flock, one herd, an organism shaped with joy. The birds flew to the rim of the moon peaks, became sylphs, streaming upward in slender flames, transforming their bodies at will as they sang the song of their beings, now larger, now small and graceful, stretching to impossible, nebulous thinness of tissue that rose and wavered in the upthrusting thermals. They touched, harmonizing waves of purple and deep green, fast approaching waves of yellow surging against them, lifting them, the following and deeper reds slowing as the songs died away.

The altar shrank back into a crescent, the beings diminished and went out like sparks, the fire faded back to a few sticks, the flames flickering shadows on the sand floor of a hogan at midnight. Across from him, Barry saw the eyes of the woman were closed. He felt light and heavy at the same time, tired and rested and very, very thirsty. The image of thirst built arroyos and dead skulls in his mind. His throat parched shut on itself, tube now clogged, shriveling away, breaking into rusty particles that fell into the echoing cavity of his body space where he wandered, mouth sealed with dust.

Something touched his arm.

"Drink," said a voice, very low, but it reverberated as if they were in a huge cavern.

He lifted the dipper, a gourd, and the smell of water overcame him, ravished his senses like the love of a woman. He drank.

The gourd passed away.

The night lay at his feet, stretching miles of empty sand to the fire that was dying down, miles of sand turning blue again and transparent, blue and a wavery floor like water

110

rising around him; he could not breathe if he could not separate again. He must separate again, but from that enormous distance he saw the dark eyes of the woman named Sarah, who looked at him and said "No" in a song he could not understand, sang "No" to him again, to both of him, so they stopped dreaming as if they were truly two because the woman had spoken to both of them at once. "No," she had said, and they must be content for the time to be one.

Time flowed away like mist before a wind. The fire drew his eyes until they felt dry and delicate in their sockets, feathery and light, as if they might drift away from his head. His eyeless face was left behind as they drifted like thistle silk across the dark, bobbing in the light breeze from the doorway, looking upward through the smoke hole while the upward burst of heat from the flames whirled them upward, out and away into the universe, where Barry still gazed from their disembodied pupils that dilated to cavernous size, seeing the drifting shoals that were galaxies, the clouds of illumined gas, the depth of the horse's head and the coal sack, the nebulae, a nova striking lines of light like humming wires between the stars, holding all together in one vast net, an interstellar spider's web. He closed his eyes.

The burst of color came with sound again, and a feeling of cool garnet color on his skin, as from a church window struck through by a shaft of moonlight, a tone made up of three semitones that he could not separate formed upon the insistent throbbing of his heart—or was it the drum? He looked inside his eyes and saw the world through a tube like a microscope, dark and glittering. He walked among the vast, buzzing hulks of the paramecia, the speeding bullets of the bacteria, the knobby whorls of molecules and the sparkling motes that were electrons appearing and disappearing, sweeping past him as he shrank through them and out again into the fields of stars, the bright banners and scarves of the universe, and a great, rust-colored moon expanding toward him. He opened his eyes.

The drum was in his hands. It felt human. The skin top was soft, sensitive, as if it would sigh when scratched. He tapped it very softly, feeling the stones around which the rawhide thongs were wrapped, like pieces of viscera under his hands, the knuckles and knobs of the living drum. He tapped with his fingers, a rhythm came from his hands and passed into the drum, and it began to speak with a whisper.

111

Then more confidently it spoke as the fingers told the drum and the drum said the words. Barry heard his voice singing words he could not understand. Was he chanting in Navajo? He heard his fingers telling the drum what to say, listened as the living skin spoke to the circle of listening people words that came by themselves and made a song. He sang.

And then it was wrong, uneasy, and his fingers no longer knew what to tell the drum. The drum sighed and stopped. A pair of hands took the drum, and a new song began.

While no time passed in the world, Barry and the Other One felt for a way to walk in singleness, a Blessed Way, somewhere to put one's feet to walk in singleness so that the Two might walk as one in another world and all be healed that was sundered and split and in pain since before time began. Barry felt the Other One beside him, traveling with him, looking at him like a brother as they circled each other with tired steps. Their eyes met, and Barry felt the ice of fear come up through his feet, up the backs of his legs as if he stood on a high place and made ready to jump. The cold ran up through his veins, icy water drowning muscles and nerves, stomach, heart, and lungs going under so he could not breathe. He began to freeze inside, seeing the Other One in agony also. He forced a long and shuddering breath.

He almost moved his elbow to tell the Indian at his side that he needed help, that he wanted out, that he could no longer breathe in this closed space where two tried to be one and that the Other One was dying also. He opened his eyes to find the dawn like white mist glowing in the doorway of the hogan.

An Indian woman he had met yesterday came stooping through the doorway with a bucket of water. She started around the circle, moving to the left, each person drinking from the gourd. When Barry drank, he felt whole again, and his dream shrank away to a tiny point of light, and vanished.

Chapter Six

"George!" She shook his arm, made him look around at her. "You're not even listening to me. I'm asking you now if this is what you want, this right here on the paper?"

"Yeah, it's all right, Mary Louise."

The tall woman with the bright blonde hair found tears welling in her eyes again. She always seemed to be crying these days, even though she was determined he would not get away with doing this to her. And now he was so wrapped up thinking about that floozie in Boston he couldn't even answer her about the house. My God, she could take it all away from him and he wouldn't even care. And that thought so moved her rage against him, so tightened her growing hatred of what he had done, of his happiness away from her, that she decided she would do it. She would take it all.

"I am going to tell Mr. Morrisey that I will fight for all of it," she said, wiping away the two tears with a quick motion. "All of it, you hear, George?"

"I never said you couldn't have it all," he said, still looking at the wall of the little paneled office. "I did you dirt, and that's little enough to pay for it."

His agreement made her even more angry, and for a minute she wanted so badly to hit him. She could imagine herself rising from the chair and hitting him with something, with one of the books on the desk beside her, with the iron bookend. Her rage made her dizzy.

"You go ahead, Mary Louise," he said, his voice still abstracted.

"You'll never find anybody that loved you like I did," she said with her face tight. "It's all you trying to be young again. The men from Rawlings told me she was just a kid, no more than nineteen or twenty. George, you are being a fool."

"I am sorry to hurt you," he said quietly in that infuriating way he had now of not getting angry. He had used to fight with her over the littlest trifles, and now he wouldn't even get mad. It was like he was still away, talking to that woman over a thousand miles' distance.

He looked at her with a sadness that made her catch her breath and turn away. "Whether there was anybody else or not, I'd have to get away."

She felt a great breath in her chest that would not come up. She would not cry again in front of him. She managed to say, "But why, George, why don't you love me anymore?" And the breath tried to come up again and almost strangled her.

"I've been close to death," he said. "I know that for a while these last couple of years I've wanted to die, and I think maybe that's why I was dying. I think I was killing myself over Charles's accident. And it wasn't really you, but the way we were . . . the way we lived was part of the whole thing. And I just got to change now."

"I could—" She started to say that she could change, but it was too much for her. She would not beg this man anymore. She was a Cahill, of the Virginia Cahills, and she was finished begging. She would not be pitied. She turned her head sharply, feeling the great sigh of breath lodged in her chest recede, allowing her to breathe again. She would not, never again, plead with this man.

"I thought you would be stubborn," she said, her voice cold now. "And Mr. Morrissey said you would, too. Do you know what he said about what you are doing, George?" She stood in the little office, ready for the parting shot, ready to see her lawyer and say she would agree to those terribly harsh conditions of divorce and alimony that he had suggested. "He said you were acting like a moonstruck adolescent."

Bo looked at his wife and nodded. He watched her face, hard and with a set frown around the mouth that she never used to have. She turned and went out the door into the next office.

The conditions were harsh, modified somewhat by Bud Hopps's indignation and the insertion of a saving clause or two modifying the payments for future support of the injured wife. Bo listened as his lawyer read through the clauses one after another, each charge against him, each

114

punitive and cutting phrase turning harmless as it hit against the screen of his abstraction from this foregone event. He kept thinking: Where was Lilly now?

Bud was reading. "Did you get that, Bo?"

"I'm sorry, what?"

"She also gets the contents of the savings accounts, and that's near two thousand dollars."

"Yeah, I thought it was about that."

"Well, Bo, I never thought I'd see you back down from a fight, but Mary Louise has knocked you out of the ring, and you're just lying there in the five-dollar seats." The lawyer slapped the long legal forms down on the table. "You're going to be paying this woman the rest of your life. You know that?"

"Yeah, sure, Bud. It's all right." Bo was thinking, it's been two weeks now since I heard. I got to do something.

"Well, I guess we're ready," Bud said, lighting a cigarette and sitting down again. "Ready to go in there and come out wearin' barrels."

After the legal proceedings had been got through, Bo saw his former wife only to get his clothes out of the house. He would not take any of the furniture or any necessities like bedding or towels. He took a couple of little things Charles had owned and loved when he was alive, and he stopped one last time in the boy's old room, as he used to do almost every night before he went to sleep. He remembered fixing it up when Charles was no more than a wiggly bundle, spitting up and squawling all night. The pictures of animals on the walls, the bed with its bright Indian-pattern spread, the Robin Hood outfit they bought for him to wear in the school play. He had been a big hit, Bo remembered, thinking of the husky, blonde-haired kid with the peaked cap and the jerkin of forest green, his bow slung across his shoulders. What a man he would have made, Bo thought. He did not feel the tears coming up now as he had so often in the past. It was now as if all the tears were gone from him, as if they had all flowed away into some quiet pool, so that now he could think back about his son with a pleasant sense of memory, just as if he were older now and his son had grown up and gone away, like any other kid, as if the accident had never happened. He had been such a good swimmer, and if he hadn't been trying to save that other kid, it wouldn't have happened, or if they hadn't sent him to camp. He was so proud of that, and of being

115

a scout, too. Jeez, Bo thought, and he smiled. What a hell of a good kid he had been. He thought, too, of that dream he'd had in Boston, of seeing Charles again out in the meadow where they used to play ball. That was real, he thought. I know you're there, Charles, he thought. I know we'll meet again. He walked back to his room, finished packing and left the house for the last time.

The following Wednesday, the first of February, as he was getting ready to leave for St. Louis, Bo received a picture postcard, forwarded to him at his new address. The picture showed a man floating high in the water of a lake while a caption under it said, "Swimming in the Great Salt Lake is easier than lying in bed." On the back was his name and address and the scrawled words:

Dearest Bo,
    She can't find the one She's looking for yet. But She's getting ready to change. I won't be here then. I'm so sorry, my darling. Goodbye. I love you always.
                                                    Lilly

His hands shook as he read the message over and over, trying to make sense out of it, trying to get more meaning from it. He looked at the tiny print at the top left side of the card: "Salt Lake City boasts wide avenues and spacious parks, and is the home of the University of Utah. It is placed in a splendid setting of the picturesque Wasatch range which rises to 12,000 feet above sea level."

He read the message again; what did she mean about getting ready to change? The Beast was changing? Or, more probably, the Beast was going to put Lilly aside and change into somebody else. But why would She do that? That was a stupid question when he didn't even know why the Beast existed at all—or sometimes *if* it did. The whole thing was so fantastic—but there was Lilly. And she was real. He knew she was as real as he was, more than he was, because she was so loving and beautiful and kind to everybody. He felt anger rising in him for the first time since he had been back home, anger at the Beast, who had saved him from death and now was consigning his sweetheart to oblivion through some unthinkable process it was going through. Why couldn't it just leave her somewhere, just go off and be somebody else and leave Lilly an ordinary human being like anybody in the world? Maybe he could find them, plead with the Beast. It was intelligent, though not in a

116

human way. He was moving even before his thoughts were completed, packing his clothes again. Lord, he thought, as he went about stuffing things into the suitcase again. I hadn't left Whitethorn for fifteen years or more, and now I'm running off at a minute's notice. Old Kneipe is going to have a fit, he thought, as he trudged through the snow to the drugstore to use the phone. In two hours he was sitting in the St. Louis-bound Rock Island Rocket thinking out plans for finding an impossible beast in a city he had never seen before. But he kept feeling the edge of the card in his breast pocket, thinking: She's in Salt Lake City, and that's where I'm going. I'll find her.

For some time now she had forgotten her own troubles, the sense of doom that held her stiffly away from people on the train. They had gone more and more slowly through the mountains as the snowdrifts on each side grew higher until the train seemed to be traveling in a tunnel of dazzling white. Once, as they crawled around the flank of a mountain, the drifts dropped away and they saw beyond the precipice a vast and distant world of snowy mountain peaks and valleys filled with conical pines set so close that they seemed a nubby green carpet far below. Then they entered the drifts again and more snow descended around them as they kept climbing. On the downgrade they stopped more and more often until word came back through the cars that they were stuck in huge drifts and would have to wait for the plows to come up from Raton to get them free. The conductors had been busy reassuring people for the first hour or so, and then when the heat began to leave the cars, everyone stopped worrying about getting to Santa Fe on time and began worrying about staying alive. It was cold enough after three hours on the mountain in the unheated cars to freeze the water in the tanks, and they had been cautioned against using the toilets more than absolutely necessary. Lilly had taken charge of three children whose mother was ill, and now they were huddled together under their coats and a blanket the conductor had brought them. The boy had a bad cold and kept coughing on her neck. She was telling them stories, the warmest ones she could think of. While she told them the story of Beauty and the Beast and the two little girls were already asleep, she was thinking with a part of her mind about the riddle that occupied the hours and days of life she might have left to her. When the boy began to nod and even stopped coughing while he slept against her, she asked her own private Beast why it was not possible.

Why must you change into someone else?

You are not suitable.

How can you have so little care? I thought you liked people.

I find people necessary to my transformation, and I like them.

You are going to take everything from me.

You had already experienced a life before I called you up.

Then why did you call me? She felt despairing again and close to tears.

The choice is dictated by the necessity of occasion.

I was suitable then? Why not now?

The time of transformation is difficult. Hard things must be done.

But I am able—

You will be in your own fate once more when I release you.

You mean I'll be dead again.

If you wish to say that, yes. But you are a Person and do not perish.

At that moment the train gave a sudden lurch backward, and a surprised cry came from the ranks of passengers, most of whom had been asleep or nearly so. The plows had dug through to them now, and they would be on their way in half an hour. The conductor, blowing white plumes of his breath, came through smiling, saying the heat would start up again soon. The three children slept around her body, and Lilly stopped asking. She could not understand the answers, except for the part about her going back to death. That was what mattered, after all. It was hard not to write to Bo again, but he would only be chasing across the country in the dead of winter and she would be gone. Well, she was over being hysterical about it. A sort of apathy had taken hold of her mind, preventing any strong action. She suspected the Beast was controlling her, but she could not feel how, nor could she fight back. It was as if she were under some kind of drug most of the time. She lay back, hugging the children to her, and after a while she slept.

Lilly was dreaming as they crossed the Continental Divide and began the long downward slope toward the Southwest, off the mountains and down toward the deserts, where, in a freezing hogan made of logs and earth, a young Indian woman panted hard to keep her breath coming. She felt the coldness of death in her legs under the blankets and the coldness of winter in the ground she lay on. There was no one else in the hogan, and for days she had lain there alone while the fever ate at her flesh. The last spasm of shivering left her, and she felt it take the last flicker of body heat. She tried to feel anger at the one who had left her here to die, but she could not find the energy even to think bad thoughts against him. And then, as the cold began to creep into her chest, she saw her grandfather standing beside the pallet of skins and blankets upon which she had lain for two weeks. His face seemed younger than when she had watched him die many winters past, and he wore the amulets and the holy shirt he had always used for the chants of healing. Now the old man held out the prayer sticks for her to see, put them back in the deerhide case that hung around his neck and held his hands out, palms up, arms spread wide. He smiled and looked upward as if accepting the blessing of the sun. At that moment the young Indian woman felt no more cold and rose to stand beside her grandfather. They raised their arms together.

The spacious sidewalks of Salt Lake City flowed with a bitter cold wind as Bo walked suitcase in hand, down from the station toward the business district where he might find a hotel. Before he found one, he had come across a tall pillar dedicated to a seagull and got a glimpse of a gigantic cathedral with a gold-plated angel on top that seemed to be nodding in the winter wind. Bo thought it must be an illusion because he was so tired and it was near dark. He stood gawking up at Moroni with his trumpet, and it certainly looked as though that angel was moving in the wind. Bo shook his head and resumed his march.

After three days he moved to a furnished room farther out, and although that made it harder to get around to the bus and train stations he was checking, he knew his money would not last more than a week at the rate he paid downtown. He tramped through the snow to five railway stations, two bus depots and an airport, asking each clerk in turn who might have been on duty in the past two weeks if he had seen a woman who looked like the picture in his wallet. Most said they saw so many people they hardly could remember one of them unless it was a freak or a bathing beauty. Bo felt she was not in the city, but he con-

119

tinued asking, hanging around the stations until police officers approached him more than once. When he told them his story, they listened sympathetically but continued to watch him. After eight days he returned to his furnished room and slept for twelve hours. When he got up on the morning of the fifteenth of February, he decided to look for work. She had been here, maybe was still here, he thought. He might even see her on the street. But something inside him felt empty, and he did not expect to run into her. Still, there was no sure place to go, and he had asked Bud back home to keep his mail for him and to let him know if any letter came from her. He dressed and walked out into the cold again, this time looking for a jewelry store.

He tried the downtown shops as he came to them, knowing each one as he walked through the door: this one had an excellent watchmaker, and this other one specialized in gem-setting and rings, and this one sold mainly silver and plate. The ones he did not recognize were the Indian curio shops, with their strings of heavy silver bracelets and chains of turquoise hanging in the windows. He stopped once to look at some of the work, hunching his shoulders against the frosty wind. The work was primitive in its weighty masses of metal and uncut stones, but there was a gracefulness to it that caught his eye repeatedly as he looked more closely at the rings and bracelets. It gave Bo a shiver almost of delight as he saw the unabashed simplicity and repetition of design. He had not felt such interest in design since his early days in the profession, those days when his imagination leaped for the impossible in metal, the spirituality of gothic captured in a simple engagement ring or the solidity of eternal love in a polished wedding band. He looked up at the sign: Navajo Smith.

He walked on to the next shop, the kind of jewelry store he was familiar with. As he entered, a silvery bell rang somewhere in the back and a short, bushy-haired man with round, gold-rimmed glasses came from behind a curtain. The shop was smaller than Bo had thought, and he almost turned to leave again, knowing it would be a one-man setup.

The bushy-haired jeweler caught his hesitation.

"What? Not leaving already? You just got here," he said, smiling so that his glasses seemed to rest on his rounded cheeks.

"I'm afraid I'd just be taking your time," Bo said. "I'm not buying. I'm selling."

"Well, so you're selling," the little man said, motioning with his hand as he walked toward the back again. "Come back here to the desk and let's see it."

Bo walked back slowly, sorry he had come in. The man misunderstood him, thought he was a salesman. "No," he said apologetically. "I mean, I'm looking for work."

"I didn't think you were with one of the big lines. Where's your sample case?" The small man sat behind a display table and motioned Bo to sit in the customer's chair opposite him. "If you come into my store, you are welcome to try to sell whatever you like. We are all salesmen, is that not so?"

Bo was put at ease by the man's smile and his easy manner. And it was obviously a slow morning, bright and cold outside this late February day and no other people in the shop. He sat down and put his hat on the floor beside him.

"There," the jeweler said. "That's better." He offered a surprisingly slender and muscular hand. "My name is Solomon McArdle. And you are?"

"George Beaumont." Bo took the hand, felt the strength in it and liked the man immediately. "I hope you aren't disappointed that I'm just in your shop looking for a job."

"I'm not disappointed yet, Mr. Beaumont, but then I don't know what you do, how much money you want to do it or if I will like it."

"Well, I see you've got a one-man operation going here, and I was thinking of getting into one of the larger places, really," Bo began. The little man's eyes were remarkably bright and protruded somewhat so that he looked almost comical when he was being serious. Perhaps that's why he smiles so much, Bo thought.

"You are so apologetic," Mr. McArdle said. "What you have to sell is not good?"

"I'm a manufacturing jeweler," Bo said, realizing he was making a terrible impression. "I have done everything: engraving, lost-wax casting, cutting and setting gemstones of all qualities. I can do any of the usual things and do them well."

"My goodness, and all this walks into my shop one cold morning and offers itself to me." Mr. McArdle lifted both his hands in mock surprise. Before Bo could take offense, the little man smiled again. "Would you like a cup of coffee?"

"Yeah, I would," said Bo, who was conserving money by eating only two meals a day now.

As McArdle got up, he said, "You are not in the Church, then."

"The Church? Oh, you mean the Mormons?"

"The Saints, they call themselves," McArdle called from behind the curtain. "They are all Saints out here." He reappeared with two cups of coffee and set them on the table. "I knew you were a stranger by your coat and your voice," he said. "Cigarette?"

"No. I gave that up. I don't usually have coffee, either," Bo said. "But it's cold and I been walking quite a while."

"So, you are looking for work in this depressed country, eh?" McArdle made slooping sounds over his coffee.

"I had a good job back in Whitethorn, Illinois . . ." Bo began, but he stopped and tried to look busy with the coffee.

"But you ran off with a tray of diamonds, and now you are in Salt Lake City," McArdle said, but he was smiling.

"I got a divorce," Bo said. "I, ah, wanted to just get away and start somewhere else. I came west."

"Yes, the marriage problems," McArdle said. "It makes us run around like squirrels in their little wheels." He smiled again. "And so, we make the world turn, is it not so?"

Bo liked the little bushy-haired man and felt a pang of good feeling inside, realizing he had not sat and talked with a friend for a long time. But he also decided discretion was better than a quick emptying out of his whole purpose in life right now. It would not do for a prospective employer to think he was on the verge of running off at the first sign of the woman he was looking for.

"Yeah, that's the truth," Bo said. He looked around at the small, neat shop, the familiar smells of rouge and solder coming from behind the curtain. He felt he would like to get back to work, to work hard and not to have so much time to think. "I'd really like to get back to work."

"I can see that, Mr. Beaumont," McArdle said, with a new, kindly note in his voice. "I will tell you what the situation is here," he said, leaning forward with his elbows on the table. "I have two shops in this city, and this one is the small one where I sometimes come to do custom work. I am not usually here in the morning, since my woman,

Mrs. Wright, opens for me and takes the trade until early afternoon." He watched Bo's surprise and smiled. "You thought this was a little bitty shop, like a corner grocery?"

"Yeah, I know a guy has a shop like this in Rockford. He has a hard time making it." Bo was puzzled now because the appearance of the man seemed to say that he was a small-time operator.

"We all have our hard times in these days, but it is getting better now." McArdle slooped his coffee again. "I think you might be a gold nugget that I am about to pick out of the street, Mr. Beaumont. Will you do something for me on trial?"

"Sure, anything," Bo said, grinning suddenly.

"Ah, that's better. You do want to work, I see," Mc-Ardle said, smiling back. "Well, there is this little engraving job, the usual thing on silver plate, cups, the loving-cup thing for the Church society, you know?"

Bo nodded. "I've done lots of that, done it for years. It's just the kind of thing I need to get back in."

"You have your tools?"

"Yeah, I got them a couple of days ago. I sent for them when I decided to stay." He paused, embarrassed. "About references, you see Mr. Kneipe, my boss in Whitethorn, was pretty upset about me leaving when I did, I was really sick and had to go to a specialist in the East, and I had to leave just when the Christmas trade was high, and—"

"And so he will not send you recommendations now," McArdle said, standing up, his hands holding the corners of his vest. "How long did you work for this Dutchman?"

"Fourteen years," Bo said, counting up. He had not realized he had been with Kneipe that long.

"Well, you couldn't have been ruining his shop for fourteen years, could you?"

"I'll guarantee my work," Bo said, reaching for his wallet.

"Of course you will," McArdle said. "But we won't talk about that before you get those cups all scratched up, will we, ha?" And he came around the little table to take Bo's hand. "And now, we are about to have a customer."

Before Bo could turn, the little bell tinkled. He looked at the jeweler with surprise.

"They were standing outside looking at the rings," McArdle whispered. "Love. The world goes around some more." And he walked briskly to the front.

In the days that followed, Bo found himself sinking

almost with pleasure into the work McArdle laid out for him. He began with the simple things and put his heart into the least little jobs, not because he wanted to impress his boss and new friend but because it comforted him. He felt each morning a little better, able to feel human again, to walk out in the large park near his furnished room and around Temple Severe at night when they turned on the floodlights and it looked like a castle in the clouds. He felt some purpose moving again in his mind, and, while he never stopped thinking of Lilly and never stopped looking for her in every way he could think of, waiting for news of her from somewhere, he began to live again. By the beginning of March, he felt more at home in Salt Lake City and looked forward to each day's work in the basement of McArdle's big store, The Ritz, on State Street. He was known as a loner, and, although he occasionally went to a movie with Tom Tingley, his fellow worker, or was invited over to McArdle's beautiful house on East Bench for dinner, he did not do much to cultivate friends.

It was a Friday night, the fourth of March, and Bo had been working up a set of designs for bracelets that he wanted to show McArdle. They showed definite Indian—or, so Bo would have said, primitive—influence and yet they were graceful and made use of flush settings and cut stones. He was excited about them and worked well after midnight before his eyes burned so badly he had to go to bed.

Lying in the dark of his room, he felt tensed up from the long hours over his worktable and tried relaxing his muscles one by one, starting with the toes, as Lilly had taught him months ago when he was sick. He practiced the three-step breathing at the same time, feeling his body respond by slowly letting go, his mind easing away from the white paper and the penciled designs he had been doing. The relaxation was proceeding into sleep, he thought, as he worked upward past his chest and shoulders, but, instead of falling asleep, he seemed to remain in that hovering condition psychologists call the hypnopompic, that sensation of almost levitating lightness that precedes sleep and that most often we pass through and downward into unconsciousness.

Bo felt light, as if his body weighed an ounce or two—a troy ounce, he thought sleepily, and the thought came slowly, as if it were mired in his body and the body was going to sleep by itself. It was a pleasant sensation to hover above sleep in this way, but he thought it was time to rest so he turned over, preparing to fall into a dream. Instead, he floated out into the darkness like a lost balloon. Bo found himself hanging a few feet from the floor, weightless. He looked back and saw his sleeping body lying on its back, one arm on the chest, the eyes closed, the breath coming slowly and regularly. It was something like the time he had left his body when he almost died back there in Boston, and, with a slow and carefully controlled thought, he remembered his visit to Charles in the meadow. But as his form began to lift toward the ceiling, he stopped the thought. He did not want that. Strangely, he felt no fear this time and felt quite right in his condition, with little desire to rejoin his sleeping body. The lightness was in every inch of his invisible form now, and he felt a slowly growing exuberance, like a light burning inside him. When the light filled his outline so that he could hold up his arm and see a transparent, glowing limb, he began to think carefully and slowly about Lilly.

As he thought of her name, he felt himself moving. He rose to the ceiling and through it with no more sensation than moving through a curtain of wind. Outside through the top of the house he moved, slipping between the molecules of joist and roofing paper and chimney brick and feeling no cold in the night air brilliant with stars. He rose higher and saw the mountains on the east and north of the city, the illuminated capitol with its golden dome and the temple glittering in the night.

"Lilly?" he said, and he began to move, south he thought, but then the movement was so fast that he could not tell. "Lilly Penfield," he said again, and the movement became a blur of speed while a sound like the sucking noise of air flowing into a tube built up around him. He kept thinking of her face and saying her name while the night changed to a total blackness and he felt a speed building up around him equal to that of light reaching through the galaxy.

Then came a sudden illumination and stasis. He was standing in a room but could not see the floor under him. The walls were there but seemed only to be sketched— like a modernistic stage setting, he thought. Against one wall was a straight chair like the ones they call ladder-back in the East, and sitting in the chair, wearing a blue travel suit and with her dark hair curled around her face, sat Lilly Penfield. Her eyes were closed and her hands were loosely folded in her lap. She appeared to have fallen asleep sitting straight up, her head slightly inclined downward. Bo looked at her for what seemed long hours before he dared to move. He tried to walk over to her but found that, although his legs moved and he could feel a floor under his feet (which seemed to be bare), he was not getting any closer. He began to run, but that was worse because the frustration became even stronger. He could not approach any closer than when he first arrived, and she did not stir, although he imagined he could see her bosom move in breathing and her eyelids twitch as if in sleep.

At last he stood still, separated from her by a dozen feet, the width of a room, and thought her name again: *Lilly*. She did not hear, and no matter how often or how loudly he said or screamed her name, she did not hear and he could approach no closer than he was. He stood and looked at her, feeling love in his whole body and mind and soul, wanting just to see her look at him, just to speak and have her hear him, just to touch her cheek one time.

When it became too much to bear he cried at her, "Lilly, this is Bo! This is Bo! George Beaumont!" He felt the wrenching at the top of his head he remembered from that time in the meadow with Charles, and the rush of sensation as he snapped back over those eons and galaxies of time and space to his own body in his room.

Heavily, on the bed again, his breathing coming suddenly short and his body stiff, he rolled over and sat up in the warm darkness, listening to the buzz of the little heater he used sometimes and seeing its warm orange cone of light. He was back.

Now that it had happened twice, Bo began to take the excursions of his soul, as he thought of it, as a reality. He had never heard anyone talk about such things, except for the few times Lilly had mentioned it, and she would not talk much about it. Such excursions seemed to be connected with death.

Certainly the first time it had happened, he felt that he had died, and meeting Charles was proof of some sort. But why had he found Lilly in that strange place of half-defined walls and floor, as if it were a sketch on paper rather than a very real place such as he had found his son? But she was not dead. Perhaps that was why he found her there. Too many questions rose in his mind for him to sleep much that night, and the next morning he walked down Second South to University and found the library at the University of Utah. It was an imposingly solid building, three stories high and built of what looked like sandstone. Bo found he would have to have a card to check out books and that a faculty member would have to sign for him. He turned away, but the woman behind the desk said, "Any established person who has lived in town for some time could probably get a card for you." He smiled his thanks and walked back toward the shop. He would ask Sol.

"Sure, I believe in self-improvement. Look what I've done to myself." The little man grinned.

It was Monday evening before Bo got back to the library, and then he wandered around most of the evening before finding one book that he wanted and locating the area where others might be. It was titled *Modern Psychical Phenomena* and was written by Hereward Carrington, Ph.D. Bo found there some discussion of experiences like his own and felt immediately as if he had discovered a new world, only to find it peopled by an advanced civilization. The author even gave precise instructions for leaving the body: the seeker who wished to project his "etheric body" should lie on his right side, relax and "will" his etheric body to come out of his chest or the lower part of his forehead. Professor Carrington also mentioned dangers in this practice, but Bo could not understand the import of the dangers, since they were simply named "material dangers . . . intellectual and moral dangers . . . hyperphysical dangers," and so on. He was astounded to find so much knowledge about a realm he had seldom heard spoken of before, and it amazed him to find this Biblical connection:

The nature of the etheric body—the "spiritual body" —of St Paul is now known; and many experiments have been conducted in an attempt to detach it from the physical body, and with some success. It is presumed that this body survives the shock of death, and that it is the seat of the consciousness. . . . (H.C., *MPP* 85)

Why had no one ever told him of this before, Bo wondered. What were the preachers in the churches doing if they couldn't tell their bereaved parishioners that a dead person was only gone to the realm of etheric bodies and that they might even be visited if one tried in the right way. But as he read on, the tone of the book came across to him and he found fewer bona fide experiences than the author had promised. He began to doubt. Maybe this professor was nothing but a crackpot. If it had not happened to him, and happened twice, Bo would have dismissed it all. The professor began to sound, for all his pronouncements, more and more like a man lost in the woods trying to convince himself that home was just over the next ridge.

In the next few days, Bo drew out and read books by William James, Rudolf Steiner and Maurice Maeterlinck. James he found most concerned with being scientific, with his careful phrasing and dismissal of events that were not substantiated by several witnesses, but he also found him cold and overly skeptical. What Bo wanted now was more than the assurance that his "etheric body" experiences were real—he pretty well believed that already. He wanted to know about that other reality, that other country, "from whose bourn no traveler returns" he heard in his mind, a fragment from school days. He wanted to know how it all fitted together, seeking closure in the most uncertain area of knowledge humans have explored.

Some comfort could be found in William James's opening remark that human beings have always known supernatural events and have simply called them by different names, but have always refused to place these events in the "real" world.

But the words of Maeterlinck gave him heart, made him feel it was reasonable:

It would be monstrous and inexplicable that we should be only what we appear to be, nothing but ourselves, whole and complete in ourselves, separated, isolated, circumscribed by our body, our mind, our consciousness, our birth and our death. We become possible and probable only on the conditions that we project beyond ourselves on every side and that we stretch in every direction throughout time and space. (M.M., *TUG*, 388)

Yes, Bo thought, writing the words out in the notebook he had bought, that's what I wanted to hear. He yearned for possibility with an almost physical thirst, recalling the woman he sought, the last sight (was it sight?) he'd had of her in the chair, her head bowed slightly, sitting straight as if she slept or were hypnotized.

He found too in the translation of Steiner the philosophy

which he was coming again to believe, a philosophy that he had forgotten last year when the disease began to ravage his body. Steiner's multi-personed system of existence was Teutonic and full of classifications, but the idea behind it he believed: we must develop the "I," the "Ego," that person whom we are; develop it and keep learning so that we do not perish. Bo wanted to believe it, wanted to believe that, like the other trials of life, this loss, too, could be conquered. The Beast had saved his life, but it was Lilly's caring that had brought him out of despair and made him live again. Now she was lost, and he was realistic enough to understand, in the middle of March with spring sometimes in the wind, that she might be gone forever. He would not say that to himself, but he felt the possibility.

That night he tried again what he had been putting off for a week or more, fearful of what he might find. He tried again to leave his body. He read until late, until his eyes were burning and he needed to lie back and rest. Then he turned off the light, stretched out on his back and began relaxing. As he breathed the full Yoga breaths and relaxed his body, the lightness invaded his limbs, pouring in with each inhalation like a glowing mist that made his silhouette a container for some airy fluid. When the sensation of being filled (or emptied, he thought calmly, the thought slow and somnolent in his mind) was complete, he tried to roll over to leave the body. Instead, he found himself moving upward—or, rather, northward, since the head of his bed faced the north—out through the top of his head. The glowing "etheric" body, as he imagined it, shot through the top of his head, through the headboard, through the brick wall into the night air some fifteen feet above the street before he felt in control again.

This time he did not feel entirely comfortable, his sight being somewhat distorted and blurred as if there were heat waves in the air around him, although he knew the air outside must be at about freezing temperature. He looked over the city as he allowed himself to rise slowly, but the landscape wavered and distorted in his vision. It's like I'm not seeing with eyes, he thought, but with some other sense, and there's static tonight. He tried to ignore the wavering landscape and said Lilly's name strongly. The movement into blackness was so sudden that he thought he had snapped back into his dark bedroom, but there was the now familiar howling sound around him in the dark, the sensation of great speed, and also a feeling of dread that was new and frightening.

At the journey's end he was in the sketchy room again, the walls only suggested, the floor invisible, and against one wall the straight chair with Lilly sitting in it, still asleep, her head bent downward slightly. But the difference made Bo's heart leap. She had a faint smile on her lips and one hand lay palm upward on the blue skirt. She was asleep yet, but she had moved. He tried again to get closer to her, because there was something in the palm of her hand. The dream sensation of frustration came over him again as he fought to get closer to her. He stood still, calmed his mind and looked harder to see what rested in her open palm. At first his wavering sight prevented it, but by concentrating on the clarity of that one part of his visual field he was able to make it come clear and even to bring it closer in a kind of magnification.

In Lilly's outstretched palm lay a silver ring with an almost square turquoise in a silver beaded setting. Bo strained with every bit of his will to bring the ring closer, for it appeared to have an inscription around the inside of the band; but it was too far away, and he could not quite make out what it said. The stone was a typical turquoise, greenish-blue and roughly cut. It was strangely marked for a gemstone, Bo thought, trying to see its pattern, which seemed for some reason to be important. He was growing very tired with all the effort, and he knew he must be using up energy inefficiently, like trying to lift a great weight from an awkward position. At last he achieved a close look: it was mottled green and brown with a prominent marking in one corner. The marking looked like a crudely drawn arrowhead pointing to the middle of the stone. He strained further to make out the inscription on the band. It came clear suddenly, but then, with an audible tearing sound, he felt his hold come loose so that Lilly and the sketchy little room and the ring disappeared. Blackness closed around him, bringing again the feeling of dread.

In the blackness he thought at first he had rejoined his body and had only to open his eyes to see the dim outline of his bedroom window. But then he felt the sensations of lightness and speed through the dark and knew he was still on his journey. The feeling of dread was like a dream he could remember having as a child, a dream where he found himself in a huge amphitheater, dark and echoing, and could hear deep voices around him speaking threats he could not quite understand. The dream returned to him with such force that he thought he must surely be asleep. And then the first one struck.

Bo let out a soundless scream as he felt something bite into his back, teeth tearing into the skin, real pain shooting up his spine. The teeth pulled away, taking some of the skin, and Bo screamed again, this time so he could hear it. He writhed in the darkness, trying to get away from the invisible thing that was biting again, this time high on his shoulder, tearing another piece of flesh away. Great God! There was another one. Teeth sank into the calf of his left leg. He thrashed around, kicking out as in dark water while vicious sharks and barracudas swarmed around him. Now he felt more bites, some of them tentative at first, some as if the creatures were prodding at him with something sharp before biting into him. And then he felt the greatest terror as something with prickly skin slapped against his back and stuck. He felt sharp things pushing through the skin into his back, felt them sinking into his body to suck out his juices. When the thing began to suck up through the tubes that were now stabbed deeply into his body, he felt the greatest terror of death he had ever experienced, even worse than when the pain ate at his guts. He cried out and thrashed around in the dense darkness, surrounded by the biting things, the stickery thing on his back with its tubes sunk in his flesh, crying out until finally it came to him—what Lilly had told him to do back when he was dying—and he cried out his own name.

"Bo! George Beaumont!" again and again, feeling pressure building inside him as he shouted the name more forcefully until power gathered like heated air around him and he felt the stickery thing torn from his body, the tubes pulling out with a horrible sucking sound and the agony of blades drawing through his flesh. And he fell, like a stone.

On his bed again in the dark bedroom, Bo was so nauseous he had to get up. He fell to his knees on the floor and crawled to the door, where he pulled himself up and managed to reel into the bathroom. On his knees by the old, stained toilet stool, he retched until his whole body felt empty. After a long time of vomiting and shuddering, he washed his face and got back to bed. Never again, he thought; my God in heaven, never again. He remembered as he lay back again what the professor, that guy Carrington, had mentioned of dangers. But he had never considered anything like that. God, those bites and that thing with the sharp tubes that were actually sucking away his life. He held tight to his pillow like a frightened child, trying to relax. The fear kept him awake until dawn turned the windows to a pale gauze. Finally he slept.

Chapter Seven

"You really had yourself a time, I guess," Johnny said, chewing on a piece of fried bread. They were lying on the sand among the spread-out congregation, who were eating, joking, talking in low tones. Occasionally one would say something to Barry in English and grin. He responded automatically, still dazed, chewing the bread with its slightly burned tang, dipping out the canned peaches with his fingers.

"Quite a time," he said absently. "Yeah. Never had anything like that."

He was silent again, unable to speak for remembering everything that seemed somewhere to be still going on, as if he had only walked away from a theater where it was all playing still, a spectacle that had not stopped, that never stopped, that he had visited for a time, for a nontime, and then had walked away from. But it was still going on somewhere. He looked around at the Indians sprawled on the sand under the willows and cottonwoods, some of the women passing among The People, giving them food, tin cups of coffee. Everyone felt good, relaxed, at one with each other and with him. Barry felt together with them, more relaxed than he had felt for a long time, even hopeful, not tired, not sleepy, although they had been awake all night. Or had it been a dream?

He looked at Johnny, who was sitting cross-legged beside him, grinning, his black hair mussed. He looked for the woman who had sat across from him in the hogan. She might have been there with her back to him, but he could not see her.

"Is it always like that?" Barry said, beginning to feel like himself again.

"I don't know what happened to you," Johnny said.
"But it's always a good experience for me. I didn't know
you could sing in Navajo."

"I sang in Navajo?"

"You said something like:

> "I call down thunder beings,
> Hear me, thunder beings,
> I call down thunder beings,
> Hear me thunder beings:
> Break me asunder
> Break me asunder
> Make me whole
> Make me whole."

The young Indian chanted it in English and then in his
own language. Barry listened to the words, but then in
Navajo he could not understand one word of the simple
litany.

He shook his head. "I said that?"

"Got a nice voice, too," Johnny said.

"I don't know a word of Navajo. I can't even understand what you're singing now."

"Well, you really became one of The People last night,"
Johnny said more seriously. "I've heard of things like that,
but this is the first time I've ever really seen it happen."

"Speaking in tongues?"

"Welcome to the Church."

"There were other things, too," Barry said, still abstracted. "Things from another world."

"You found your paradise?"

"I don't know if it was that, but I never suspected I
had all that inside me." He thought a minute as he took a
swallow of coffee. "And there were some things I guess I
did know I had inside me."

Barry felt extraordinarily good for a couple of hours
after the informal ritual breakfast, talking with some of
the people who had been at the ceremony and taking notes
on their responses. None of the ones he talked to told
stories of anything like the experience he had had, most
of them speaking of feelings rather than images, saying it
was a Blessing Way made successfully, speaking of their
own prayers and translating some of the songs that had
been sung during the night. One older woman said she

had watched the spirits of her ancestors moving through the hogan blessing everyone, and she said, too, she had seen the Bear-that-walks-like-a-man standing over the fire with his head in the smoke hole, and that he also blessed them. But for the most part their stories were of the songs, their feelings and the blessing.

About noon Barry sat down under a stand of willows, looking through his notes and watching a group of children working among the garden plots, pulling weeds and chopping at the wild grass. He looked up at the high blueness of the sky above the canyon rim, closed his eyes against the glare and fell soundly asleep.

When he woke, lying full length on the sand and cramped from being doubled up, the sun had left the canyon, bringing early dusk, and he could smell meat cooking. He slept well that night too, and it was as if the ceremony had extended over a day and two nights, for when he woke on the following day he felt it had only just ended.

I have had to wait a long while tonight before coming out. The old Indian man, Albert Chee, has been in and out of the shelter several times. He speaks in his language, walks around in the rocks mumbling to himself and comes back to lie down again. Finally he falls asleep. I slip out into the late moonlight and shift.

Tonight I will not venture downstream but explore the top of the cliffs. I find the trail and go leaping up it in the deep shadows, eager to gain the top and the moonlight which awaits me there. At the top of the trail I see Barry's car still sitting on the edge of the cliff and sit down behind a juniper to get my breath back. The mesa at this point is thinly forested with piñon and juniper, nothing more than twenty feet high, but enough to give cover. It might be a good place to hunt. I lie on the gravelly ground listening to the night noises, feeling to the limits of my spatial sense, watching the moon shadows beneath the stunted little trees. It is very quiet, late in the night, perhaps two hours before dawn.

Do you hear, Big Pussycat?

I am startled by the sudden voice. It has been a long time since Mina communicated with me in that way, and her voice is so much stronger than it used to be. I look for the position of the half-moon. It is low on the horizon now in the west. We will only have a few minutes to talk.

I hear you, Mina.

Mommy's asleep, but I'm out in the yard in the tire swing and the moon's almost gone already. Are you and Daddy all right?

Yes, dear Mina, we are doing very well.

Why are you in two places, Big Pussycat?

There is no mistaking what she has said. I think for a moment.

I don't understand, Mina. I am lying at the edge of the canyon by myself.

There's two of you.

I look around me, feeling suddenly alert, my spatial sense coming alive to everything within range. Small animals, one larger animal nearby. I rise to my feet cautiously and sense about again. It is not as large as me. Then I scent it. A deer.

There is only me here, I say back to her.

I am talking with both of you, Mina says, puzzled, an emotion of surprise coming through to me.

?

She says she can't talk to you yet because you're not awake, the little girl says across the distance. It is as if she is inside my head, but far back in the darkness. Her words are clear and sharp, but far away. I strain to hear something else. Is someone else speaking?

I don't understand.

She says you will pretty soon.

Who is this you are talking to, Mina?

She's like you, Big Pussycat, but she's not able to talk to you like I do.

Now I am thoroughly aroused and frustrated. If there is another of my kind I must know it. My skin prickles at the thought. I recall what the coyote said.

Mina, tell me where she is.

I can't tell. And now she's gone.

What did she say, Mina, exactly?

She said you would wake up pretty soon and then you could talk.

But I am awake, I say, frustration making me pace about and feel anger.

Her voice becomes faint then, and I notice the moon is near the far horizon. It must be out of sight now from where she is in Albuquerque. Why our talking depends

136

on the moon being up I do not know, but it was that way last summer. I ask her again, but her reply is so faint that I cannot make out the words. I tell her goodbye and begin trotting along the edge of the cliff in an upstream direction. Another like myself! The thought makes me almost miss my footing at one point and I move back from the edge to run just inside the line of junipers. A fall from there would be inconceivable. I wonder absently as I trot between the little trees if I could shift in time to a winged creature in order to save myself—and that brings memories of the peyote ritual last night. I push those thoughts out of my mind, for they are in some way painful to me. I will think about that later. What I need now is action.

I sense a large animal to my right at the same time as it scents or hears me, and it goes leaping away. I turn suddenly and take out after it. The deer. I am so close at the start that his musky odor, something like that of a very clean fox, is hot in my nostrils. But he is clever, and within two hundred yards I have lost him. I pause, not breathing, feeling in all directions, listening. Wise animal. He has stopped not a hundred feet away, down inside a dry arroyo with only his young antlers sticking out.

I stay still, suppressing my breath and scent. He is still as stone for another minute, then he moves slightly, turns his head from side to side. I am quiet and frozen. The deer thinks he has eluded me and walks out of the little arroyo, doubles back and comes past me on the right. I wait until he is as close as he will be to me and with a sudden leap to the side am after him.

He is so fast that I miss him with the blow I thought would knock him to the ground. He has leaped almost straight up in the air and turned away at the same time and is off again through the little trees faster than anything I have ever chased. I am excited by his scent now, running heedlessly through the trees, through cactus patches, breaking branches from the trees in my rage to catch him. I am almost on him again when he swerves impossibly to the left as I strike and only graze his hindquarters. What a fast animal! But I can turn almost as short as he can. The sand cascades up around us, and he leaps away. I get in another swipe, drawing blood from his right hind leg this time.

I have extra traction in this soft sand and am gaining on him as he leaps wildly toward the cliff edge. I am aware he is heading for the cliff and slow down. The crazy thing may leap off into space, but I do not wish to try my powers that way. He gains a bit from my delay, but then he reaches the edge and has to turn sharply on the bare rocks. Almost he loses hold and goes over into the canyon as I come racing out of the trees toward him. Between two deaths, the young buck deer scrabbles away from the fall, his hindquarters slipping over the edge. It delays him, and when he turns downstream it is the wrong way. I have outguessed him and catch him by a foreleg.

His antlers swing down toward me, but I have already changed my hold and have his throat. He is down and killed before he can bring the horns near my face. His blood pumps out, hot, carrying the last breath from his body. He looks up at me with one dark wide eye before death takes him. I pick him up by the neck and straddle-drag him back into the junipers, where I lie across the quiet body that was a few minutes ago the swiftest game I had ever tried.

In the midst of the pleasant business of taking apart my meal, I sense a large animal at the edge of my perceptual field. I pause, the liver half eaten, listening for confirmation. Yes, a coyote or lynx, probably, from the size and movement. I remember the creature outside of Albuquerque that night last week, that miserable shape-changer. I throw a query at him.

Is that you, coward?

?

The reply is not in words, but it is a declared thought that no dumb animal is capable of. I get up from the carcass, licking my lips. I would give much if it were the same creature and I could get my claws into him.

Come have some, if you dare.

I am hungry, not stupid.

I feel rage inside me, not a pleasant sensation when one is eating.

Are you the one I have met before?

Come over here, Big Kitty. I have another lesson for you.

I cannot stand his mocking voice. How can he have come this far just to taunt me? Is he the one who was talking with Mina? I stand for a minute or two, torn between finishing my meal, which that coward will not dare to disturb, and trying to catch the rascal and tear him up first. I decide I cannot eat when he is mocking me like that and take out after him.

138

Three times I believe I have his miserable carcass in my grasp, but he is too quick with his changes. After finally cornering him, I go into my rush only to have him shift into an eagle and fly up again, mocking me. I have no practice being a bird. He would destroy me in the air. I send a taunting challenge up to him and trot back to enjoy my meal. I arrive at the place where it was to find it dragged away, a bloody trail leading off to the cliff edge. That rotten, tricky coyote has had help. I leap after whoever has stolen my kill and find two other miserable wild dogs just pushing the deer carcass over the edge into the canyon. I skid to a stop, roaring at them as they leap away in opposite directions. The deer carcass slides down the steep sandstone butte, the limp antlered head dragging back and forth as if nodding goodbye, and then it reaches the point where the stone curves under and falls out of sight into the dark canyon.

What terrible creatures these coyotes are to take a meal away and destroy it rather than letting me have it. But then I realize that it is near dawn and I will never be able to stay in my shape long enough to find the deer a thousand feet down and a mile or more up the canyon. By that time it would be dawn, and I will have to resume my Person or be seen in daylight. The coyote is clever, knows my limitations. He and his pack will take their time. They know the canyon, the trails, and they will find my deer soon enough to enjoy it. I look up into the night sky that is growing light in the east, the stars fading, leaving the one bright morning star to illumine the dawn.

Damn you, coyote!

I sit down on the stones to clean my muzzle before going back toward the trail I know. For all its beauty, this canyon has been a very frustrating place for me.

Barry had been sleeping in the Chees' summer house, eating their food, and he was acutely aware of what this must cost an Indian family who appeared on the bare edge of subsistence. As he and Johnny walked out early in the morning to relieve themselves over by the cliff, he said, "I'd like to pay for my grub since I've been here, Johnny."

"My mother would never let you do that, you know," he said as they stood in the cool air listening to the birds tuning up.

"She wouldn't mind if I made a gift in friendship?"

"That would be acceptable."

"Say twenty bucks or so?"

"Too much."

"How about some stuff from the trading post?"

"A new big kettle and a couple of fry pans would be nice."

"Done."

Back at the shelter they waited outside for a few minutes, hearing Albert Chee and his wife having a before-breakfast argument. Johnny walked away up stream, hands in pockets, and Barry followed. So, even the Indians had problems with marriage, Barry was thinking. He said something to that effect, and Johnny turned on him with an angry look.

"Sure. And getting pushed around on your own land doesn't help," he said.

They walked on for a way out of earshot of the shelter and sat down.

"He'll be out in a minute," Johnny said. "Probably go into Chinle and get drunk."

When the short, rather bowlegged Indian man emerged from the shelter, it was more than even Johnny had expected. Albert Chee came storming out, breaking away part of the brush wall as he came, a large old forty-four revolver in his hand. He shouted something and fired the weapon into the air with a boom that reverberated from the canyon walls, back and forth like a whole platoon having firing practice. At the noise, a gaunt mongrel dog that had been hanging around the shelter, and apparently was a stray, leaped out from behind a rock and stood looking at the man with fear, its back hunched.

"Hey," Johnny yelled, and said something in Navajo. His uncle ignored him. He pointed the long revolver at the dog and fired again, the noise echoing as before. But now he was firing again and again, the weapon jumping in his hand, dust kicking up around the dog. The noise was like a cannonade. When the revolver was empty the dog lay on the rocks with blood spattered around it. Barry and Johnny watched in disbelief as the older man put the weapon in his belt and strode away toward the little corral against the far side of the canyon. He saddled a big brown mare and was away before the other two men could stop him.

Johnny shook his head and said nothing.

"What the hell was that all about?" Barry said, looking at the body of the dog where it lay still now.

"Blowing off steam, I guess," Johnny said. "Hell, let it go."

Barry decided the less said the better, and they walked back to the shelter for breakfast.

Later that morning, Johnny suggested that his friend from the city take a tour down the canyon to a historic ruin that was nearby before he left. Barry would be going back to Albuquerque alone, since Johnny Strong Horse was needed at home now. The pinto pony was tractable for a beginning rider, Johnny said, saddling the little horse. Barry got on her and went pacing, then trotting off down the canyon on the hard-packed sand and flat sandstone that was almost like a roadway in some places. Johnny had said even a white man could not miss the ruin down there, and that he could climb up to the cliff house if he went to the far side and was careful.

Barry held the little horse to a walk, breathing the cool morning air, riding in the shadow and watching several wild canaries that were flying ahead of him from one cottonwood to the next, thinking probably that he was after them. They were like little yellow projectiles, little butter bullets, Barry thought, feeling almost perfect in his happiness. He would make a trip to the trading post this afternoon, sleep again in the summer house tonight and get an early start in the morning for home. Johnny had said he would find it easier going down to Gallup and straight home along US 89 since it would be almost all paved once he got to the state route and turned south. The pony picked up her pace as they rounded a bend in the canyon, and Barry saw that the canyon widened out again into grassy benches high on each side of the stream, with clumps of trees that looked as though they might have been a cultivated orchard at one time.

Scattered through this area were hundreds of sheep, peacefully grazing, widely spread but none of them by itself. Barry looked around for the shepherd, wondering if it would be one of Johnny's sisters or someone he had met in the previous days, but he saw no one. He walked his horse past them and almost missed what Johnny said he couldn't. He chanced to look up to his right and there was the ruin. A hollowed-out space under the beetling cliff was partly filled with small stone houses that came right to the edge of a forty- or fifty-foot drop. He got off

the pony and tied her to a willow, then splashed through
the shallow rivulet to get a closer look at the cliff dwelling.
At the foot of the cliff was a splayed-out and desiccated
ruin of some houses, perhaps even older than the ones up
in the cliff, which still looked pretty much intact. He
walked along the sunny base of the cliff looking for a
way up, but it was all sheer. He looked up, leaning back,
wondering how the hell the Indians had got up there in
the first place, much less carried enough stone up there
to build that set of apartments.

"Come along to your left," said a voice from above him.

It was a feminine voice. Barry grinned. The shepherd
had found a good place to be lazy. He walked around as
directed, and beyond the end of the sheer rock, where it
appeared to join the rest of the cliff, was a steep little
stairway cut into the stone. He clambered up without
much trouble and, with a final jump, found himself level
with the cliff dwellings. Looking out across the valley, he
saw the pinto tied to the willow and nibbling the leaves,
the herd of sheep grazing among the little fruit trees and
the slope of the valley that narrowed and turned again
less than a half mile further down. Then he thought to
look for the shepherd.

"I think this is the most beautiful place in the whole
canyon," the woman said. She was sitting in bright sun
on a partly ruined stone wall, swinging her legs like a
schoolgirl. It was Sarah Lakuchai, smiling as if she had
arranged a very pretty trap.

Barry felt a flush rising up his neck and into his face.

"You are taking care of the sheep?" he said, feeling
stupid.

She nodded. "Sometimes I do it for my little sisters.
Did you enjoy the ceremony of Blessing?"

"Very much." He walked over to the wall she was sitting on and leaned against it. Might as well be friendly, he
thought. After all, we're both responsible adults.

"I asked a lot of people afterwards, but they didn't experience the same things I did," he said. "I had—visions,
I guess you'd call them." He felt distinctly uncomfortable
near the Indian woman, whose eyes never left his face.

"Maybe because it was your first time with peyote," she
said, and her smile was kind. She was not at all shy or
embarrassed as were the other Indian women.

They talked of peyote, the tactics of the whites in
reducing the herds, and then came a silence. Damn it,

Barry thought, I do feel like a school kid. And he flushed again. The woman was too self-possessed to be an Indian, he thought. She acted wholly in command of things, waiting for him to make a move of some kind.

Well, he thought almost angrily, I'm not going to make a move. She's a damned lovely woman, and I know I'm attracted to her, but this is silly. He turned to Sarah, straightening his back and stretching his arms at his sides, getting loosened up to leave.

She looked at him, her eyes sparkling, and he remembered how he had looked into her eyes across the fire in the hogan; his nerve left him.

"I guess I'd better be getting along," he said. He did not move.

"I feel we know each other very well, Barry," Sarah said. Her tone had dropped from the conversational to an intimate one. This is not going to happen, Barry thought, working up some anger. I will not let this happen. I am going home tomorrow. I am not a weak, philandering gigolo. But he looked at the woman, smiled as she was smiling, felt her eyes moving over his face, looked away guiltily and then back at her.

"You are——" he began, and his voice sounded like a frog croaking. He cleared his throat and laughed self-consciously. "I find you a very attractive woman, Miss Lakuchai," he got out finally. "I think I'd better be on my way."

She slid down from the sunny wall and took his hand in her cool, smooth fingers, leading him as she ducked under a low linteled doorway into one of the old stone houses.

"You see here, Mr. Golden," she said, as if she were giving him a guided tour, "one of the four rooms in this house. It is the grain storage room. And in here"—she led him on, still holding on to his hand and pulling him along as she stepped through another stone doorway—"you see the place for preparing food. You would call it the kitchen in English, or *la cocina* in Spanish." They stepped through the last doorway into a room that had no roof; the sunlight slanted in and turned the stones of the wall a light ochre color. Barry could feel warmth reflecting from the wall. The floor was drifted with sand. He felt as though he were standing in a shallow well, open to the sky, dry and empty. He was acutely conscious of the smooth fingers, warm now and pressing his hand as they stood in the

143

roofless room. His mind refused to attend to the woman, although she was close to him, looking at his face, her breath slow and even. She let go of his fingers and quite deliberately stroked his cheeks with both her hands. He flushed, and a thrill flashed down his spine, as if he had just lost all his body heat. He stood with arms down, looking at the blue-black hair smoothly braided with strips of wool into a gleaming knot lying on her neck. Her hands moved across his face, one finger now behind his left ear. He managed to look down at her face. She was smiling faintly, her lips turned up at the corners, just a flash of white teeth showing between her lips. He shuddered with a convulsive movement, aware that his body was reacting to her hands on his face and neck.

"Stop it now, Miss Lakuchai," he said, and again his voice sounded strange, as if it came from someone else. He began to be aware that the Beast inside of him was awake and rising to the surface. He would not let this happen, Barry thought desperately.

"I will not let—" he began.

Her hands gripped into the hair at the sides and back of his head. She pulled his face down to hers and her lips moved across his own, sending another thrill down his spine and making his legs shiver. She began to kiss his lips, licking them lightly, holding firmly to his hair. He could not move his head without being violent. He felt the enjoyment of the Other One inside, and his own body responding, felt the revulsion fading away. A rationalization formed in his mind, something about the accident of time and place, but he could not concentrate on it, so insistent was the woman. He had not touched her with his hands, but he felt the rising of great desire and knew it was not merely his own desire but the Other One inside of him desiring, and he shivered, wondering at the strength of that lust now flooding upon him like swiftly rising water.

She was unbuttoning his shirt, moving her hands on his chest, and he was aroused now, his own breath growing shorter, as did the woman's. Delicately, her fingers touched him in ways he did not know about, ways that made his head sing and his mouth salivate like a dog's. She played him as an experienced lover does a young virgin, and he felt even more helpless with his reticence, still wanting not to do this thing, not to have done it, perhaps to do it and deny it, but to somehow be beyond this point of decision. Her fingertips brushed across his nipples, bringing

144

gooseflesh to his skin. He dared not look down into her face.

"Touch me," she commanded, taking one of his hands and putting it to her cheek. "Touch me." His hand felt the smooth, brown cheek, the neck and shoulder. His other hand came up of its own accord and pulled the woman's slender body against his so that all her body, its curves and hollows, pressed against his own, moved into his own and made fire begin wherever they touched. Barry groaned, gritted his teeth and pulled the woman's body to him, unable not to as the power of the Other One came over him, and he gave in to that vast and insatiable lust roaring through him.

Then, with a violence he had never experienced, he tore the clothes from them both, the woman tearing with him. They bit and panted as they raged to put their bodies together, clawing at each other like cats as they rolled in the sand of the floor, writhing across their discarded clothing, pulling at each other's flesh, kisses turning into bites, embraces becoming terrible grips on the other's body, cries coming from both as they seemed to fight for the right of power over the other. The madness blanked his mind. Barry groaned and cried out, pulling at the woman's slender brown body, catlike, otterlike, smooth and slippery under him, climbing around him like a serpent as he fought with her in mindless passion until she was on top of him, scratching at his belly, finding what she wanted and thrusting herself down onto him in a simulation of rape that Barry would remember later, would want somehow to be true. He found himself at the ultimate point helpless of volition, mad with lust, carried on the passion of the Beast, who rioted inside him and yet could not come out, was held somehow in abeyance. Barry could feel him raging to get out at any cost, to *Be Self* in this fight with the Indian woman. And it would not, or could not, the power it exerted drowning Barry in its passion as the woman pounded on his body with her hands, scratched him, bit his shoulders until they bled, and he writhed under her, his passion and that more powerful force of the Beast rising intolerably inside him. He thought he would explode into hot fragments.

And she suddenly stopped, held him in some way. One hand reached beneath her, held him so tightly the passion that would explode, but now could not, began to spread out through his body, sideways through his flesh like

145

molten metal under his skin. His eyes bulged as he looked at her gazing down at him, the smooth brown breasts with their nipples hard, the belly rising and falling with her rapid breath. Her eyes sought something in his, the hand prevented his completion.

"Now we will try again," she said, releasing him so that he felt a sudden surge and began to move up hard against her again. She moved with him again, more slowly but gaining speed, moving in slow circles as he heaved against her, helpless in his lust that now pulsed upward toward the peak again. He wanted it more than anything in life, felt the agony of the Beast inside him forcing his body past its limits as he felt the pressure building intolerably again, and this time it would go. . . .

She stopped him again, holding as before, smiling down at him as she panted, her face and body glistening with sweat, the blue-black hair cascading over her shoulders and shining like the darkest night. She held him so tightly, a grip he could not believe. He was afraid to try to dislodge her, and the passion spread out again, burning his insides, putting him in agony that would not be stilled. When he moved, she squeezed slightly, and he had to stop for the pressure shooting pain into his guts. And when it had spread through his flesh again, it seemed she was inside his body, listening and feeling what his body was doing, in touch with every nerve and muscle, monitoring each pulse beat, watching the slowing of the neurons as their glow faded. She released him again.

Each time it was like that, and each time she stopped him, sometimes raking his chest with her claws as she held him, reminding him of his captivity. The Beast inside was in a state bordering on madness, and Barry feared for both their lives, panting, sweating, swinging his head from side to side, his mind gone, eyes staring up at the slender brown woman as she began once more. He felt the power coming back again, stronger and stronger. Even she would not stop it this time. And then she did, easily, as if he were a tiny child holding to her hand, pleading with her—and he heard his voice pleading, begging her, weeping, the tears running down his face, his arms and legs limp as she would begin again, and his body responded again, helpless in her grip.

"Now my love, my loves," she said softly to the mindless one beneath who slobbered and thrashed like a beast in a trap. "Now you may have it, my only one." She brought him again to the high brink of passion, held him there but did not seize him this time as she had, held him and held him, like a little child being urged to leap from a precipice, unwilling now to let the wave break, afraid while the body surged with great heaving undulations like a stricken animal. As it broke, as he leaped out into space and felt himself exploding, his sensibilities fragmenting from their center, he heard the cry that burst from his throat, a howl that could not be made with human voice, the howl of the Beast suddenly present as the two of them burst the final bonds of energy and hurtled outward in a violent explosion that drove out his senses like a bursting of the nerves from the flesh. Returning to his own form, Barry clutched at the woman as heaves of passion shook his body. She screamed, and he, blind with ecstasy, clawed at her, and the Beast writhing to escape again and unable to, screaming from the man's throat so that the two voices, the man's and the Beast's, mingled in an eerie wail, blending into an unearthly chord.

Then the silence, the breathing of the man and woman coalescing and parting as the woman lay across his heaving body, their bloods mingling from the lacerations they had done to each other, blind, deafened, gone from the world.

The sun had moved up the wall, so only the top of the room was brilliantly lighted now, making it seem more than before like a well. Barry looked up into the slanted, deep, velvet-black eyes of the Indian woman. Her hair was loose, hanging around her face and over her shoulders, the delicate, high cheekbones giving her expression an ethereal quality now that the passion had gone from it. She seemed emptied of personality, a transparency of woman with something behind it that he could not see, some inner force pulsing within. He realized that he was afraid of her, and he had never been afraid of a woman, but now he was afraid.

She did not speak, only got to her knees and moved off of his body to the rumpled mess of their clothes, mangled and kneaded into the sandy floor. He pushed himself to one elbow, his mind slowly coming back. A slow horror began to build in his mind, the beginning of guilt. He felt more than drained from the release of passion, more than the dregs of an ecstasy that had almost been to the death. He felt he had been possessed. The fear was almost stronger than his mind could manage, for he was looking at the brown-skinned woman—a lovely woman, a delicate woman with exotic, almost oriental features and slender hands and arms, small breasts bobbing lightly as she searched through the clothes to begin dressing. He was afraid, and the Beast was afraid also. Barry felt fear inside that made him tremble, for he had never felt that one's fear before. He had endured the dangers, the pains, the survival needs, the chances taken, but never this fear. He looked down to find his clothes, and his hands shook, scattering the sand.

Standing on shaky legs, he looked down at his body, scratched as if he had been dragged down a mountain through a cactus patch. His back smarted with scratches that had got sand in them. The woman, too, had long excoriations down her hips and legs, scratches across her belly and one on her cheek. They had fought each other like wild animals. Barry could not think about what had happened, but the fear that rose inside him was like the secret knowledge of a mortal wound.

When they had dressed and stepped back out to the wall where they had met, the sun had moved on past, leaving it dark gray stone again. Out in the valley the sheep had gathered against the far side of the canyon to be out of the sun. The pinto stood with her head down, switching her tail at the flies.

"You are going home today?" The woman was expertly braiding her hair back with the strips of wool again.

"Yes. I mean, no. I am going to the trading post to get a gift for the Chee family. I will go home in the morning —tomorrow." He shook his pant legs to get more of the sand out. Nothing would make him look presentable again, and the woman looked also as if she had just stepped out of a barroom fight. He felt miserable, wanted to be angry with her, but was actually afraid to be. He could not understand that. The woman was a head shorter and certainly fifty pounds lighter than he, and he was afraid. He put out a hand to steady himself as he looked over the edge of the cliff. He felt a warm, smooth hand take his.

"I am sorry, Barry," she said. "I have tried to do some things this morning; maybe it was wrong." She smiled at him as if nothing had happened. "You will understand more sometime." With that cryptic remark she slipped lightly down the stony pathway to the floor of the valley, while he stood watching, and walked across to the shaded side where the sheep lay. A little yellow dog that Barry had not noticed before got up from his nest under a cottonwood and trotted along with her. From this distance she looked like any Indian woman, more slender than some, skirt a bit shorter and swinging as she walked, but just an Indian woman. He made his way down the pathway, slipping once so that he hit his elbow hard.

Chapter Eight

"Such a solid, dependable workman as you are, Bo," Sol said. "Who would think you believed in such things?"

"I just wondered if you knew anybody who could help," Bo said, embarrassed.

"Do I know any crazy people?" Sol put his hand on Bo's shoulder and smiled. "I know one. He's a maverick, like us in this Mormon homeland." He sat down beside Bo, who was eating lunch at his workbench in the basement of The Ritz. "You know, these Saints . . . they call *me* a gentile."

Bo looked up and grinned. "Yeah, I feel like a lost soul out here, too. But at least I don't have to go looking for a liquor store or a tobacco shop anymore."

"Ah ha!" Sol said. "You see how sensible you are—even more than me, a poor Irish-Catholic Jew who can't do without a little wine in the evening." He looked serious for a minute, and, as a result, his face took on that comical air that Bo had noticed when he first met the man.

"You have really been dreaming about leaving your body?"

"It's happened more than once," Bo said. "But last time it really got scary, and I think I'd better get some help."

"Can you come for dinner Sunday?"

"Sure, that'd be great."

"You come. I will introduce you to a crazy man. He's just like you." But Sol was smiling again now.

Nicholas Wiedemann had such a profusion of pure white hair and beard that Bo thought he looked like a man peering out of a snowy hedge. All one could see of the man were his eyes and the huge, downturned beak of a nose, but that was enough for most people. The eyes were so dark brown that they looked to be all pupil, full of blackness and mystery, hanging like black moons under the half-closed lids. His nose had a predatory look about it, Bo thought, like an enormous owl. He was almost as tall as Bo but seemed shorter because he stooped. He appeared to have some spinal defect that was not bad enough to be called a hump.

The three men sat in front of the broad marble fireplace in Sol's living room sipping after-dinner coffee. Sol's wife sat quietly in a chair to one side, listening and glancing up occasionally but not speaking. The house was quiet except for the slow ticking of a grandfather clock in one corner of the room.

"You are not an adept, then," Wiedemann said. His voice was husky, almost a resonant whisper.

"I guess I'm just a beginner," Bo said, somewhat abashed by the bearded man's air of wisdom.

"The demons could have drained you dry," Wiedemann said.

"Let me ask just one thing," Sol said, raising his slender hand. "Why do you two healthy American men with good jobs and in good health want to get involved with demons?"

Wiedemann turned his head toward Sol, and his beard parted slightly in what might have been a smile behind the bushes. "No one wants to be involved with demons," he said. "But if one is careless"—he turned to Bo—"or if one is an amateur, then the demons arrive."

"But I had been there before," Bo said, "and one time I even went to see my boy—in heaven," he added, looking sideways at Sol, who raised his hands and waved them in the air before putting them back on his coffee cup.

"You have told me you visited the dead on three occasions," Wiedemann said, as if Bo had not spoken at all.

"No, just that once, when I saw Charles," Bo said.

"But what you described is the journey to the dead— the rushing noises, the blackness, the bright radiance. That is the way to the land of the dead, Mr. Beaumont."

"But I went to visit Lilly, and she was there, but she's alive." His face underwent a spasm of emotion as he realized what might have happened. Could she be dead? Could that be why he couldn't touch, couldn't talk to her? But he had talked to his son, and Charles had been gone for two years.

"Impossible," Wiedemann said, sipping his coffee. "The

astral body may journey across the earth or it may visit the realm of the dead spirits under certain circumstances. It appears that you have never journeyed except in the realm of the spirits." He looked at Bo from the huge dark eyes that were like black wells half hidden by his eyelids. "Interesting," he said.

"Why would she be there?" Bo muttered, half aloud.

"There is a way to find out," the bearded man said softly.

"You mean if she's dead?"

"Precisely. You must refrain from entering the spiritual realm and journey only in our dimension. If she is on this earth you will find her. If she is not, you will be drawn into the spiritual realm, and there"—he said, leaning forward and fixing Bo with his gaze—"there, you must be most careful."

"Yeah, I know," Bo said.

"The adept," Wiedemann said, "can give nourishment to the demons and emerge with more power. The amateur may lose his life because he does not know how to control them."

The evening was a strange one, the talk becoming so abstract to Sol that he looked at his wife, who glanced back at him and rolled her eyes upward. They got up quietly and retired to her sewing room, where they talked while their two visitors continued about the techniques of astral travel in the two realms.

"The astral body is, for our purposes, wholly controlled by thought," Wiedemann said. "Until we leave our bodies in this dimension forever"—he nodded as Bo said, "When we die?"—and went on, "then we will come under another form of control. But until that time, we are tied to our earthly envelope by the binding thread." The bearded man looked up, and Bo thought he could detect a smile again. "One might compare this thread to the umbilicus of the foetus."

"That's how we're able to come back so quick," Bo said.

"Precisely. However, in traveling to the realm of spirits, this thread is severely strained. The aura must be maintained in its full brightness at all times if one is not to be endangered by the creatures of darkness—what we refer to as demons."

Bo thought back to that terrible night. He had strained so hard to understand what it was that Lilly was holding, and it was then, just as he saw it clearly, that he fell back into the darkness. He had let his energy get too low—run out of gas, he thought—and got attacked by the animals out in the boondocks.

"They are of myriad form and capability," Wiedemann was saying as Bo began paying attention again. "And they are called by many names: Abaddon, Ashtaroth, Asmodeus, Beelzebub and so on down the alphabet. But they have only one purpose." He paused, leaning forward so that his face was close to Bo's. "To steal your life force."

"You mean my soul?"

"You might call it that, though that would be an erroneous name for what they are taking from you." He wiped his hand along his leg, as if the very thought of the demons made him feel unclean. "They are, according to some ancient writers, the souls of the fallen angels. And for others they are simply creatures indigenous to the darkness between the worlds. Whatever one supposes of their origins, they desire—no, they *lust* for—one thing: energy."

"But if they're spirits," Bo said, "they can go where they please just by thinking about it, can't they?"

"After eons of such existence, even the spiritual body becomes worn away. They must, therefore, prey on the unwary souls whose life force is dispersed or tied to inappropriate objects."

"You mean like the souls of the damned?"

"Again, the terminology is not precise, but yes, those are the ones demons depend on for their energy."

Bo was thoughtful, listening to this and trying to place it in his childhood theological world of heaven and hell, with a benevolent but stern Father and an implacable Satan who waited below in fire. He looked at the other man, seeing the unchanged, bearded face. It was as if Wiedemann did not live in time like other people. He did not look tired or any different from three hours before when they had begun the conversation.

"Then they are in what people call hell?"

"Wouldn't you describe it so?" The beard parted slightly.

"Yeah, that's true. Hell couldn't be any worse than that."

As they talked into the evening and the fire died down and finally was no more than embers among the white ashes, the adept Wiedemann described the techniques for passing through the realm of demons into the land of the dead spirits. He also told Bo how to avoid that realm altogether by keeping his thoughts fixed on this world and traveling only across its surface, as if on a flying carpet or in an airplane.

"In that way," he said softly, as the old clock ticked on in the corner, "you cannot be attacked. Of course"—he shrugged—"if the one you seek is actually not in this world, you will be unable to find her. Your wish to visit her, the saying of her name, will result only in an aimless wandering. You will know after a time that she is no longer with us."

Bo felt so tired as he heard the old clock chime once for 1:00 A.M. that he felt the demons might get him right there in his chair in Sol's house if he stayed another minute; but he had to get one more thing from this man.

"I was trying to figure out a message," Bo said. "At least, I think it must have been a message, when I got caught by the demons." He took out his pocket notebook and a pen and drew the diagram he remembered from the ring Lilly had been holding. "It was a heavy silver ring, an Indian piece," Bo said as he drew. "It had a turquoise stone that was square, or just about, and had a little flaw in it. It was this flaw that seemed important. It looked like this."

Wiedemann took the offered piece of paper and looked at the simple design. He handed it back.

"You can't tell anything about it?" Bo asked, disappointed.

"You are the only one who can tell what it means," the bearded man said, almost in a whisper. "The spirits may sometimes have to speak in symbols, in cryptograms, in parables. It is left to the kindred spirit to render their message plain."

"Well, do you think it's an arrow pointing into the box?"

"As you have drawn it, yes, it resembles an arrow," Wiedemann said. He turned his head and did a strange

154

thing. The beard parted widely and a large, pink yawn appeared.

Bo almost laughed as he stuffed the paper into his pocket. On his way home in the chilly night air of spring, he resolved to make another try at finding Lilly in that dangerous realm. But at the thought of the demons, he shivered and looked around as if to reassure himself that he was walking a real street under the stars of his own universe.

Perhaps because he was frightened, the next three times he tried to leave his body Bo found himself unable to do it. Once he even fell asleep trying and only dreamed he had journeyed. The dream was so different and so indistinct in comparison with the actual experience that he knew it had been a failure. The fourth time he waited until quite late, after midnight, reassuring himself by writing instructions on a piece of paper beside the bed. He would remain in this world and merely journey across the surface of the earth so that there would be no dangers from the realm of spirits.

The relaxation took all his concentration, but he could feel when he had succeeded in loosening the muscles of his chest that this time he would make it. The sensation of floating came easily and without fear. He rolled from the bed and felt the airy lightness of what he now thought of as his etheric body floating in the semidarkness of his bedroom. This time he waited purposely, familiarizing himself with the room, floating up to the ceiling and putting his glowing hand and arm through the plaster and lath as if it were so much smoke. At last, feeling confident that he would remain in this world, he thought about going outside and floated through the roof of the house.

The sparkling city extended around him, the flat expanse of the Great Salt Lake off to the west with a mountain rising out of it. He thought very carefully of finding Lilly Penfield if she were on this earth, thinking her name only within a context of her activities as a living person. He continued to float above the city, feeling the hard points of the stars over him in the mild spring night. It was the end of March now, and the trees in the parks were budding; some had leaves already. He said her name, being careful to surround it with the context of this world. Slowly he felt a wafting movement, as if a slight breeze had touched his cheek. He checked a feeling of elation as he began to move south, away from the city. Her name came to his mind again, unbidden this time, and he moved more rapidly over the desert, southeastward now, the patches of vegetation where towns grew in the desert slipping past as if he remained still and the world turned beneath him.

The stark shadows of Monument Valley flashed below him, and the lights of a town could be seen away to the left as he continued south. He was not sure what state he would be in now, whether it was still Utah or Arizona, or maybe New Mexico. He would have to bring a map next time, he thought happily, looking downward like an aerial tourist on the furrowed and mountained land. He began to drop toward the earth, and his heart felt a great anticipation growing. Lilly was in this world, after all, for he had come these ways to find her. She has to be alive, he thought, as his etheric body slowed and he found himself hanging in the darkness above a land strewn with black stones.

He hung there a long time, wondering where she could be in this desert that stretched away in every direction like the surface of the moon. The anticipation he had felt waned, faded away as he saw nothing, heard nothing. He thought of her name again, more strongly, but his etheric body only moved aimlessly about as if it were looking for a more convenient piece of sagebrush or more interesting pile of yellow and black rocks. Bo was about to return to his body by saying his name when he saw, or rather felt, the glowing of some life near him. At first he was certain it was an illusion, for it was a cold glow, like the light of a glowworm, but it was moving at great speed along an erratic track. The glowing thing dashed over humps of rock and leaped bushes, flew into and out of the dry arroyos and finally, in a flurry of sand, stopped. The glow grew stronger for an instant and then settled into a dark red gleaming. Bo willed himself to move closer and tried to look, to see with eyes that were not eyes at all.

The ruddy glow enclosed a creature that Bo could now recognize. The lines of the body were those of a long-legged cat without a tail, a tiger, blue-gray furred and with strange, almost human hands. It lay on the desert floor devouring a jackrabbit, its body glowing like an overheated furnace. Bo came close, seeing the jaws carefully disassembling the rabbit, the paws carefully holding the body. He could feel the satisfaction emanating from the great body like the heat of its chase, which still surrounded it in a fiery aura. He was fascinated to see it eat. This was the Beast that held Lilly its prisoner, the Beast that had healed him of a deadly and incurable disease. And it tore out the rabbit's liver as delicately as a surgeon, chewing it with audible pleasure.

Bo called out to the Beast, but it did not respond. He called to Lilly, but could get no sort of feeling that she was there at all. The Beast finished the rabbit and began cleaning itself much as any cat would, licking its large front paws, its eyes slitted comfortably. He had about decided just to follow it until it changed back when he was startled by the Beast's looking directly at him. From where he "stood" on, or perhaps just above, the desert ground, the Beast had been sitting sideways to him. It had turned to face him so quickly that he involuntarily felt fear and shot upward into the night air. From this vantage point, he watched the blue-gray animal below as it padded about, sniffing, holding its head up in a strange way, looking around for the thing that it had perceived. Bo willed himself down to the earth again, telling himself how ridiculous it was to be afraid of the Beast when he was a completely impalpable etheric body.

But it was unnerving to stand there as the Beast approached, its huge eyes glowing in the darkness, the teeth showing behind the black lips. Bo tried to speak to it, calling out as loudly as he could, but the animal walked past him, turned and walked past again. Clearly it felt something in the area, but it could not identify or find a trace of what it perceived. At last the animal seemed satisfied that it had been mistaken and turned away. Bo followed by floating just above the ground as the big cat loped across the mesa toward a group of squat, almost round huts made of logs. Near the huts ran a small dry watercourse lined with straggly trees. Off to the right in the darkness, Bo could sense a large group of animals, sheep, in some sort of rough enclosure. He saw the Beast stop at the door of one of the huts and willed himself to that spot.

To his etheric perceptions, whether they were sight and sound in the usual sense or some other mode, there came a burst of brilliant light that almost blinded him. The Beast was gone, and there appeared a dark-haired woman in a long skirt and velvet blouse cinched with a silver belt. Bo stepped forward, saying, "Lilly, it's me," but the woman only paused to listen for any sound that might indicate she had been discovered and then stooped to enter the hut and was gone.

Bo felt dazed, his senses in disarray. He had seen her face from a close distance: the dark, almost Oriental eyes, the long black hair of the Indian braided with a blue strip of cloth, the mouth held in a straight line. It was not Lilly.

"I am ignoring my better judgment again," Sol said. He looked comically serious, patting Bo's shoulder and glancing up into the bigger man's face as he spoke. After Sol's treat at lunch, they had stopped in the park before returning to The Ritz.

"You've been better to me in three months than old Kneipe was in fourteen years," Bo said, feeling embarrassed and pleased at the same time.

"A good jeweler does not throw pearls away because the string is broken," Sol said, shaking his head.

"I can't promise that I'll even be back at all," Bo said.

"If and when, my boy," the little man said, "you can step right into your job again." He smiled. "And if you bring some good designs back, as you say you are going to do, so much the better. For myself, I think it's more likely you will teach those dumb Indians how to work silver and stones."

Bo felt overwhelmed by this man's trust. He was a person who had always shied away from close friendships, but Sol got to be close without ever trying, without any of the demands that closeness had always seemed to put on Bo in the past. It was more like he was a relative, Bo thought, maybe even a father. He thought then of his own father, the thin, nervous, aimless man his father had become before he died of grief over his dead wife. Very unlike a father, he thought then, but a good friend. The sun was hot on their shoulders now, the pigeons wheeling in great inclines over the people who fed them in the park. Sol looked at the stubble on Bo's face.

"You haven't been standing close enough to your razor these mornings," he grinned.

"It's just something I feel like doing," Bo said. "Maybe your friend Wiedemann impressed me with his foliage."

"No, no, I was kidding about you two being alike. He's a silly man. He lives somewhere else, not in the world. You, now," Sol said, squinting against the bright sun, "you are of this earth."

The two men—the short, bushy-haired one and the tall, gaunt one in the battered hat—began slowly walking back toward Main Street.

"If you don't find her, my friend," Sol said. "There's other fish in the sea, remember."

"If Lilly taught me anything," Bo said, "she taught me that life is here to be lived and not to grieve over what you can't ever have. But I won't stop looking until I'm sure she can't be found anywhere in this world."

"Well, the good fight, the great quest." Solomon McArdle waved his arms vaguely in the air as if frightening the pigeons. "Love, the great leveler." He grinned at Bo, who seemed deep in thought. "You didn't get my joke?"

Bo burst out laughing. He wanted to hug the little jeweler, but instead he put his hands on Sol's shoulders; and the two men laughed until there were tears in the eyes of them both.

Chapter Nine

The road along the rim of the canyon that led to the village of Chinle was not much better than the horse track Johnny had directed him over several days ago. Barry cursed the rocks and the sand while the Model A steamed along for more than twenty miles until the road turned to gravel and he saw a sign that said Chinle was two miles ahead. The village turned out to be larger than he had expected, with a big stone schoolhouse and an administration building for the Indian Service. After his few days in totally primitive surroundings, the gravel streets and stone and timber houses appeared the height of civilization. He even found a gas station where his little car was well treated and filled up with all the liquids it would hold.

"Where's the trading post here?" he asked the Indian who was pouring water into the car's radiator while steam billowed out.

"Hubbel's or the Sanchez post?"

"Why, I guess the biggest one."

"Hubbel's, down there." The skinny brown man pointed to a timber and stone building with a pitched roof. Several Indians in black hats leaned against the wall near the door.

Barry found the store almost sumptuous after the post he had visited with Johnny on the way in. It seemed to have everything one might need, including such luxuries as Coleman lanterns and stoves and tents of all kinds. Barry felt like one of the Indians now and took his time browsing around the counters, looking up at the hanging utensils to get the best cooking pot he could afford for Mrs. Chee. In one corner of the store an area was set off by a low railing, and behind it two men worked at benches making silver and turquoise jewelry. One of them was a

Navajo of indeterminate old age, a red band around his hair. The other was, surprisingly, a white man with a short black beard and hair sprinkled with gray. His face as he looked up at Barry seemed calm, but his gaze was intent, almost searching. He laid down the little hammer he had been using on a miniature anvil and smiled at Barry.

"Interested in some jewelry?" he asked.

"I thought only the Navajo worked silver around here," Barry said, smiling. He liked the man immediately, for some reason.

"I'm just learning some of their tricks," the bearded man said, standing up and holding out his hand. "George Beaumont," he said.

"Barry Golden." They shook hands, Barry feeling the strength in the handclasp. He stepped back. "Maybe I could look at something to take home to my wife and kids."

"Sure." Beaumont said a word in Navajo to the old Indian working at the bench. The Indian grunted but did not look up. "Here's what we got in bracelets," he said, taking a tray from beneath a glass countertop. "Now these are old, out-of-pawn stuff," he said, pointing to some heavier pieces. "And these are some that Red Hand and I have been making here in the post."

Barry looked at the different designs, the weight of the stones and metal in the bracelets, how they felt when he picked them up. The newer ones were more delicately made, but the designs were traditional and the stones set with great solidity in the metal. He was afraid they would be awfully expensive and said so.

"Well, now," Beaumont said, hefting one of the old pieces, "there's quite a few ounces of pure silver in this kind of thing, and that stone's a pretty piece, too. This would cost you upwards of a hundred dollars in Phoenix. Here it's forty-nine dollars flat." He grinned. "Low overhead."

Barry smiled, liking the older man's comfortable air.

"Well, how about some of the newer pieces. I kind of like that one." He pointed to a twisted wire bracelet with stones set all the way around it.

"Yeah. Red Hand made that one. That's a beauty. It's got coral mixed in with the turquoise, see? The price on that is . . . let's see. Sixteen bucks."

Barry made a deal on a bracelet for Renee, a ring for

Mina with a lovely flat stone in it that Beaumont had set and a tiny silver pin in the shape of a wild turkey with feathers of petrified wood, coral and turquoise for little Martin. They concluded the deal, and Barry bought the pots and pans he had come for as a present for Mrs. Chee. He remarked on this to Beaumont, who raised his head sharply.

"That wouldn't be Albert Chee's wife?" the gaunt, bearded man said, his face suddenly grave.

"Yeah. I been staying with them up in the canyon for a couple of days. Friend of mine . . ." Barry was going on, but the other man had turned to the trading post proprietor, who was getting out penny candies for some Indian kids.

"Sam? Fella here is a friend of Albert Chee," Beaumont said, his face in a frown.

The proprietor handed the candy to the kids and came over, also frowning. He was a large man with a big belly and wore his hat all the time.

"You hear about Albert?" the fat man said, leaning over the counter to look at Barry.

"No," Barry said. "I left there this morning, late . . . I guess around noon or a little later." He felt guilty about all that had happened that morning and stammered, as if he had committed a crime.

"He killed a man this morning," Sam said, picking up a toothpick from the counter and digging at his teeth. "Down at the ranger station. Shot him clean through the heart with an old pistol."

Barry recalled Albert coming out of the shelter that morning and killing the dog. He must have gone crazy. "Was he drunk?"

"Yeah, I 'spect he was," Sam said. "These people get a little liquor in 'em, look out." He looked at Barry with a deprecating nod. "You're a friend of his, you better see the sheriff. Maybe you can help find him." Sam moved off to wait on a white couple who had just walked into the store.

"Where can I find the sheriff?" Barry asked the bearded man, who seemed as full of sympathy as Sam had been of indifference.

"Come on," Beaumont said. "I'm going out to the canyon anyway." He called a couple of words in Navajo to Red Hand, who again just grunted.

"How long it take you to learn to speak Indian?" Barry said as they walked down the dirt street.

"I don't speak it, really," Beaumont said. "Red Hand taught me a few words, but I can't really understand it. I'm trying, but I'm not all that good at languages."

The sheriff was not in his office, and the deputy said the whole bunch, probably half a dozen men, was out looking for Chee to bring him back. "They all gone up del Muerto," the deputy said.

"Where is that?" Barry asked as they walked back to the station where his car waited.

"Why, that's where you came from," Beaumont said. "If you were staying with the Chee family."

"I thought it was Canyon de Chelly," Barry said. "That's what Johnny called it. He said it a little different . . . sort of *tseh-i*, something like that."

"Well, you see there's really three canyons," Beaumont said. He held up his hand with three fingers extended. "This one on the left is Canyon del Muerto, the middle one is de Chelly, and this one on the right is Monument Canyon." He smiled for some reason and said, "You see, they make a sort of arrow shape, pointing into Arizona."

"Canyon of the Dead?"

"Yeah. Good name, too. There was a massacre up there back in the last century. About a hundred Indians, mostly women and kids, holed up in a cave back there. The Spaniards killed every one of them except one old man who told the story. Place's not very far from where the Chees live, if I remember right."

"You know the canyon pretty well, I suppose," Barry said as they got into the Model A.

"I only been here a couple of months, but I walk it all the time. Yeah, it's so big that nobody knows it really, not even the people who were born here, but I got a rough idea of the place and some of the people."

They rode along talking for the twenty miles or so of the rim road, and by the time they got to the trail down, which Barry recognized by landmarks he had picked out earlier, they had gotten to know each other about as well as if they had been neighbors in a small town. But there was, in each of the men, an element of mystery that both recognized. It seemed to Barry he had met a man who shared his view of the world. They started down the trail together after looking into the canyon and noting no unusual activity below that they could see.

163

"Hey," Barry said, "there weren't any other cars up there. If the sheriff came out this way, wouldn't he have come by car?"

"I doubt it," said Beaumont. "They most likely rode horses up Chinle wash looking for Albert's trail. They couldn't have got here yet. Maybe they've caught him down stream a ways. He was on horseback, wasn't he?"

"Yeah, I guess he was." Barry hardly noticed the beauty of the trail or the canyon, now turning ruddy with evening light again. His mind was on the Chee family and their disaster.

Barry found himself in the awkward position of bringing bad news to the Chee family, for no one in the camp had heard anything from Chinle. Albert had evidently not come back since early that morning. He tried to make Mrs. Chee understand, and Beaumont tried also, but they only succeeded in making her think that Albert was dead. She sent one of her daughters up to the permanent camp to get Johnny, her face drawn and terrible looking. She would not believe anything, obviously, until she could hear it in her own language. When Johnny came running down the edge of the stream, it was obvious he had been told by the little girl what was the matter. He looked at Barry for confirmation.

"True?" he panted, his hat in his hand. "My uncle killed a man?"

"That's what they said in Chinle," Barry said, feeling intensely the agony of his friend.

Johnny put his arms around his "mother" and led her into the shelter, talking softly in Navajo. After a moment the men waiting outside heard the woman's voice raise in a wail, a moaning that rose to a crescendo and fell again to rise again with the next breath. They were startled by the arrival of several people from the upstream camp, the women ducking to go into the shelter as Johnny came out putting his hat on. One of the women who went into the shelter was Sarah Lakuchai. She paused to look at Barry before ducking through the doorway, but it was George Beaumont Barry was looking at.

Beaumont looked at Sarah and his face went white under the beard, his eyes starting out. He stood like a stone on the spot until she disappeared into the shelter.

"Bo?" Barry said to the older man, feeling a chill run through him. "What's the matter? You look like somebody's holding a gun to your head."

Beaumont emerged from his trance and stared hard at Barry, as if trying to remember who he was. His voice was harsh. "Who was that?"

"The young woman? A relative of the Chees—Sarah Lakuchai, I think her name is." Barry felt uncomfortable. All of this going on, he thought, and I have to think about that, too.

"She was not here last month," Beaumont said, his eyes squinted up as if he were thinking hard or trying to look through a stone. "I was here, and she was not here."

Barry felt that his new friend had suddenly gone crazy also. He thought first that Bo also had come under the Indian woman's power—but no, that was silly.

"Well, I wish you'd let me in on it," Barry said impatiently. "I met her at the peyote ceremony, among a lot of others." He looked closely at Bo.

"It's her," the older man whispered. "And now what do I do?"

Barry turned away. It was too much for him to fathom, and the irritating abstraction Beaumont had fallen into was not to be dealt with. He walked over to where Johnny was standing, talking with some of the men from the upstream camp. He could understand nothing of what they were saying, of course, which only added to his frustration. He stood there helplessly for a few minutes, waiting for Johnny to realize he was there. Finally the young Indian turned to him, his face a noncommittal mask.

"He killed a white man then?" Johnny said.

"That's what they said." Barry hated the difference of race now. He felt suddenly an alien in the camp. "They said he was drunk and the man insulted him or something. But the man he shot had a knife. It might have been self-defense."

"A white?" Johnny said, his face impassive. "Murder." Johnny said a few more words to the men around him. They nodded and the group broke up, heading back upstream.

"We'll try to find him," Johnny said. "Some of the men thought of places he might go to hide, and I've got an idea myself."

"You're going to turn him over to the sheriff?"

"It's a white matter, but even the tribal cops would shoot him first and then bring him in. Yeah, we've got to find him."

Johnny and two other young men headed down the canyon on horseback in the deepening dusk while Bo and Barry took some meat and fried bread one of the women brought them and headed back up the trail to the top. Barry was surprised to find the sun still in the sky when they emerged from the canyon.

"We're not going to be much help up here," he said as they threw their blankets and food in the back seat.

"Well, we can move faster and see farther, at least as long as we can see," Beaumont said. "We can locate the sheriff's bunch, maybe, and see if they've found him yet."

But even that was no easy task, for the canyon was cut into many side canyons of varying depth and length, some of which it was impossible to get near in a car. They spent the evening tramping along the rim of the canyon, peering down into its deepening gloom for signs of activity. They saw Johnny and the other two Indians trotting along the streambed far below and then drove on down a mile or so and got out to look again.

"This place is a lot bigger than I thought," Barry said. They stood on the edge of a thousand-foot-deep chasm sometime later.

"They used to think the Navajo had a big fortress up here," Bo said as he shaded his eyes to look down the sheer rock. "But it was just the canyons themselves that scared people."

They drove another mile and looked down again, seeing only the scattered hogans and shelters of another settlement.

"Maybe those people would know something," Barry said.

"If they did, they likely wouldn't tell us," Bo said. "We better let your friend Johnny take care of the asking."

At their next stop, with the sun resting on the horizon, Bo pointed down and to the right of the cliff they were standing on. "Right under us here is what they call Massacre Cave, I think, if my memory is good. It's a couple hundred feet down, but there's no path to get there from the top. I never saw anybody climb it from the bottom, but they say there's a trail that goes to it. I've looked at it from the canyon floor, and it's about seven hundred feet straight up."

"You think it's possible for him to have got up there?" Barry was trying to visualize a cave seven hundred feet up a sheer cliff.

"There's so many ruins and caves in these canyons," Bo said, shaking his head. "He could be anywhere."

"Maybe we should go down there and check," Barry said. "Isn't there a trail down near here?"

"Oh, yeah, I think there is one going to a bunch of hogans up ahead," Bo said. "But we might better locate the sheriff before it gets really dark. You see there's so many side canyons, too. There's Many Cherry and Twin Trail, and Black Rock Canyon between here and the junction with de Chelly, and then there's others: Tunnel Canyon and Cottonwood Canyon before you get onto the wash where it comes out above Chinle."

But they did not find the sheriff's party by full dark, and they finally gave up and made camp on top among the junipers. The fire was more for its comforting blaze than any necessity of cooking. They had not brought coffee, and Barry missed that, but they had bread, meat, dried fruit and a bag of water.

"I doubt that posse will be traveling at night," Bo said, as he got his blanket out of the car.

"Maybe we should get down in the canyon tomorrow morning and see if they've gone by us," Barry said. He was extraordinarily tired and felt a discomfort inside him. The Beast stirred about near the surface of his mind, making it hard for him to think about anything.

"We're about across from Twin Trail," Bo said. "The main canyon is nearly a mile wide here. There's some hogans down there, I believe." He rolled up in his blanket under the edge of the juniper branches.

Barry made sure the fire was safe and burning low, and he spread his blanket on a soft patch of sand. The stars flared with their accustomed brilliance, and a waxing moon rode just above the eastern horizon. He tried not to think about this day, to put everything out of his mind, and for once he succeeded.

The fire burned on for an hour or more as the two men breathed evenly in sleep. As the last embers were blowing in the faint night wind, a creature the size of a full-grown tiger slipped out of the blanket that had been around it and padded away into the dark.

As I ease through the door of the hogan, I hear the women moaning in unison from the hut they use for their religious services. They are keening the death of Albert Chee, whom they believe is already with his fathers. Sarah

167

would have been with them, but I exerted control and had her plead sickness. This night I feel it is nearly time. Certainly it must be soon, or I will have to seek another. My time is limited now, a new sensation. I have always ignored time, thought it was only humans who fought its passing. Now I know its necessity. I trot away from the camp, keeping to the rocks to avoid tracks, and soon I can break into a full run downstream. I ignore the perceptions around me of the night animals, the penned sheep, the slinking coyotes, one of whom is a failed Outsider. Him I give a wide berth as I run, not wanting to arouse his interest. He is what in a human society would be called insane, perhaps perverted, a perfect specimen out of the Navajo legend. Such a creature has missed his time and will never have a second chance, a terrible fate for one who has awakened and knows what is possible after The Leap has been made.

At the holy spot near the ruin, where I attempted to waken the Other with human passion, I pause and walk carefully around the hidden burial pit to avoid anguish caused by the relics. The power of such objects is in their absorbing and holding intact the time-space structure of some highly charged event, sometimes even that of a Conjunction. This burial pit must contain such a charm, for it is powerful indeed. I feel it calling to me as I walk warily around the perimeter of its force. The relic draws its power from the Outside through a kind of permanent opening. It is not a thing I wish to deal with. Ahead somewhere is the one I seek, the one I must awaken soon or let him be lost like the coyote, a beast, trapped on this world.

Several miles down the canyon, after slipping past two settlements of permanent hogans, I sense the three Indian men from my own camp. They are in their blankets under some cottonwoods, the horses hobbled nearby. The one named Johnny is awake, but he does not hear me as I make a wide detour of their camp. His anxiety affects me, and I feel compassion for his trouble, wondering if it might be possible to locate his uncle before he is found and killed by the whites. Perhaps I will catch his scent. It will not hinder my purpose to be aware of it. The canyon grows very wide here, and against the high cliffs I see white moonlight striking, turning the edge of the canyon to a gleaming tracery in the night. A light wind flows down the canyon, carrying my scent, for I am allowing myself to be known. I pause to rest beside some fallen boulders near the east wall, feeling out to the limit of my perceptual field for him. If I could only speak. But that is impossible until he wakens.

For what seemed hours, Bo lay on the sand just under the juniper branches, talking himself into it, telling himself he had done it many times before and he could do it now. But it was too early, or he was not tired enough, or he was in unfamiliar surroundings and worried by the night sounds of owls and wind in the trees. He could not get the relaxation going, and finally he slipped off to sleep by mistake. He woke what seemed only instants later, but the moon had leaped up the sky, so he knew he had been asleep more than an hour. He concentrated again and this time felt the relaxation beginning in his legs.

Carefully rolling out of his body when he felt the lightness, he stood above the moonlit desert, seeing the glow throughout his body, gazing around him with the peculiarly distorted vision typical of looking without eyes at the things of this world. He was intent on his guest but noticed Barry's blanket was empty as he rose into the dark air and said the Indian woman's name firmly to himself.

With a part of his mind, he wondered about the other man, but then he was startled by the direction of his movement. Instead of moving back up the canyon, as he had thought he would, he was hovering over the edge and moving directly downward along the cliff now luminous with moonlight. Could she be down the canyon this far? His glowing form settled into the darkness of the canyon as if he were some ocean denizen losing its buoyancy and drifting down to the floor of the sea. He said the woman's name again to hasten the travel, but he did not move faster, only settled more and more slowly. And then he knew why, for just below him was the blue-gray Beast, lying under a tree, alert but unmoving. She has come down-canyon in that form, he thought, hovering above the big, tailless cat. But why?

He could not communicate with her. He had tried that before, but he could watch and perhaps learn something of her purpose down here. With more than starlight and reflected moonlight from the canyon walls, the Beast glowed faintly to Bo's perceptions. It was her aura he was seeing, the glow of life surrounding her like the halo of a saint in some medieval painting. Bo settled his mind, thinking of nothing so he would not move from the spot. He would find out what brought the creature here. Perhaps there could yet be a confrontation and a solution.

But the etheric body is not a stable entity in the material world, and Bo had trouble just waiting. He could not keep his mind still and found himself drifting not only in the canyon but dangerously near to lifting out of this world altogether. He feared that more than any danger he had ever faced, including the threat of death, and he struggled to keep his thoughts channeled on the Indian woman. The Beast lay below him as if she had all the time in the world, and Bo finally decided he must move or go back to his body, so dangerous did it seem to try holding still with his thoughts constantly turning toward the one he sought.

Then he felt a hot rush of shame come over him. He had forgotten about the man they were hunting. He could find the Indian by simply saying his name. But before he had said it, he caught himself. What if Albert Chee was dead and the command of his name sent Bo hurtling off into the darkness between worlds where terrible fanged creatures hungered for souls? He held himself over the Beast below that seemed as peaceful as a genuine big cat lying in the sand thinking of nothing but its next meal. Without worrying more about it, he said the name: Albert Chee.

Thank God, Bo thought, as he felt his etheric body rising and moving up the canyon at increasing speed. He must be alive. But how could he be *up* the canyon? Bo held himself in tightly, ready for any swerve that might indicate a plunge into the realm of the dead, but he only moved steadily and easily up the canyon that was now filled with moonlight in the east-west stretches. The walls became higher as he sailed back toward the camp he had been at earlier that evening, and he recognized the cliff that held the hollowed-out place called Massacre Cave. Sure enough, he thought, as he floated upward until the valley was far beneath him. At the lip of the cave, which was indeed formed something like a mouth with a protruding lower lip, he paused and could see the glow of a human aura. Albert Chee lay curled up in the far corner, away from the white sticks and blotches that were bones and skulls scattered across the back of the cave, remnants of the people killed there a hundred and thirty years ago. Albert was alive, and a very brave or very desperate Indian to sleep in this place of uneasy spirits. Bo knew how desperate the man must be, for the Navajo have an almost ineradicable fear of night and of the dead they are so afraid that often they will abandon a house where a relative has died and move away rather than live there with the spirit.

Albert's breath came in short, uneasy gasps. He was not asleep, Bo realized, but lying curled up to keep warm, probably frightened almost to death to be there. Bo allowed his etheric body to drift back out over the lip of the cave, trying to pick out the toe and finger holds in the almost vertical cliff that Albert must have used to get up here. Sometimes there was a tiny ledge or outcrop that a man might hang to, but for most of the distance up the cliff there seemed to be only little pockmarks and cracks that a bird would have had trouble hanging on to.

He knew now where to look. It would be simple for the searchers in the morning. With the solution to that problem in his insubstantial hands, Bo felt relief that he could now get back to the Beast and his quest for Lilly. Without the necessary care as this thought occurred to him in other than words, he found himself burning with the need to find her now that he felt so close to the goal, and her name leaped into his mind. Instantly he felt as if, in his physical body, he had toppled backward and was falling down the face of that terrible cliff. Vertigo pulled his mind out of shape, the blackness closed around him with a crescendo of roaring. Fear surrounded his etheric body like a damning aura to draw demons from every dimension. He felt them like sharks around him as he fell into blackness, waited for the first bite while he tried to get his mind in place, tried to say his own name in the whirl of infinity where the fragments of his personality fell like wreckage into the deep.

As I pick my way down the trail toward the bottom of the canyon, I find myself wondering over my motives. Certainly I would help Barry and his friends find this Indian, but I feel more than that altruistic impulse driving me down into the darkness. Time presses on my mind, as if I were a human running to catch a train. I do not recall ever feeling such urgings in my life.

A scent catches me off guard, a scent so pungent and beautiful that I miss my footing and roll down a hundred feet in a cloud of dust and loose rock. I scramble to my feet and cast about to find that smell again. I trot down the easier slopes near the bottom of the cliff now. Ah, there it is again, a thread of absolute beauty. I have to stop, lift my muzzle and savor that scent. It is languid yet dynamic, like my own odor but intensified into almost a palpable drift, like a warmer shelf of water within the cold water of a lake. I cannot tell what direction it comes from, but the wind is blowing gently downstream, so it must be back that way.

I angle across the sandy bottom of the gorge, my nose picking out the nuances of the scent so that I can home in on the source. But it is a peculiarly elusive trace. After going through its vapors three or more times in one crossing of the valley, I realize it will be nearly impossible to track directly. It has dispersed from some source, perhaps far upstream, and now is hanging in the night air in several different strands of odor, like gossamer trailing in the wind, invisible and yet unmistakable as it touches the skin. I listen and cast about with my spatial sense. The usual night creatures are moving about, a large owl sits on a cottonwood limb up ahead, there are no sheep or settlements within my range, but there are some large animals—coyotes, just on the edge of my perception, over in the open space that marks the beginning of another canyon. I believe Beaumont called it Twin Trail Canyon. But they are inconsequential to me now. I am frustrated by the nondirectional scent. It surrounds me rather than simply flowing to me from a source. It is maddening to smell this intriguing thing and not be able to find it.

After what might be hours, I find myself half a mile up the side canyon, still with that scent in my nostrils, still unable to find its source. I have not even gotten upwind of it. And then, as I trot zigzag up Twin Trails Canyon, it fades. I am about to turn and go back when a different perception catches me unaware. There is a camp of men and horses not more than a thousand feet ahead up this side canyon. As for the scent, I feel I can get back to it again. It has so frustrated me that my mind feels charred from thinking about it. I shake my head and trot on up the side canyon, keeping the men's camp in my spatial sense. There are half a dozen horses hobbled off in the grassy slope to the left, and around a small fire in a hollow are lying the men who have come with the sheriff to find Albert Chee. I will take a minute here before going back to that elusive odor.

Two of the men are sitting with their back to a large boulder smoking cigarettes. Four or five are wrapped in their blankets, asleep near the fire. I creep close enough to hear their talk as the cigarette ends glow and subside. But they are talking of women and other things inconsequential to me. The jokes are softly told—crude, like schoolboy tales. I listen for a time and am prepared to move away when they stop their desultory conversation and one stands up and stretches.

"Go get Curtis. I got to get me some sleep."

"Yeah, me, too. Hey, we goin' on back in the morning, you think."

"Nah. We got to see if that old boy is at home. That's the least we can do after riding all over this damn canyon."

"He ain't there," says the voice of the one still sitting down. "He left that pony and went up on top. He's in Gallup by now."

"I dunno. He's as tricky as any other Indian, and he ain't likely to take off for the city like a white man would."

"They wasn't any tracks, Buddy said."

"Hell, he didn't look long enough up there, I tol' the sheriff I ought to gone with him. Buddy don't give a shit. That old boy coulda walked along the edge on the rocks or something. I say he's gone home or hidin' out somewhere up in del Muerto."

The other man stood and stepped on his cigarette. They walked back to the fire and wakened another man, who then got up to sit behind the same boulder and smoke his cigarettes. I moved back down the side canyon into the open space at the junction. So, Albert had left his horse in the side canyon and gone on foot in some unknown direction. But the feeling seemed to be that the sheriff would want to follow the main canyon back to Chee's home in the morning.

In the wide opening that is almost a mile across and flat sand for most of that distance, the moon is now flooding the whole valley with silver. I trot out across the sand, my muzzle up to catch the scent. I cross the entire valley and start back, but not a trace of it can I find. How strange that it would completely disappear in the few minutes I have been up the side canyon. It is frustrating, and I run back and forth like a stupid dog in the broad, sandy area, trying to pick it up from the ground or in the air; but nowhere can I find the trace. It seems now like a dream, something only in my mind. Finally I give it up and begin trotting upstream. Perhaps I can pick up Albert's scent. It would not be difficult if he had walked this way, but I suspect he did not come through the canyon, for I cannot catch anything like his odor, even though I traverse the canyon floor wall to wall several times.

Hours have passed this night with nothing accomplished. The maddening scent has completely disappeared, I have found nothing more about Albert. I have located the sheriff and his bunch of men, but they would have made themselves obvious in the morning anyway. All I have done tonight is wear myself out and establish to my own satisfaction that Albert has not walked through this part of the canyon. I find the trail up again and climb it wearily. Something drops down inside my mind like a heavy weight falling against a closed door that might have been opened. I feel more than tired—depressed, I suppose. I am not used to feeling like this and think it might have something to do with that elusive and beautiful scent that I have lost.

Dawn is not far away when I approach the sleeping Beaumont and the blanket where Barry will sleep again. As I walk by the other man, I notice he is very still, and in my spatial perception I am startled to find that his vibrations are almost nonexistent. Is he dead? I walk over to him cautiously, sniff at his form. He smells sick, or . . . no, like something not quite alive. I touch him with my nose and he is cool, inert. Something is definitely wrong.

I shift.

"Bo!" Barry shook the big man's shoulder. He was limp, like one dead. "George, George Beaumont, hey, George!"

To Barry's intense relief, the older man's eyes fluttered and came open. They had no life in them for a minute or so, and then the man's chest gave a great heave as he drew in his breath. He uttered a strangled sound, as if he was trying to scream while someone choked him.

"Bo? Hey, wake up. What the hell is the matter?" Barry was scared now. Was the man an epileptic?

But then his eyes came alive again and he gave a great burst of breath, his arms coming up to his face, covering his eyes.

"Oh, ah, God," Bo said.

"Hey, now, come on out of it," Barry said, his hands on the man's shoulders.

"All right, all right, okay, now," Bo said, finally seeming

awake. He sat up, holding his head in his hands, his eyes wild and looking around in the faint dawn.

Barry sat beside him, looking at the stricken, white face. Off in the trees some birds were quarreling about waking up so early.

"I think you saved my life," Bo said, looking at Barry with haggard eyes.

Barry thought the older man looked as if he had been climbing mountains all night. "That must have been some nightmare."

"Yeah, that's what it was all right." Bo lay back, breathing hard through his nose. "I'll be okay now. Tell you about it later."

"Well, if it was just a dream, I guess it'll keep," Barry said, grinning.

"More," Bo said. "More. But one thing I found out." He raised himself to one elbow.

"What's that?"

"I know where Albert Chee is."

In this night when spirits and beasts and men creep about the canyon, there are others who move with purpose through the late moonlight. Below the house ruin where Barry and Sarah spent yesterday morning lies a hidden burial pit, round, sided with flat sandstones set on end, covered with a basketweave of saplings that have held the earth for a thousand years. In the dry pit lies the body of a chief, doubled on itself, the skin and rags of clothing long withered and ready to fall into dust, the bones lying in the foetal position, a pair of new sandals for feet that have never moved again. And in a clay pot, itself inside a basket, lies a bag of magic tools: feathers, bone whistles, carved stones. Among these dusty objects is a finely carved figure that looks like mother of pearl. It glistens as the moonlight strikes it, the iridescence of the ocean in its facets and planes. Dirt falls around it as rapid pairs of paws dig away stones and saplings and sharp teeth tear into the basket and the pot itself. The figure gleams as it is laid bare to the light of the moon it has not seen in a thousand years. Heedless paws scatter the bones of the chief as they scramble about in the pit. They are purposeful, these two coyotes, acting on the orders of another who stands a hundred yards away, his tongue hanging out as if he were grinning. One of the subordinates picks up the carved figure and trots off down the stream with it in his mouth. The one who has stayed back keeps his distance, trotting along behind. When they find a trail to the top of the canyon, they go up, purposeful in the late moonlight.

After a sketchy breakfast, the two men shook out their blankets and prepared to drive back up the canyon to the trail near Massacre Cave. Barry had just rolled up the blanket and turned toward the car when Bo cried out.

"Hey, what's this?" He walked over to pick up something at Barry's feet. "It fell out of your blanket, or maybe it was under you in the dirt. Look at that." The jeweler held up the glittering, pearly object for Barry to see.

"It's nothing I ever saw before," Barry said, holding his blanket in a roll against his chest and peering at the figurine. "Pretty, isn't it?"

"I'll say. It's a real beauty." Bo turned it over and over in his hands. The figure was of some standing animal, bear probably, with its muzzle lifted, head thrown back as if crying out. The carving included a portion of rough, grayish shell that formed the back of the figure, dark and knobby as tree bark. Around the middle of the animal ran a band of lighter color, like a belt cinched around it. The forepaws of the animal appeared to be held down by the belt.

"Let's see," Barry said. He took the figure and at once felt a light buzzing in the shell, as if it were in very rapid vibration. Startled, he dropped it in the sand and had to pick it up again. The delicate vibration continued as he turned it over and looked at it more closely.

"Hey, what do you suppose makes it feel like that?"

"That's probably abalone shell," Bo said, "slick from being handled so much. I'll bet it's really old."

"No," Barry said. "I mean that kind of buzzing you feel. What makes it feel like that?"

Bo looked at the other man, puzzled. He reached for the figure again, and Barry handed it to him. "Buzzing?" he mumbled, holding it, feeling only the slickness of abalone shell.

"Yeah, it kind of vibrates . . . buzzes, or something," Barry said, and then he stopped as something inside him, some far-back image, almost a memory but more like a dream, came into his mind. A figure, a standing bear with a belt around it and its muzzle lifted to howl. A word: amulet.

"It just feels like shell to me," Bo said. He held the

176

figure out to Barry. "It was under your blanket; I guess it's yours."

Barry could tell that the jeweler wanted the piece, admired it and wanted it as any craftsman wants a fine piece in his own line, but he reached for the figure and put it in the pocket of his Levi's jacket. "Yeah, I think I'd like to keep it for a while," he said, his face absent with thought.

Bo was disappointed, but he said nothing more. They got in the little car and bounced around over some roots and rocks and started back along the edge of the canyon.

"This dream you had about Albert," Barry said, as they drove along the dirt track between the trees. "You pretty sure about that?"

Bo sat silent for a minute and then decided to tell it. "I'm able to do what they call astral projection," he said loudly over the noise of the motor. It sounded absurd shouted out in daylight like this, he thought.

Barry looked sideways at the other man, the black beard and gaunt face. "You went there with your spirit?" He looked back at the track they were traveling on, half caught up in his own reveries, trying to place the memory of the amulet.

"It's something I did for the first time when I almost died, and I learned how to do it. But it's dangerous." He stopped, not wanting to tell the rest.

Barry was half aware of what the other man was saying. He was interested, and yet he could feel the faint tingling of the stone in his breast pocket. Why was it so important? He roused to what Bo had said.

"What do you do? Just get out and fly around?"

Bo was relieved to find that Barry did not scoff, but he could not tell it all. Where he had gone last night had been too much to think about. What he had found—or, rather, what he had not found—frightened him. He blocked out the memory of the darkness and the creatures who had waited for him there. But beyond, in that other place, the light shining through everything, the translucent room with its stagelike setting, the ladder-back chair, the window: there had been no one there. The chair was empty. He could not even think what that might mean.

"Sometimes," he answered. "Anyway, I got a look at Albert Chee, and he's in Massacre Cave. I'm sure of that."

"Good enough for me," Barry said.

Half an hour later, Bo said to turn right so they could look at the edge of the canyon, that there ought to be a trail down along there somewhere. When impatient, search more carefully, someone ought to have said to the two men who crashed through piñon and scrub oak to find themselves at a sheer cliff time after time. It was mid-morning by the time they found the trail down. In the east, huge thunderheads built their castles against the blue over the bare slopes of the Chuska Mountains.

Chapter Ten

From the level floor of Canyon del Muerto, four men watched a tiny figure moving up the almost vertical red cliff. The figure was hatless and might have been barefoot. It was an Indian, as were two of the watching men. Barry shaded his eyes, feeling his stomach go empty at the thought of hanging to those tiny dents and projections hundreds of feet above the rocky floor.

"Why did he have to go up?" Barry said to one of the Indians who spoke some English.

"His family," the Indian said.

"How do you know Chee is up there?" Bo said. They had arrived on the scene when Johnny was already halfway up the cliff.

"They saw him," the Indian said, shrugging and pointing down the canyon.

"I guess the people at that camp down there," Bo said. But Barry was tensely watching now as Johnny reached the lip of the cave, pulled himself over the edge and disappeared. In a minute or two the tiny figure's face appeared over the edge and a voice floated down to them. Barry could not make out what he was saying but supposed the Indians could, since they began talking in low tones to each other.

"What's the matter?" Bo said.

"Albert Chee." The Indian paused. "He is sick."

"He needs help?" Barry said.

Without answering, the two Indians walked over to their horses, mounted and rode downstream at a rapid trot.

"What the hell?" Barry said.

"I caught one word," Bo said. "Rope. Maybe they're going to let down a rope from the top." He squinted up at the cliff edge, which appeared to recede and to be covered with scrub oak and piñon. "Might be pretty tough that way."

"Well, I wish we knew what to do to lend a hand," Barry said, and then he gave a gasp. "Hey, he's coming down."

The tiny figure was on the lip of the cave again, carefully starting down the invisible toe and fingerholds. In a matter of minutes he was a third of the way down. He stopped on a ledge and hollered down to the two men. It sounded like he said, "Go meet them."

"Did you get that?" Bo said.

"I think he said 'meet them'," Barry said, looking downstream where the cottonwoods along the wash extended from wall to wall of the canyon. "Did he mean his friends from the camp?"

But his question was answered when out of the cottonwoods burst a group of horsemen at a gallop. It looked, Barry thought, just like a scene out of a Buck Jones movie, with the posse chasing the bad men in a cloud of dust. And at that moment the memory of the night before, a memory that had somehow been obscured, came clear and he knew where the sheriff's men had been.

The horsemen had seen the figure on the cliff, which now decided to go back to the cave and started up the wall again. Bo saw one of the men draw a carbine from his saddle scabbard, but he could not believe it until the sound of the shot boomed and echoed between the canyon walls like thunder. Up on the face of the cliff, the tiny figure in blue Levi's and jacket jerked as if he were hanging suspended from a wire. For a second, Barry thought he would see his Indian friend fall from the cliff, but then the man spread his arms as if to hug the mountain and was still.

The sheriff, a heavy man with a small brimmed hat with conchos on it, hollered, "Who the hell did that?" He turned to the man with the carbine.

"Put that goddamned thing away. You dumb sonofabitch. I asked you to help me track a man, not kill him."

The man with the rifle held it across his saddle, not putting it back in the scabbard. "You see him up there?" he said, squinting up at the cliff where the figure still spread its body flat against the stone. "He's gettin' away, and I'll bet anything that's him."

"That's Johnny Strong Horse," Barry said. He was too

shocked at the shot being fired so suddenly to react to the man who did it. "He's Albert Chee's relative. Albert is in the cave."

"Well, he'll come down when he gets thirsty," said one of the men.

"Yeah," said another. "Let's put a bottle of whiskey down at the bottom. That'll fetch him." He laughed, and several of the men joined in.

Bo was telling them about the other Indians and that they had some plan to get the man down, but Barry wasn't listening. He shucked off his shoes and Levi's jacket and trotted across the rock to the base of the cliff. The rock felt warm and solid to his bare toes.

"Hey," the sheriff yelled. "Where the hell you think you're going?"

Barry did not answer, only put his foot in the first shallow indentation and started up. For the first hundred feet, he shivered as if he had ice water running down his back, his hands and feet quivering against the sandstone that he clutched. He watched the toe and finger holds go past his eyes, not looking down except to place his next step. He did not consciously hear the men shouting below him, nor did he look down. His heart thumped and boomed as he climbed higher, his mind turned wholly to the task, feeling the stones. He found a crack in the cliff face that was like a sudden broad avenue and that he could stick his whole instep into and stood with one foot in the crack for a minute, breath blowing, heart pounding. Sweat ran into his eyes and ears, and he felt every muscle standing out with strain. A pressed-down fear blanked out his mind into a purity of purpose he had never felt before. He would not acknowledge the terror that held him tightly. He looked up, but the cliff leaned inward a hundred feet up and he could not yet see Johnny.

It did not occur to him that if his friend fell, he would probably hit Barry and take them both to their deaths. The trail was too demanding. Nothing went on in Barry's mind but the solidity of each hand- and foothold. He took a breath and went on up, taking each stone into account, noticing when he entered the blackened area where minerals had been washed down the cliff from torrential summer rains, remembering that the black area was more than halfway. But it did not register as a fact that had any significance. Only the next handhold was important. He came to a tiny ledge and rested again, pressed against the wall, feeling yesterday afternoon's heat still seeping out of the solid rock. He chanced a look upward and could see the blue-jeaned figure flattened against the cliff as Barry was. Another hundred feet. He called, almost under his breath, "I'm coming, Johnny. Hang on."

The holds got better up this far, not as weathered for some reason, and as Barry came up under the wounded man, there was a ledge wide enough to stand one foot sideways on. He got to where he could touch Johnny's bare brown foot. One pant leg and foot were soaked with blood, which dripped and ran down the blackened rock.

"Can you make it up?" Barry said, his breath coming so short he could barely make out the words himself.

"Leg won't work."

"I'll help."

"Get away. I'm losing my hold."

Barry did not answer, but crawled up another notch. His face was even with the back of Johnny's knees now, and he could smell the blood, see the hole in the back of the man's thigh. If that was a deer rifle the deputy had used, the hole in the front of the leg would be a lot worse. He could not advance another inch, it seemed. He looked along the cliff on both sides and upward at the edge of the cave that now seemed impossibly far away.

"Look left," Johnny said through his teeth.

Barry looked at the stone, the irregular black indentations, but at first could see nothing. Then he saw the crack, almost vertical and about a handspan broad. It angled off to the left, but if he could get a foot in it he might help Johnny up to the next ledge. He inched up, got his left hand in the crack, his muscles snapping as he levered his way up behind the Indian until his toes gripped onto the same ledge as Johnny's bloody foot rested on. Now his face was next to Johnny's and the Indian turned to look at him, so close that his eyes were out of focus.

"Feels like my leg is gone."

"It's there, but it's got a hole in it."

Barry was trying to get his left leg up high enough to wedge his foot in that crack.

"Like a crab," Johnny breathed.

Barry saw what he meant and inched his right foot across until it was against Johnny's. Then he gripped into the crack with his left hand and hopped, terribly jumped across the intervening space, his foot leaving the toehold, swinging out and hitting the cliff face again, feeling desperately for the toehold where Johnny's other foot was. It held. Barry lifted himself with his arms until he could get his left foot solidly in the crack. There. Now he put a hand across Johnny's back and under the armpit, pulling as he whispered, "Now. Try it."

They moved up a notch. Then two notches. And then the crack got too far away from the toeholds to be of use. Johnny rested, holding his body against the rock while Barry got behind him again, covering him like a protective shield. The two men panted together for minutes while voices floated up from below. Neither of them paid any attention.

"Now," Barry panted into his friend's left ear, "I'll hold the bad leg while you raise the good one."

Johnny's nod was very slight. His breathing came shallow and fast. He let his weight sag onto Barry's arm and raised his left foot to the next toehold. Then they both pushed upward and Barry followed. By doing this each time, they made slow progress to the ledge just under the lip of the cave. Barry's whole body was shaking with fatigue and terror now. He felt the emptiness beneath him as if it were a door opening out of his back, the long airy drop that demanded wings.

The two men panted together, Johnny's head just below the slight overhang at the cave edge.

"Albert?" Barry called, hoping the older man could come help them. He felt he could not make the final effort, his arms and legs shaking so badly now that he was afraid they would collapse without warning. The cliff was nearly vertical at this point, though it sloped inward some ways back.

"He can't," Johnny said, his voice faint. "Sick. Bad."

"We'll do it," Barry said, surprised at the loud sound of his own voice. "Now, let's go."

"Nothing left," Johnny said, and suddenly his whole weight sagged down against Barry's body, pushing outward, threatening to tear loose his hands that held to the ledge.

"Johnny?" Barry's voice was high with fright. He felt his hands being pulled loose, knew that his friend had fainted. He tried to change his grip, lost it, right hand coming away from the rock and waving in the air inches from the ledge. His body began to swing, the right foot slipping from the ledge. The other man's body slumped heavily against his legs. Barry felt panic as he tried to twist back, his right hand clutching air farther from the ledge, and then his left leg took the full weight of the unconscious body, and his left foot snapped out of the toehold. He fell, a tiny grunt escaping his lips, fingers sliding down the rushing sandstone.

I shift.

Claws are better than broken fingernails, but not much better until they hit a ledge of rock on the sloping area some fifty feet down the cliff. The Indian's body is still on my shoulders. I have it pinned between me and the cliff. If I let it fall, I could make it, I know. I might even shift into bird form, get away. For the first time I can remember, I am certain death is possible. But I will not let the body go. One foot, claws fully extended, is solidly on a tiny ledge. I grope about with the other foot, trying to get a purchase. I think about scratching holes in the rock with my claws, gnawing holes with my teeth. My mind is running wildly, facing dissolution. I force the fear away, force my mind to slow, my muscles to stop more strain than is necessary. The slowness is better. I have one foot secure. I can hold this man's body with one arm. Do not think of the watchers so far below us.

Now it is slower. The fear is blanked out. With every sense, I feel the rock around me for holes, cracks, ledges, the little toeholds pecked in the stone by Indians hundreds, maybe thousands, of years ago. I find them, sensing them as glowing dots and cracks in the stone with my spatial sense. I feel more confident now, raising myself and the unconscious body whose blood is still dripping from the wounded leg. I will complete this trial, I tell myself, raising up to take another step, and another.

The lip of the cave is in front of me. I throw one arm over it, the claws anchoring in the dusty stone cave floor. With the other arm I pull the Indian's body off my shoulder and slide it into the cave. The next second I am in the cave. It is shallow, filled with dust, the ceiling low and bulging downward. In the corners are old bones and skulls. Albert Chee lies doubled up against the near wall, his eyes closed, breath shallow. I sniff the wound in Johnny Strong Horse's thigh. It is torn open, the muscles and bone visible as the blood continues to pump out slowly. This will kill him in a short time if it is not stopped. I need help.

And then the door opens in my mind. The door I had not realized would open, or even that it was there. Like a child entering a garden—or perhaps coming out of a small enclosure—I go through the door. The world expands.

Unbelievable.

When the blind see for the first time, the deaf hear, the lame spring up and run across a sloping lawn, the bird finds its new wings: These are comparisons that occur to me, but none describes the expansion, the flooding in of sensation and knowledge and purpose that then, like an explosion of brightness, makes me alive to myself. I know what to do, where she is, what we are here for. The possibilities are infinite now, and I crouch in the narrow little cave with two sick men, feeling my self for the first time. Energy floods into me. I call.

She answers. I know her thought, the gladness, her love. She will be here in minutes. Over the lip of the cave I peer cautiously. What a drop that is. I had not looked down. Inside, I feel Barry cringing back from the sensation that looking from that height brings. It is much higher than I had thought. Down on the floor of the canyon something is causing the men and horses to scatter in all directions. I hear their shouting.

Another sound approaches from up the canyon. I look in that direction to see a low brown mass moving down the streambed, expanding in the flat places, pressing together again where the stream flows through close walls. A stand of willows goes under the brown frothing wall of water, and now the sound comes up to me, a low rumbling, crashing noise as the flash-flood waters come roaring down the streambed. In the wide area below me, though, I am thinking, the water will surely dissipate in the sand. And as I watch, it reaches the mile-wide sand delta and spreads out, losing force but rising to several feet around the cottonwoods and willows on the canyon floor.

The rain must have been far back in the mountains, for the sky remains clear, the sun brilliant on the opposite cliff. Below, the men and horses have disappeared downstream, gone somewhere in the heavier stand of trees. I watch as the flood loses force and spreads out evenly over the sands. And then she arrives.

The bird appears over the edge of the far cliff, sailing directly at the cave mouth like a graceful diver. I watch her, knowing it is she, feel her words in my mind as she approaches across the abyss of air. She lands with a thunderous flapping of great wings and shifts into her own lovely self, the blue-gray fur glinting like an evening sky

185

full of stars. She greets me, we touch muzzles and she goes to work on the wounded man. I have never seen a healer operate, never known there were such things until now. I follow her thoughts, the intense kinetic probing that goes inside the man's flesh from her mind, the careful arranging of tissues, the heat of regeneration. It is miraculous, but nothing more than any healer could do. The blood stops as the arteries are joined again. The bone ends are in place and lightly fused, as much as the man's body can stand at this moment. The flesh is cleansed and joined. She makes a bandage of the man's shirt and ties it around the wound.

She moves to the older man, whose body has not stirred.

He is shocked, she tells me. *His Self has closed up.*

Can you help?

I can wake him, but his own will must complete. He must want to live.

She probes at the man. He opens his eyes, sits up in the dust, looks at us with blank eyes. There is no surprise. He is not in his mind.

The humans are cared for as well as we can do it. We are together for long moments, saying, listening, feeling in our own minds each the self of the other. We prepare in this way for the joining that will be possible now, the Conjunction.

Voices drift down to us from overhead. Then a rope appears at the cave mouth. We consider whether to shift, or whether she should leave for a time. I cannot think of being alone. She will stay, but we must shift until our humans are cared for.

We shift.

Barry looked at the Indian woman with whom only yesterday he had been as physically intimate as it is possible for humans to be. She looked back at him, smiled. They felt at once like friends and strangers.

"Now you see," she said.

"You must be very close to your Beast," Barry said, feeling great fatigue from the climb now.

"She has been kind to me."

Barry thought about that. Yes, it was possible to say that his Beast had also been kind, but then he had not asked to be taken out of his life and put into this double form. He noticed the rope switching back and forth outside the cave mouth. Bo's voice came down from above.

"Hey, Barry!"

"Yeah, I got it," Barry said, reaching out over that terrible drop to get the rope and drag it back into the cave. When he glanced down, the fear he felt shoot along his spine made him jerk back and sit heavily on the dusty cave floor. God in heaven. He had climbed that! He must have been out of his mind. Cold sweat sprang out on his forehead, and he felt like being sick. But the rope was pulling strongly in his hands now. Someone was climbing down. The Indian had skinned his hands getting around the slope of the stone as he came into the cave, but he let his bloody hands dangle as he looked with amazement at Sarah. He said a few words in Navajo and she answered, her look noncommittal. Then she said something else, indicating Johnny. The Indian nodded and began tying the rope securely around Johnny's waist and shoulders.

Johnny and his uncle had been hoisted out of the cave, the Indian rescuer leaning perilously out over the long drop to get their unconscious bodies safely around the overhang. He looked at Sarah and Barry sitting near the opening, said something to her in their language and then began climbing up the rope, bracing his bare feet on the stone. He was out of sight in seconds.

"Now?" Barry asked, wondering at the change inside him, the new sensation of fullness and joy he felt from the Beast. What would happen to him now? He recognized some hold the Beast was exerting over his mind. It was hard for him to think about his survival with that pressure on his mind, as if he were under some strong tranquilizing drug.

"I'm coming down," was shouted from outside the cave. It was Bo.

The two humans stood uncertainly as the rope jerked back and forth. Barry grabbed the end of it to make the climb down easier. Beaumont's feet came into view, bare as had been the Indian's, then his long, gaunt body, the black beard. He swung down to the cave floor, looking at Sarah with no surprise.

"Why'd you do that?" Barry asked.

Bo took the figurine from his pocket, the carved piece of abalone shell that had been in Barry's jacket pocket. He grinned at Sarah.

"In case you're wondering"—he looked at Barry also—"I know about the two of you."

He stood, his legs apart, as if ready for a battle. In his

hand the figurine glistened: the carved bear, muzzle in the air as if crying out in pain. Lifting it in his fingers, he held it toward the man and then the woman.

"I know this has some power over you creatures in your natural form," he said, grinning. "If you want to take on your other forms, go ahead." He stood, waiting. The two people looked at each other. Sarah spoke first.

"Bo, what do you want? We are almost finished here."

"I want—" The tall man paused, swallowed. "You damn well know what I want."

Barry looked at the woman as he felt his existence fading, felt the two Beasts in their completeness taking form. It was like knowing when you are falling asleep, he thought, as his self faded away into something larger, something so powerful he could not comprehend its limits. Yes, like falling asleep and being aware as the landscape of dream takes form, and you yourself become something else. . . .

We shift.

The two great cats sat on their haunches, the one tawny, the other blue-gray. They were similar but not identical. They did not need to look at each other now, for they were already one in their minds.

"You're beautiful, all right," Bo said, holding the figurine at arm's length in front of him. He was frightened in spite of himself, muscles quivering behind his knees.

You want a Person, we say.

"I want Lilly," Bo said.

Do you know your son was a Person of ours once?

Bo stepped back, hit his head on the low, overhanging ceiling and half fell, half crouched among the scattered bones of those a century dead. He looked at the two Beasts, the hand holding the figurine faltering. "My son?"

Charles Cahill, whose full name did not come through at the time of his being called—Charles Cahill Beaumont, a fine young man, my second Person, I say, remembering in my self for a moment that heroic young man and his ignominious end caused by my own childish reactions.

"What?" the black-bearded man said, his face sagging. The amulet had fallen into the dust and lay glittering among the bones. "My son? He's dead," he whispered.

All of our Persons are chosen from the newly dead, we say. *It is our method of assuming humanity for our purposes. Our kind must mature in a different life form, and so we are able to draw on those Persons who hold in-terim positions in the adjoining space.*

"You can call back the dead?" Bo's eyes are dull and full of pain now. "Then Lilly was dead, too?"

You know she was. You have been there.

"She said one time," he whispered, "that she remem-bered it."

We can use the amulet you have. It is an opening, or you might think of it as a time-stop. It opens into ad-joining spaces and allows energy to be transferred through its timeless structure. It may be used to add energy to any time-bound form.

"What are you saying?" Bo said, seeming to come back to life.

That together we can draw energy from Outside, but our ability to do so is limited.

"Can you bring them back?"

We can each create a separate structure with our own life energy. Together we can bring in only two Persons without injuring ourselves.

"Well, bring them back, then," Bo said. He stood up again, carefully, stooping under the low ceiling. "Lilly, and my son, too," he added with a note of triumph. He bent to pick up the amulet again.

It is not possible to bring them both. Barry will be brought in as a separate Person. That is one. You must choose the other.

"Between Charles and Lilly?" Bo screamed. "You can't be saying that. I can't make that choice, condemn one of them to death. That's horrible!" He took a step forward, the amulet held before him. Both of the Beasts rose to their feet and backed away a step or two.

Please. Do not threaten us. We might leave you at any moment.

"Okay, okay, but if you can bring back one . . ."

It is not possible to bring back both.

"Why does he . . . I mean Barry . . . why does he—" Bo stopped, his head dropped. He turned away and put one hand against the stone wall. "I don't mean that," he said softly. He stood for a long time, or perhaps it was only a few seconds. Time in the cave did not move in a normal way. The dusty bones might have stood up again, fleshed as they were in the last century, alive and speaking with each other as they waited in the cold for the Spanish with their guns.

When the man turned, his face looked old. There seemed more gray in his hair and beard. "I understand," he said. He closed his eyes, and from under the lids two tears came and ran down his cheeks. He said, "Charles."

Barry sat on the fender of the Model A gazing along one edge of the canyon where the piñons and yuccas ended and the sandstone began. Down in the depths it was evening, although the sun would not set for at least another hour. From the corner of his eye he could see Bo and his son standing beneath one of the taller cedar trees. They had been talking, hugging each other, walking about for maybe an hour, Barry thought. He grinned, and in spite of his happiness he felt tears in his eyes. Hell, they could take all night if they wanted to. He felt firmly himself now, fitted to this world, not doubled and torn in opposing directions or given to strange hungers and powers. This was his world.

Before, in that terrible time when he had never been alone, when the Power had been always with him, he had not known of his past, his human life. Now it was clear; even the death, the blaze of brightness from which he had been pulled back by the power of those creatures united with what seemed accidental events. The amulet that coyote had meant as a malicious trick on the Beast, the fact of Mina's extrasensory powers and George Beaumont's abilities, too: all of these had somehow been brought together into a web of power. In those few seconds, Barry had shared with the creatures and had learned something he would not ever tell his two friends standing over there in the evening light.

—Barry comes through Mina's power and his own life force.

—Charles can be brought back because his father's love held the boy in an interim space.

—The others continue on their way as imperishable Persons.

Barry remembered the brightness clearing to reveal the Indian woman, Sarah, a little boy, a slightly built young woman with short, dark hair and other people he did not recognize. They rose then, as on an updraft of light energy, disappearing into the brightness.

—The young woman could not be brought back.

—She had been released on her way.

—He does not know he had no choice.

No, Barry thought, he will never know that.

A sudden shout from the two standing under the cedar tree jerked Barry from his reverie. They were pointing out over the canyon. He jumped to the ground and ran to where they stood watching the birds lift out of the dusky canyon like meteors rising from the earth.

"God!" Bo said, his hand shading his eyes. "Look at that!"

"They're almost too bright to look at," Charles said, his hand also at his forehead.

The two flying creatures, for they were not really birds, rose from the canyon into sunlight, circling about each other, scintillating with color: aquamarine, crimson, turquoise, a deep coral red, color flowing back from them. They trailed a fluttering rainbow as they rose into the evening sky. The brilliant winged beings circled, approached in graceful curves, seemed to fuse with flashings of white light, circled again, always rising higher into the deep blue sky.

Barry watched, his mind opening to the beauty of their color and movement. Parts of the peyote ritual came back to him, the vision of a home world where these were in their natural surroundings, a world of shifting forms. I have been so fortunate, he thought, as the two flying creatures came together again and the light blazed out from them.

And then the spot of light exploded, showering fragments of rainbow down into the canyon. And a second later the detonation hit them, a loud crack, as of close lightning. The sky was clear, deep blue again and empty.

"Damn," Bo said, turning his dazed face to look at Barry. "They blew up."

Barry looked at Charles, who was smiling. "No," he said. "That was the Leap."

Later, as the little Ford bounced along toward Chinle, Barry still felt some of that joyful glow, the farewell of those creatures whose life imperative was a progressive change of form, as simple as the tadpole and the moth. From the back seat came the happy voices of Bo and Charles.

"Well, can we, Dad?"

"Sure. I just got to stop off in Salt Lake City to see a guy I know and make some arrangements." Bo's voice picked up, grew more confident. "I bet your mom would like that town."

"We can talk her into it, can't we, Dad?"

"Sure," Bo said. "You know we can."

Barry switched on the headlights as the sunset glowed deep red like embers in the west. He was going home, too, really home this time. A movement caught his eyes as they bumped out of an arroyo, and he noticed a large, lean coyote trotting off at an angle between the junipers. The wild dog cast a quick look toward the car and turned sharply away into the growing darkness. Poor coyote, Barry thought. Even his meanness was put to good use. A person could say that's how coyote got such a bad name among the Navajo, or could say that's how the Indians came up with the Thunderbird symbol. But the truth is, he thought, settling his arm on the window and sniffing the evening breeze, the truth is, we'd be better off attending to the important things. He grinned. Like getting home.